The Dog Collar Murders

An Inspector Angel Mystery

By the same author

IN THE MIDST OF LIFE

CHOKER

THE MAN IN THE PINK SUIT

THE IMPORTANCE OF BEING HONEST

MANTRAP

SALAMANDER

SHAM

THE UMBRELLA MAN

THE MAN WHO COULDN'T LOSE

THE CURIOUS MIND OF INSPECTOR ANGEL

FIND THE LADY

THE WIG MAKER

MURDER IN BARE FEET

WILD ABOUT HARRY

THE CUCKOO CLOCK SCAM

SHRINE TO MURDER

THE SNUFFBOX MURDERS

The Dog Collar Murders

An Inspector Angel Mystery

Roger Silverwood

ROBERT HALE · LONDON

© Roger Silverwood 2011
First published in Great Britain 2011

ISBN 978-0-7090-9208-7

Robert Hale Limited
Clerkenwell House
Clerkenwell Green
London EC1R 0HT

www.halebooks.com

2 4 6 8 10 9 7 5 3 1

Typeset in 10.5/13.5pt Sabon
Printed in Great Britain by the MPG Books Group,
Bodmin and King's Lynn

ONE

It was one of those days when the birds were coughing, the Rottweilers were barking and the police cars were screaming down the streets of Bromersley, while in the kitchen in St Joseph's Vicarage, Bromersley, South Yorkshire, a brother and sister were having breakfast together.

'Oh Tom, you'll be the death of me,' Phoebe Wilkinson said as she lowered her cup into the saucer. She snatched up a big black shopping bag from the floor at the side of her chair and rummaged around inside it. The bag was always with her, and was always full and bulging.

Tom Wilkinson put down his cup, reached out for the last piece of toast and said, 'What are you looking for, Phoebe?'

'My pen. I have a pen in here somewhere.'

'Why do you want to hump that big bag of rubbish about with you everywhere you go? It's twice as big as you are, and you can never find anything in there.'

She snorted and dug even deeper. 'I have told you before that I have all my things in here ... things that are important to me ... things that I may want ... at a moment's notice.'

'You know, Phoebe, I'm sure some of the congregation look at you and think you're the vicar's batty sister.'

Her nose was in the bag. She glanced out at him momentarily and said, 'I'm too old to care what anybody thinks.'

'I care. They are my people. They expect me to set them an example. They might start thinking that I'm batty too.'

She ignored him and continued to rummage.

'What do you want a pen for?' he said.

'To write all this down. I shall never remember everything.'

'Look, Phoebe, you needn't worry. Elaine knows all about the arrangements. And the times and dates are in the diary.'

Her fists tightened but she soon released them. The arthritis in her fingers was painful that morning. 'I don't want to be dependent on somebody else *all* the time,' she said. 'I want to know it for myself.'

'Well, borrow *my* pen.'

She waved him away. 'I have my own pen in here somewhere, *and* my notebook.'

Phoebe Wilkinson almost turned the bag inside out to no avail, and then she suddenly found it, held it up and waved it at him, triumphantly. 'I knew it was here.'

Then she returned to pushing the mish-mash of stuff around the bag again. A wrapped sweet, a single glove, a bottle of pills and a photograph of Frankie Dettori fell on to the carpet. She quickly rescued them and pushed them back in. Eventually she produced a small notebook. 'There!'

Tom Wilkinson put the slice of buttered toast to his mouth and took a bite.

'Now, when does the plane take off?' she said.

'Monday morning. I am taking the services here, tomorrow, as usual, of course, then on Monday at 10.15, Quentin is collecting me to take me to Leeds airport. I should be in Rome for teatime.'

She pulled a face like an alligator. 'How very nice for you.'

'You'll be perfectly all right, Phoebe.'

'It's not right that you're leaving me when winter is just setting in. And Rome is such a long way away.'

'It's my work, Phoebe. The bishop wants me to go to represent him. There are all sorts of meetings and discussions over there he wants me to attend. And it will be the last opportunity I shall have before I retire.'

She sniffed then said, 'With champagne receptions in noble palaces, I expect.'

'Some of those too, I hope. Now don't be difficult, dear. You are going to be perfectly all right. I have tried to anticipate all eventualities. I have arranged for Elaine to come in *every* day, and Quentin to pop in about seven o'clock daily to check that you're all right and to lock the door.'

'What if I go dizzy again and have one of my falls?'

'You've got your personal alarm phone. You know exactly what to do. I've been through it often enough with you. You press the button, there's a nurse on duty at the other end 24/7 as they say. You just tell her what the trouble is.'

'And what if your plane crashes? What am I going to do then?'

'It won't crash and if it did, I'd be in paradise a bit early, that's all. You'd *still* be all right. Everything is in order.'

'Huh. I don't want to have to deal with the solicitors. They don't speak intelligible English any more. And what if they sell The Grange?'

'I am only going for two weeks. It'll keep while I get back.'

'When will I be able to get my share of the money?'

He glanced up momentarily at the ceiling. 'You're always on about that. Soon. Very soon. As soon as a purchaser has completed. And I shall pay Elaine before I go, so you won't have anything to pay out.'

She glared up at him. 'I haven't *got* anything to pay out *with*. You've got it all. I ought to have *some*thing in my purse.'

'Don't let's go through all that again. I put it in the bank for you. You know that you just lose money. And you don't know what you've done with it. And you've nothing to show for it. It's happened so many times.'

'It's just my memory, Tom. That's all. I don't remember things.'

'Well ... remember to be nice to young Robin Roebuck, if you see anything of him. He'll be taking some of my services. He'll be returning those vestments he borrowed. Tell Elaine some of them might need laundering. The thing is, just keep everything ticking over until I get back.'

She looked down at the carpet and shaking her head said, 'I can't keep answering the phone, Tom. I don't know what to say to people. They say they know me but I have no idea who they are. And sometimes it rings all evening.'

'Everybody wanting me will know that I'm away, Phoebe. There was a piece about it in the magazine, on the pew sheets and I mentioned it in the notices. Anybody who rings up, just tell them I'm away and give them Robin Roebuck's number, that's all.'

'As long as it doesn't ring during *Casualty*.'

He looked at his watch, then stood up. 'Gone nine. Must get cracking, sis. I've morning prayers in fifty-eight minutes, and I haven't prepared a thing.'

He went out.

She drained the cup of the last drop of tea. Then she pushed hard on the arms of the carver and stood precariously holding on to the table. She looked round, then bent down to pick up the black bag. By leaning on furniture and grabbing strategically placed handles, she made her way to the door into the hall and through another door into the sitting room. She was making her way across the room when she heard the front door slam shut. She stopped abruptly and looked back.

A voice called out, 'It's only me, Miss Wilkinson. It's Elaine. Where are you?'

'In here,' she called. 'Sitting room, dear.'

A young woman in a blue overall came in, looked across at her, smiled and said, 'What are you trying to do?'

'Get to my chair.'

Elaine put a hand under Phoebe Wilkinson's arm and supported her to the electrically operated lounger chair by the fireplace. She lowered her into it and then handed her the control panel.

'There you are,' Elaine said. 'Now I'll get you a nice hot water bottle.'

'Thank you, dear. No rush,' she said as she pressed a button on the control panel which started the buzz of a small motor in the chair and caused the leg rest to rise slowly. When it reached a comfortable position, she stopped pressing the button, put the control on the chair arm, straightened her dress, looked up at Elaine and said, 'Did you have a nice evening then?'

'Yes, thank you, Miss Wilkinson. Did you?'

'The usual. At my age, Elaine, one vicarage dinner with your brother and the church wardens and their wives is pretty well much like another.'

Elaine spotted a copy of the local newspaper on top of other papers and magazines on the little table at the side of the chair. 'You've read the *Chronicle* then? I looked for The Grange again but it is not advertised. It *must* have been sold.'

Phoebe Wilkinson blinked. Her face brightened. 'Do you think so?'

'Most likely.'

She smiled. 'Half of that money is mine, you know.'

'I hope they got a good price for you, Miss Wilkinson,' Elaine said. 'What are you going to do with your half?'

'Not sure, Elaine. I'm really not sure. Haven't made my mind up. There are so many good causes. My brother said we might have to take a low price because of the recession. But you know him, always the pessimist.'

Elaine's eyes glowed. 'Some people say the recession is over. I heard that some really good houses are fetching big money. Your father's house is a lovely house in an expensive area. Probably fetched millions. Imagine all that money to do whatever you like with.'

Phoebe Wilkinson did not need Elaine to draw her any word pictures.

'Whatever it is, imagine all that in cash,' Elaine said.

Phoebe Wilkinson shook her head. 'It'll come in a cheque or a warrant or something like that, I suppose. It'll just be so much paper.'

Elaine said, 'I heard on the news that they're talking about doing away with cheques? Some shops won't take them now. It's back to old-fashioned cash. My father still buys everything with cash. Doesn't have a bank account. Doesn't trust banks. Is there any wonder? Well, who does *these* days, I ask you? Huh.'

'Well, I haven't a cheque book now,' Phoebe Wilkinson said, then she shook her head. 'Think of it. Had one since I was twenty-one. All those years, then last April, my brother wouldn't let me replace it because I lost it between here and the chemists. If I want any money for anything now, I have to ask *him* for it.'

Elaine didn't think that was right, but she knew that she oughtn't to say so. She patted the old lady's hand and said, 'I'll fill you a hot water bottle, Miss Wilkinson, then I'll make you a *nice* cup of coffee.'

'Lovely, dear. Thank you.'

Elaine went out and closed the door.

Phoebe Wilkinson half closed her watery blue eyes and slowly rubbed her chin. There was something on her mind. Something was troubling her. After a minute or so, she made a decision. She blinked several times thoughtfully as she reached out for the phone book. She soon found the number she wanted and underlined it with her ballpoint pen. Then she reached out for the phone and tapped out the number. As it rang out, her lips moved silently as she rehearsed what she intended to say.

It rang for a long time and then it was answered by a man who sounded startled. 'Er ... hello?'

Phoebe Wilkinson frowned and said, 'Is that Mace and Hall, solicitors?'

'Well, yes, but the office is closed,' the voice said. 'It's Saturday, you know. I wouldn't normally be here. I just called in because I had forgotten something.'

'I know it is Saturday, young man. Nevertheless, this is Miss Wilkinson here. Miss Phoebe Wilkinson, and as you happen to be there perhaps you would be kind enough to assist me?'

'Oh, yes. Miss Wilkinson. If I can I will, Miss Wilkinson,' the young man said.

'Would you kindly tell me what progress you have made with the sale of my late father's house, The Grange, Duxberry Road?'

'Oh yes, Miss Wilkinson. Good morning to you. The Grange? Oh yes. In its own grounds. Natural lake. Five bedrooms. I remember. It's not my department actually, but I seem to remember that there was a lot of interest shown in it. At the price, it is rather an exclusive property ... and there are not many potential buyers who have immediate access to that amount of ready cash in this financial climate. They may be in the process of trying to raise the money from the banks or building societies. This snow and ice and bad weather may have slowed down people's intentions. Though it might be getting warmer soon.'

'I don't want a weather forecast, young man. I simply want to know if it is sold. Can you please confirm *that* for me?'

'I really don't know, Miss Wilkinson.'

'It *could* be, then?'

'Oh yes. If it was a cash sale it very well could be.'

'A *cash* sale? I see. Ah well, how soon could I expect to receive payment?'

'We don't hang on to clients' funds longer than necessary, Miss Wilkinson. In such circumstances, fees and disbursements are quickly worked out and deducted and the balance paid out by our cashier in a very few days.'

'A few days?'

'Earlier if there were special circumstances.'

'Yes, well, please tell your cashier there *are* special circumstances ...'

'I certainly will, Miss Wilkinson.'

30 Park Street, Forest Hill Estate, Bromersley, South Yorkshire, UK.
7.10 a.m., Monday, 11 January 2010

Detective Inspector Angel was at the bathroom sink lathering up his face with a new badger-hair shaving brush he had had bought for Christmas.

His wife Mary came into the bathroom with an opened letter in her hand.

'Michael,' she said, rubbing her temple, 'I have been reading that letter from Lolly again.'

He squinted at the mirror. References to Lolly, Mary's sister, tended to irritate him. She reminded him of a butterfly that fluttered about the place seemingly unable to decide where to land and when it did, it settled by a burning flame and singed a wing.

He picked up the razor, rinsed it under the hot tap and applied it to his lathered cheek.

'Can I read the bit I mean?' Mary said.

His eyebrows went up. 'Do I have a choice?'

She glared at him momentarily and then looked down at the letter. 'It's the last bit. She says, "Mary, darling, you are my only sister and we used to be so close. We had such fun. Do you remember when we all used to go to Grandpa's in the summer and stay for simply ages? You and I used to go down to the pond and paddle and fish and sunbathe. That's where we met the Simpson boys. Barnaby had a crush on you. And Nigel had the hots for me. Happy days! I know that I miss you terribly. I would love for us to spend some time together again. We could have a really great time when Michael is at the office doing his murders and things. It would be simply great if we could get together again. I would love to come over and see you.

I hear there are some great shops in Leeds these days. I wonder what happened to Nigel. As it happens, my apartment is being decorated the first two weeks in January and will pong of fresh paint for a week or two after that. If you could do with me about then, it would be great. We haven't seen each other since Pa's funeral, and I haven't seen you since you moved into your new bungalow. It would be great to give you a big hug. And Michael, of course. Lots of kisses. Love you. Lolly."'

Angel growled and then said, 'What about it? She wants to come here for a holiday and to get some clean Yorkshire air in her lungs.'

Mary's eyes flashed. 'It's to see us and get away from the smell of fresh *paint*.'

'Those foreigners smell of onions.'

'It's the garlic. I keep telling you. And my sister isn't foreign.'

'I don't care what it is. I don't like it. *She* probably smells of garlic now. She's been living over there long enough.'

'Don't be ridiculous. She smells perfectly … clean.'

He was making a long downward stroke with the razor. He broke off and said, 'They can't help it. They eat a plateful of garlic, swill it down with a bottle of house red, and then dance a few choruses of the Can Can. Then they begin to sweat … it comes out through their skin.'

Mary's face went scarlet. '*All right, all right!*' she yelled. 'I'll write and tell her she *can't* come, because she smells.'

She turned and made for the door.

Angel, realizing he had gone too far, stopped shaving mid-stroke and said, 'Besides, there's nowhere she can sleep.'

There was a second's delay.

Mary turned back. Her voice softened. 'That back bedroom is spotless. It just needs clearing out, the curtains cleaning and the paint washing. All it needs is a new bed.'

'There *is* a bed. There's that bed in the summerhouse that came from your mother's.'

'She can't sleep in *that*. It's about a hundred years old.'

'It's a valuable antique. It'll be cosy.'

'It'll smell.'

'She'll never notice.'

She breathed in rapidly and said, 'Michael. We *need* a new bed.'

He rinsed the brush out vigorously and put it in its stand to dry.

'It can go on my credit card,' she added. 'We'll hardly notice.'

His eyebrows shot up again. 'It'll still have to be paid for. It won't come free because it's on *your* credit card. The gas bill's due, and the half-year rate bill is overdue. Forget it, love.'

'We need a new bed, Michael, and then if anybody wants to visit us, we've the accommodation.'

'Why?' he said through the towel. 'Are we going into competition with The Feathers?'

She glared at him again, then stormed out of the bathroom.

Northern Bank, Bromersley, South Yorkshire, UK. 10 a.m., Monday, 11 January 2010

The First Security Delivery Services van driver and his mate came out of the Northern Bank on to Main Street, dropped the boxes they had collected through the slot in the side of the van, locked it and then climbed into the cab. The next point of call was the Yorkshire and Lancashire Building Society on Market Street, so the driver carefully drove the van along to Western Bank then turned right down into Almsgate, a tiny one-way back street, manoeuvred his way through the line of parked cars and delivery vans and suddenly discovered a large black furniture van slewed across the road blocking the way. The FSDS driver had just applied the brake when there was a thunderous bang on the cab roof. It resounded in their ears. The vehicle rocked and the roof collapsed several inches. The two men gasped and crouched down as they thought it might cave in completely and kill them. Then through the windscreen they saw a giant metal claw pierce the radiator. The sight of the advancing claw made the driver's mate's blood run cold.

'What the hell?' he said.

Steam hissed and billowed over the bonnet. The windscreen shattered. Their vision ahead was entirely blocked. The driver struggled to open the cab door to make his escape but he could not budge it. They heard the crunch of metal behind them as the van sides were being pierced by two other giant metal claws. The noise grated on their ear drums.

The vehicle was on the move upwards. It was swinging from side to side.

'God. What's happening?' the driver said, his chest banging like a Salvation Army drum.

'Press the automatic raid transmission advice, John,' he managed to remember to say.

The driver's mate pressed a red button on the radio transmission set. It was programmed to send a standard recorded emergency message that the vehicle was being raided to the branch office in Sheffield. There was already an automatic live twenty-four-hour satellite navigation system link that advised them of the vehicle's location at all times.

The van then suddenly rose upwards.

The two men looked at each other. Their eyes showed stark fear.

The van swung to one side, clipped a parked car then rushed straight upwards as if it was a bouncing ball on the rebound. The men's stomachs dropped as it gained momentum. Through a broken side window the driver could see some first-floor office windows. The van was swinging away from them. They were sailing through the air as if in a hot-air balloon.

They stared at each other, their mouths open and their eyes the size of traffic lights. 'What's happening?'

There was the screech of torn metal as the giant claws opened to release their grip.

The van was in freefall.

'Hold tight, John.'

'God help us.'

The driver grabbed hold of the steering wheel. His mate grabbed the door and the handbrake cowling, preparing himself for a hard landing. The front of the van landed first. It made a hell of a racket and jarred every bone they had. But they were back on the ground. They were grateful for that, but their arms and hands were shaking. They tried to open the cab doors. They had to push and kick them. It was hard work but they eventually prised their way out. The van was a wreck. They looked round. They were in a small private walled car park, but there were no cars there and the gate was closed. The crane grabber was rapidly retreating into the sky. Several men in balaclavas and carrying guns were busy at the back of the van. One of them saw them, left the back of the van and dashed up to them. They knew he meant business. He herded them together to the corner of the car park well away from the mangled van. He told them to take off their helmets and lie face down on the ground. It was cold and hard. The van driver looked back to try to see what was happening.

He felt a gun in his back.

'Look down!' an angry voice yelled.

Suddenly, there was a loud explosion. They felt it through the ground.

A few seconds later, men's voices shouted jubilantly.

One of the men said, 'Fill that case. Hurry up.'

There was a lot of activity and noise. Heaving and banging, metal on metal. A few moments later, the same voice said, 'Don't mess about. Come on.'

Another man came across to the van driver and his mate. He had a roll of two-inch-wide black sticky tape. He quickly wrapped it tightly round the two FSDS men's wrists behind their backs, their ankles and across their mouths and eyes.

'Come on,' the voice said. 'Two minutes forty-five. It's time we were out of here.'

And they were gone.

It was only a very short time afterwards that police cars screeched up to the car park, and five uniformed officers and three in plain clothes battered their way through the old wooden gate, rushed to the two men tied up in the corner and cut them free.

DI Michael Angel was the senior officer there and quickly took in the scene. 'Are you men all right?'

'Think so,' the FSDS driver said, rubbing his wrists.

'Yes,' the driver's mate said, getting to his feet. His hands were still shaking.

Angel looked round the car park. 'What happened? How did you get here?'

The FSDS driver pointed up in the sky. 'That crane. The van with us inside was lifted out of the street, over the wall and dropped – literally – here.'

Angel blinked, then stared briefly at the massive builder's crane towering above the super structure of the multi-storey hotel building in progress two streets away.

He called across to one of the patrolmen, and pointing towards the construction site, said, 'Quick, Sean. Get the man who has been driving that crane.'

Patrolman Donohue nodded and rushed off.

Angel glanced at the FSDS van and saw that one of the rear doors was hanging precariously on one hinge and the other was on the ground twelve feet away. In the side of the van there was a black hole. He knew it must have taken four sticks of dynamite at least to have caused that much damage. The van was a write-off.

Angel looked at the FSDS driver. 'How many were there?'

'Four or five. They had guns.'

Angel's eyebrows shot up. 'Can you give me a description of them?'

'Don't know. Ordinary. Wearing balaclavas. Jeans, T-shirts, dark jackets or overcoats and trainers. One was in a dark suit. Black shoes.'

'Did they have a car? Which way did they go?'

'Didn't see. Don't know.'

'How long have they been gone?'

'A couple of minutes before you arrived.'

Angel turned away and addressed the patrolmen. 'Right, lads. Not much to go on. See if you find any of them. Anybody who looks guilty, or starts to run when you get near. Concentrate on the town centre for a start. Then work outwards. Constable Weightman, take the bus station. Hurry up. But be careful. They are armed. I don't want anybody hurt.'

The patrolmen ran to their cars.

Angel dived into his pocket and pulled out a mobile phone. He tapped a number into it. It was soon answered.

'PC Ahmed Ahaz, sir.'

'Ahmed. I'm in a private car park on Almsgate. It's empty. It was all locked up. Had to force open outside doors. The offices are unoccupied. It's that narrow little twisty lane at the back of Western Avenue ... a sort of service road. I want some transport urgently to take two men to hospital. Phone Transport. Speak to Sergeant Mallin. Also, I want you to contact Don Taylor in the SOCO office and tell him I want him down here pronto, to look at a security van that's been hijacked. All right?'

16

'Right, sir.'

Angel closed the phone and shoved it in his pocket. He glanced at the sad excuse for a van. There was very little bodywork that was unmarked. All the windows were shattered. The front wheels were at unseemly angles. Wisps of smoke were still filtering out of the black hole in the back. A trickle of water was running down the car park from its radiator.

He went back up to the two FSDS men.

'The van safe is empty. How much was in there?' he said.

'Over four million,' the driver replied.

Angel frowned then shook his head. After a moment, he said, 'It's a lot of money to be dragging around the streets. Was it all paper money?'

'Yes. All sterling paper currency, fifties, twenties, tens and fivers. All used notes. No coins,' the driver said. 'It's not usually that much. It's because people have spent their Christmas money and because of the sales, I expect.'

'No chance of finding out any numbers on any of the notes?'

The driver shook his head. 'Sorry. It was all used notes.'

Angel wrinkled his nose. 'Yes. Mmm,' he said. He went quiet for a few moments, then he said, 'Did you hear any of the villains speak?'

'One of them told us to come into this corner, to take off our helmets and lie on the ground,' the driver said.

'Did you recognize any accent?'

'I never noticed. I had a lot on my mind. It all happened faster than it takes to tell it.'

'Must have been local or Yorkshire anyway. You would have noticed if it was Cockney or Irish or something like that, wouldn't you?'

'I suppose I would.'

His mate said, 'I heard one man call out instructions to the others to fill a case. I suppose he meant them to put the money in it.'

Angel's face brightened. 'You mean in a suitcase?'

'I don't know. Could have been.'

Angel's eyes narrowed and he rubbed his chin. 'A suitcase,' he said. Then, suddenly, he reached into his pocket, took out his mobile, ran down his directory, found the name PC John Weightman and clicked on it.

A few seconds later, a voice answered, 'Yes, sir.'

'John. Where are you?'

'Bus station, sir. Nothing suspicious to report.'

'Witness says one of the men could be carrying a suitcase, John.'

'A suitcase?' Weightman said.

'Take a look at the rail station next door. A suitcase might blend better in a railway station.'

TWO

Detective Inspector Angel's office, Police Station, Bromersley, South Yorkshire, UK. 3 p.m., Monday, 11 January 2010

There was a knock at the door.

'Come in,' Angel called.

It was DS Carter, one of Angel's two sergeants. She had joined his team six months earlier. He much preferred men on his team but Flora Carter had proved herself to be both intelligent and brave, so he forgave her for smelling sweetly of soap, frequently wearing a smile and for being invariably optimistic.

'You wanted me, sir?' she said.

'Aye. Where's Trevor Crisp?'

'Don't know, sir. Haven't seen him.'

Angel wasn't pleased. DS Crisp, his other sergeant, always seemed to be missing when there was an emergency. He was also remarkably good at providing excuses.

'The patrolmen I sent out round the town looking for the robbers are now phoning in,' Angel said. 'Not *one* of them has seen anything.'

Flora nodded sympathetically.

'Get them together,' Angel said, 'and organize a door to door on Almsgate. There are a lot of windows looking down on the road as well as the car park where the van was lifted.'

'Right, sir,' she said and dashed off.

Angel reached out to the phone and tapped in a number. It was to DS Don Taylor, head of SOCO at Bromersley force, who was at the crime scene on Almsgate.

'What have you got, Don?'

19

Taylor was reluctant to answer. 'They haven't left anything here, sir.'

Angel's face tightened. He ran his hand through his hair. 'Nothing, Don?' he said.

'The villains seem to have worn gloves throughout, sir,' Taylor said. 'No blood, urine, saliva. Also, being outside, it is much more difficult to find samples positively attributable to the crime.'

Angel grunted then said, 'No DNA then?'

'And the ground is hard and bone dry, so there are no footprints either.'

Angel frowned. It wasn't looking good.

'Wonderful,' he said, wrinkling his nose. 'So what's the use of that expensive training you've had and all that sophisticated and pricey equipment you've got down there in that glorified lavatory?'

'The explosive charge was dynamite, sir,' DS Taylor said. 'About four sticks, I should say.'

Angel frowned. 'I knew that from the smell,' he said. 'Where did these smart boys get four sticks of dynamite from, Don? A few years back we could say that they'd been lifted from a local coalmine, but now there are no mines left. And none have reported any missing. And they all have to account for every stick.'

'It's easy enough to fiddle, sir.'

It was true enough. Nobody knew exactly how many sticks would be required to execute a particular job.

'All right, Don. When you've finished there, go to the driver's cab of that big crane you can see behind you. The driver may have been careless, thinking we wouldn't bother looking up there. You might get prints from the controls. It'll be a bit of a climb. And while you're there, find out how a villain was able to gain access to it and operate it. Doesn't expensive machinery like that require a key to start it up?'

Taylor was suddenly silent. The idea of climbing up into the cold, blue sky was obviously not being greeted with joy.

Angel visualized him looking up at the crane driver's control cab.

'Sean Donohue missed the man by only a minute or two,' Angel said.

'It's a helluva way up there,' Taylor said.

'If you find anything interesting, give me a ring,' he said. He replaced the phone, leaned right back in the chair and stared at the ceiling. He was thinking about the likely characters who would pull such a brazen robbery as that in broad daylight and not leave any DNA behind. It would have taken some planning. He couldn't think of anybody. All the brains for jobs like that were behind bars. It must have been a new face pushing his luck.

There was a sudden knock at the door.

Angel leaned forward and called, 'Come in.'

It was DS Crisp. The Don Juan of his team. He came in with a bright face and all smiles. 'You wanted me, sir?'

Angel screwed up his face and eyed him closely. 'Where the hell have you been?'

'I got stuck with Peter King.'

'I never get stuck with anybody I don't want to get stuck with, except the super and the chief constable.'

Peter King was a local man who occasionally confessed to committing murder even though he was completely innocent. It was his hobby ... a very dangerous hobby. One day he was going to be found guilty of some serious crime he didn't do.

Angel's face relaxed. 'What's he confessing to *this* time?'

'Murder of that prostitute in Leeds, just before Christmas.'

'Why didn't you kick him out?'

'I couldn't find a suitable question about something that was *not* in the newspapers. The reporters had been very thorough ... reported every detail. And Peter had certainly done his homework. Anyway, I eventually caught him out, then I took a written confession statement from him, emailed it to Leeds and put him in the reception cell with a cup of tea.'

Angel shook his head. 'All very time-consuming to achieve nowt. Leeds CID had better come back soon. The super won't want to be giving him hospitality a moment longer than necessary.'

Crisp said, 'Democracy at work, sir.'

Angel sighed and slowly rubbed his chin. 'Now, lad, I've got a job for you.' He quickly briefed Crisp about the robbery of the security van, then said, 'I want you to find out about the black furniture van that was slung across Almsgate, the one that blocked up the road and brought the FSDS van to a halt. And I want to know *everything* about it. Absolutely *everything*. Got it?'

Crisp nodded pensively. 'Right, sir,' he said and went out of the office.

Angel sat back in the chair for a couple of minutes, his eyes almost closed, his fingers clasped. Then he leaned forward, reached out for the phone and tapped in a number.

'Yes, sir,' Ahmed said.

'See if you can find a quarry or a demolition contractor or ... really anybody who has reported the stealing or loss of any sticks of dynamite in the last few weeks or days.'

'Just locally, sir?'

'No. The whole country,' he said and replaced the phone. It rang as soon as it hit its cradle. He blinked in surprise and snatched it up. 'Angel.'

It was Superintendent Harker, breathing heavily. 'It's a triple nine, lad,' he said. 'A clerk at the railway ticket office at the station. Shot in the chest by a man with a handgun.'

Angel looked up and sucked in air.

'Ambulance on its way,' Harker said. 'There is a witness. A woman. A Zoe Costello. She's waiting down there for you.'

'Right, sir,' he said and slammed down the phone.

He didn't like shooting any time. In broad daylight in the town centre it was damned audacious – like Chicago in the twenties. But it was great to have a witness.

He dashed out into the green corridor, leaned through the open doorway of the CID room and caught Ahmed's eye.

'Come with me, lad.'

Ahmed turned away from his computer and grabbed his hat. He was delighted to be escaping the office; made a change from routine filing, dealing with ad hoc inquiries and being general dogsbody. In addition, it made him feel important to be with Angel. He wasn't quite so pleased when he realized it was because almost everybody else on the team was taken up with inquiries to do with the security van raid.

As Angel raced the BMW through the streets with Ahmed sitting next to him hanging on to the seatbelt and his helmet, he repeated the message he'd had from the superintendent, and told Ahmed to contact DI Asquith on his mobile. 'Give him my compliments, lad. Tell him we have a possible murder situation at the railway station

and ask him for immediate uniformed assistance there. Then phone
Don Taylor, tell him the same and that his services are also urgently
required, then phone DC Scrivens and tell him I want him there
smartly, also. Right?'

'Right, sir.'

They had arrived. Angel followed an ambulance into the small yard.
Its red brake lights suddenly shone. It stopped on double yellow lines
under the 'Bromersley Station' sign. Angel stopped three yards behind
it and ran after the two paramedics who dashed into the small covered
entrance way, pushing their way through a crowd of fifteen or so
people, and past two windows to the ticket-office door.

A man in a blue uniform with the word 'Stationmaster' on his hat
opened the office door to meet them. His face was red and his eyes
moist. He looked at the men in the green paramedic clothes, stepped
back and pulled the door wide open.

'He's in here,' the stationmaster said.

The paramedics rushed in with blue canvas valises, followed by
Angel holding up his warrant card.

'Police,' Angel said.

The stationmaster looked at it, blinked, nodded, and closed the
door after them.

The paramedics rushed over to a bundle of clothes in a pool of blood.

Angel looked round the small office and saw a woman sitting
uncomfortably on a high stool at the far end of the little office. She
was dabbing her face with a tissue. That must be the witness. 'You
saw the man who shot this young man, miss?' he said.

She gulped and said, 'Yes.'

'Did you see which way he went?'

She shook her head.

He screwed up his face. 'Be with you in a minute,' he said.

Angel buttonholed the stationmaster. 'Did you see which way he
went?'

'No, sir. I was on the platform checking on some goods for the down
train. I heard a bang. I thought it was a gunshot from somewhere near
the ticket office. I couldn't believe my ears. I ran towards the office,
unlocked the door and found young Harry Weston on the floor, blood
rushing out of his shirt front ...'

The man's face creased. He couldn't speak any more. He turned away towards an old iron fireplace in the corner littered with Silk Cut cigarette packets and cigarette ends.

'Has anything been taken? Cash? Tickets?'

Without turning round, the stationmaster shook his head.

'Do you have any CCTV anywhere? Covering the platforms, the trains, the ticket office?'

The stationmaster shook his head.

Angel patted him gently on the shoulder and said, 'That's all for now. Will you come down to the station with me later … make a statement?'

He nodded.

Angel crossed to the corner of the office where the paramedics were kneeling. They had rolled the blood-soaked young man over. His face was still and white.

'What's his name?' one of the paramedics said.

'Harry Weston,' the stationmaster said.

The paramedic put the working end of a stethoscope on the young man's neck and after a few seconds looked up. 'There's a pulse,' he said quietly.

The stationmaster licked his lips, took a few deeper breaths and tried to smile.

Angel's heart seemed to rise, open out and float in his chest. He did not know the young man, but it was great news.

The man pulled the stethoscope away from his ears to let it hang round his neck. He ran out.

The other paramedic promptly found a suitable vein in the back of the wounded man's hand, introduced an intravenous line into it then held up a plastic bottle.

Angel realized the injured man wasn't able to talk, so he returned to the young woman. 'I am Detective Inspector Angel,' he said.

'Zoe Costello,' she said.

'Did you see what happened?'

'Yes, Inspector. A man. A vicar. A priest. Well, a man in a dog collar was at the ticket window shouting at the clerk inside … then suddenly he pulled a gun out of his pocket, just like on the films, and shot him.'

'You actually *saw* him?'

'Well, yes. Briefly. Very briefly.'

24

Angel's heart leaped. She had actually seen the gunman. He nodded encouragingly. 'Did he see you?'

'Don't think so.' She thought a moment then shuddered. 'No,' she said.

'Did he come back on to the platform?' he said.

'No, he didn't pass *me*. I was on the platform, you see. Waiting for a train.'

Angel rubbed his chin. He frowned. 'He must have gone the other way ... out of the station, into the town then.'

'I suppose so,' she said.

Angel nodded at her and said, 'Right. Do you mind waiting here for a few minutes, then coming to the station and having a look at some videos? That gunman might be already known to us.'

'Of course,' she said.

The paramedics were lifting the injured man on to a stretcher, the stationmaster now holding the drip.

Angel dashed over, opened the door, went out ahead of them and called out, 'Make way, please. You may save this man's life if you get out of the way. Everybody move away, please. Thank you. Thank you.'

Ahmed came up to him, saw what was happening and joined in the job of moving the crowd back.

The crowd obligingly eased back but craned their heads to look at the injured man's face as the stretcher was whisked past them.

As soon as the ambulance had driven away, Angel addressed the crowd, which had increased to around thirty by then, and said, 'I am a police officer. I believe a man was shot here a few minutes ago. Did anybody here see what happened? Did anybody here see a priest? A vicar? A man wearing a dog collar? Did anybody see which way he went? Did anybody see anything at all unusual?'

Nobody said a word.

'If anybody saw anything, please come forward. Let's try and catch the man with the gun who shot that young man.'

Still silence.

'If you saw nothing and *can't* assist the police, then please move on. There's nothing more to see here. Thank you very much.'

Angel watched them, but nobody made a move to leave. Everybody looked as if they'd been planted where they stood.

Passers by coming out of the bus station stopped, looked at the crowd, saw the police uniforms and stood around adding to the numbers. An ice-cream van pulled up. Its siren played a few discordant notes and a glass window opened for business.

Angel turned, grabbed hold of Ahmed's cuff, and quietly said, 'Start taking their names and addresses. That's a sure-fire way of getting them to leave.'

Ahmed nodded and reached into his pocket for his notebook and ballpoint.

At that moment, two marked police Range Rovers arrived, sirens blaring and lights flashing.

Angel's face went scarlet. His eyes flashed. He rushed out to the front to meet them. 'Switch that racket off! This isn't a ruddy funfair. Your blue flashers are more than enough. I'm trying to get rid of a crowd, not drum one up.'

'Sorry, sir. Sorry, sir.'

'Get rid of these people and that ice-cream van, tape round and then check with DS Taylor. He should be here any second. When he arrives, I'm off.'

He turned away. SOCO's van arrived. He stopped, turned back and quickly briefed DS Taylor. Then DC Edward Scrivens arrived.

'What can I do, sir?'

'Find Ahmed and send him to me, then somewhere around is the stationmaster. Take him to the nick. Put him in an interview room. Give him a cup of tea and make him as comfortable as you can.'

'Right, sir.'

Angel went back into the ticket office. Zoe Costello saw him and eased herself off the stool.

'Right, Miss Costello. My car's outside. Let's go.'

Interview room one. Police Station, Bromersley, South Yorkshire, UK.
5 p.m., Monday, 11 January 2010

'Yes, I'd love a cup of tea, Inspector,' Zoe Costello said.

Angel looked up at Ahmed. 'Two teas, lad. And see if you can find those pot cups and saucers we used to use before they put that machine in that makes everything taste of cardboard.'

Ahmed's eyes narrowed. He had a feeling that that china had gone upstairs to the chief constable's suite. 'I'll do what I can, sir.'

'And will you let me have a laptop and the disc with the new videos of our rogues' gallery?'

'Yes, sir.'

He went out.

'Now then, Miss Costello,' Angel said, 'please tell me everything that happened from when you arrived at the station this afternoon. What time did you get there?'

'I got there at three o'clock. I was going to catch the 3.05 to Meadowhall. Do a quick bit of shopping and then dash back home. I went up to the window for a ticket, and bought a day return. The clerk would have been the lovely young man who was shot.'

'What do you remember about him? What was he like?'

'I've been trying to think back, but there was nothing special about him. He had fair hair, I think … and he wasn't very old. That's about all I remember. The business of getting a ticket took only a few seconds. You see, I had the right money …'

'Was there a queue? Did you see who was in front of you, or behind you?'

'No. There was no queue, Inspector. It wasn't busy at all when I went there.'

'So you went through to the platform?'

'Yes. On my way to the platform I passed the priest coming off the platform. I didn't take much notice but a dog collar makes you look again, if you know what I mean.'

Angel's heart leaped. She had seen the priest *from the front*. He nodded encouragingly. 'Would you describe him?' he said.

She shrugged. 'A typical, average, middle-aged man in a dark suit, with a dog collar and black shirt and, I think, black shoes.'

'How tall was he?'

'Say, about five foot eight.'

'What was his hair like? Did he have a moustache or a beard? And was he wearing specs?'

'I only saw him for two seconds, Inspector. But I don't think he had any facial hair, and he wasn't wearing spectacles. His hairline was average, I suppose. To tell the truth, I can't remember. There was nothing striking about his face or his hair. It must have been brown or black. He was just ... ordinary. Except for the dog collar, everything about him was ... very ordinary.'

Angel nodded.

'I must say,' she said, 'he looked very much like a priest. Smart, intelligent and sober. He could be a *real* priest.'

Angel considered it. She was right, of course, but what a dreadful thought! 'Mmm. Then what happened?'

'I went on to the platform.'

'Did you see anybody on the platform ... either platform?'

'There were a few people ... fifteen or twenty ... all sorts of people ...'

'Can you describe any of them?'

'No. There were people of all kinds. Looked like workmen, students, housewives doing what I was doing, shopping and so on ...'

'So where do you think the gunman came from? Which direction?'

'He definitely came from the direction of the platforms. Don't ask me which platform. I didn't see.'

'Then what happened?'

'I could hear my train coming in the distance. I looked down the platform for it. Then I heard a loud, angry voice behind me. It was from the ticket office. I was only a few yards away from the barrier. He shouted something like, "Where was he going? That's what I want to know." I think that's what he said. If the clerk replied, I didn't hear him. I thought it was unusual, so I turned round, stepped up the platform to the barrier and peered round the corner. My train was almost at the platform. The brakes shrieked. Carriage doors slammed. I saw the priest reach down into his right pocket – well, I assume that's what he did. It was his right-hand side. I could only see his left-hand side. Anyway, up came his hand with the gun in it. He pointed the gun at the window and then there was a very loud bang. It was *very* loud. I pulled back round the corner before he saw me. I went all shivery and leaned back against the wall. Then the stationmaster rushed past me. My heart was pounding. He had been on the platform. He was making for the ticket office. I recovered myself and looked round the corner again, but there was no sign of the man with the gun. The stationmaster was having trouble unlocking the ticket-office door. The key seemed to be stuck. He was very upset. I helped him. We went in together and found the ticket clerk on the floor bleeding profusely from his chest.'

She stopped and reached in her pocket for a tissue.

'Then you phoned for an ambulance and the police?' Angel said.

Her mouth turned down. A tear rolled down her cheek. She nodded.

Angel stood up. 'Well, thank you. We'll take a little break, shall we?'

She nodded again.

'Won't be a minute,' he said, making for the door. 'I'll see what's happened to that tea.'

He came out into the passageway. He looked up at the green corridor. It was very quiet, then he heard the rattle of pots. Ahmed came round the corner with a tin tray holding cups, saucers and teapot.

'I thought you must have gone to Bombay for that tea, lad,' Angel said. 'Take it straight in. Then bring in the laptop with the videos of the rogues' gallery. Then you'd better phone the hospital and see how Harry Weston is and if it is possible that I could have a few words with him.'

'Right, sir.'

Angel went into interview room two, next door. DC Scrivens and the stationmaster were seated opposite each other at the table. Scrivens jumped to his feet.

Angel gestured to him to sit down. He looked at the stationmaster. 'Are you all right, sir?'

'Well, yes,' he said quietly. 'But I would like to know how Harry Weston is. And I would like to get home.'

Angel knew the feeling. He felt exactly the same. The remains of yesterday's topside of roast beef, cold with pickles, were waiting for him.

'Won't be long now, sir. By the way, the lad that's been shot, Harry Weston. I need to know his next of kin.'

The stationmaster jumped to his feet, his bottom lip quivering. 'Why? Have you heard from the hospital?' he said. He looked very grim, expecting the worst. 'What's the news?'

Angel shook his head. 'No, I haven't heard anything yet, sir. Need to inform his family, that's all.'

The stationmaster slumped back down in the chair.

'Don't worry,' Angel said. 'He's in good hands.'

The stationmaster looked up at Angel and nodded. He knew it was true. Then he frowned and said, 'He's not married. Never has been. And I know his father and mother are dead.'

'Right. Thank you,' Angel said. 'I'll be back in five minutes.' He closed the door and returned to interview room one.

He was pleased to see Zoe Costello holding a florally decorated saucer with one hand and sipping tea from a matching cup with the other. She looked across at him and smiled. 'I hope that your tea is still hot, Inspector,' she said, pointing to the cup on the tray.

'Thank you, Miss Costello,' he said. He closed the door, sat down, reached out for the cup and took a gulp. He put the cup down and licked his lips. 'I've been waiting for that,' he said.

On the table he noticed the laptop that Ahmed must have brought in. He plugged it in and lifted the lid. The video had twenty-four of the worst-known-gun-toting thugs at liberty in the UK at that moment. It showed front face, left profile, right profile and front face again. He set the video running and watched for her reaction.

After five minutes, the show was over.

'He's not there, Inspector,' she said. 'Sorry.'

Angel wrinkled his nose. He wasn't pleased. He wasn't surprised either. Nobody had ever said that catching murderers was easy.

'Thank you very much, Miss Costello,' he said. 'I won't keep you any longer. I'll arrange for you to have a lift home. Thank you for your cooperation. I'll be in touch.'

He then unplugged the laptop and carried it next door.

Scrivens stood up as he came through the door. He looked at Angel with raised eyebrows.

Angel said, 'Get Transport to organize the safe delivery of Miss Costello home, Ted. And Ahmed is still around somewhere. Send him to me, then sign out and get yourself off home.'

Scrivens was pleased. He smiled, nodded and went out, closing the door.

Angel looked at the stationmaster, who was very quiet. It had

THE DOG COLLAR MURDERS

been a long day. 'Won't be long now, sir. By the way, what *is* your name?' he said as he plugged in the laptop and opened the lid.

'Evans, Deri Evans,' the stationmaster said.

'Well, Mr Evans, I just want you to look at this short video of known villains. See if you can pick out anybody you may have seen today. Please take your time. This is very important. Then I'll arrange for you to be taken home.'

'Thank you.'

He started the CD. 'Now then, do you recognize any of these charmers?'

'You know I didn't see the man actually pull the trigger, Inspector,' he said as the first video picture arrived on the screen.

'I understand that, Mr Evans, but you might have seen the man on the platform or hanging around the station?'

There was a knock at the door.

'Come in.'

It was Ahmed. 'You wanted me, sir?'

'Aye. We've almost finished here, lad. Arrange with Transport to take Mr Evans home and be sure to take his address. Go and sign out, then collect him from here and get the driver to drop you off on his way back.'

'I'll stay on and assist you, sir, if you want me to.'

'Nice of you, lad. But no need. Besides, your mother will wonder where you are at this time.'

'Right, sir. I'll be back for Mr Evans in a few minutes then.'

He went out.

Angel turned back to the stationmaster.

'Any joy, Mr Evans?'

''Fraid not.'

The picture show ended.

'Sorry, inspector,' Evans said.

Angel sighed and said, 'Thank you, Mr Evans. I hope you have a good night.'

Angel then went to his office and slumped in the chair. He looked up the Intensive Care ward phone number at Bromersley General and tapped it out. He hoped he might be able to see Harry Weston briefly and ask him if he could name or describe his assailant.

'Intensive Care,' a soft woman's voice said.

'Bromersley Police,' he said. 'I am inquiring about Harry Weston. Would it be possible to see him briefly tonight?'

'No. He's in theatre.'

'I'm the police officer investigating his attempted murder. It is important that I speak to him as soon as ever possible.'

'I understand that, but he won't be permitted visitors for at least twelve hours. Maybe not even then. I'm sorry.'

'Thank you,' he said and replaced the phone. He rubbed his chin. Nothing there then. He looked round the office. There was nothing else that needed doing that couldn't wait until the morning. He looked at his watch. It was eight o'clock. He'd known worse days.

He was home for 8.10.

Mary glowered at him. 'Why didn't you ring me and let me know?' she said.

'I couldn't. It was an attempted murder case. I was expecting a breakthrough.'

'Huh,' she said. 'If you'd got your breakthrough you wouldn't have been here now.'

It was true. He was stuck for an answer. 'Is there any tea?' he said.

'It's in front of you.'

He took off the cover plate. Underneath were three thick slices of cold roast beef and a big spoonful of cold cauliflower and potato. The pickle jar on a saucer stood prominently in front of him. He picked up the knife and fork.

Mary slumped down in the chair opposite him. 'I married you for companionship but I never see you,' she said.

'You had me all weekend to argue with,' he said.

She glared at his plate. 'You can't eat that meat now. It's all dried up.'

He looked round the table. 'It'll be all right,' he said. 'Any bread and butter?'

She frowned. 'Bread and butter? You never have bread and butter with cold meat.'

'Is there any bread and butter?' he repeated slowly.

She stood up. 'I'll get it,' she said and went into the kitchen. 'What do you want to drink?' she called.

'I'll have a beer while you're by the fridge.'

32

He heard her take a sharp intake of breath. 'If you have alcohol now, it'll make you sleepy.'

'Yes, well, that's what I want to do, sleep.'

'You'd be better off with tea or coffee.'

He banged the cutlery down on the table. '*Mary*! Do you have to argue about every single thing?'

'I am only thinking of your welfare.'

'My welfare would be best served by you letting me decide for myself what I would like to eat. If you have *no* objection.'

'I don't care what you eat. You can eat yourself silly if you want to. But if you're ill, I will be the one who will have to look after you.'

He frowned.

Mary arrived with the butter dish, butter knife and a packet of sliced brown bread. She banged them down on the table.

He looked up at her as she turned away to the kitchen.

'Thank you,' he said without meaning it.

She then returned with a can of beer and a glass. She banged them down on the table.

Angel opened the pickle jar in silence and helped himself to several onions and a large piece of cauliflower.

She looked at the pickles on his plate then watched him replace the lid on the jar, screw it tight and put it back on its saucer.

'Do you know how much that jar of pickles cost?' she said.

His lips tightened back against his teeth. 'No, but I know I am destined to find out.'

'£1.68,' she said. '£1.68! It's daylight robbery.'

In silence, Angel reached out for the pickle jar, unscrewed the lid and, with his fork, picked up the pickle from his plate, a piece at a time, and ceremoniously returned it all to the jar. Then he screwed the lid on, put the jar back on the saucer and pushed the saucer away to the middle of the table.

Mary had watched his every move and she stared at him for several seconds with her mouth open.

Meanwhile, Angel picked up the knife and fork and began to cut into the beef.

Eventually she said, 'What did you do that for?'

'The pickles are obviously far too good for me.'

Her lips tightened.

'You can be so ridiculous,' she said. 'You *know* I didn't mean that.'

Angel shook his head. 'Mary,' he said, 'half the time I don't know what you *do* mean. Don't you think, to save any more misunderstandings, and so that I can get on with my supper, we should stop arguing and switch on the telly?'

Mary ran the tip of her tongue thoughtfully over her bottom lip, then said, 'Was there some programme you especially wanted to see?'

'No,' he said, buttering a slice of the brown bread. 'No,' he repeated. He had no idea what was on.

She leaned over towards him. After a few seconds she said, 'I want to talk to you, Michael. Seriously. I've something to say.'

He stared at her. He wondered what was coming next. 'You don't have to *announce* it, Mary. You can just come right out with it and *say* it.'

'You know how you were saying that we hadn't a decent bed for Lolly when she comes ...'

Angel looked heavenward. So that's what it was all about. He knew that there had to be something strange going on but he hadn't linked it to his dizzy sister–in–law and Mary's sudden wish to make accommodation available for her. He had thought that that subject had been discussed and closed that morning. He looked at her and frowned.

'I didn't say that we hadn't a decent bed for Lolly. *You* said that.'

'Well,' Mary continued, 'I have gone into my mother's money and bought one. It'll be here in a couple of days.'

Angel held his hands upwards. He didn't approve of her hacking lumps off the few thousand pounds her mother had left her. He reckoned that they could happily manage on his salary if matters were sensibly managed. He had considered that Mary's mother's money was hers exclusively and hardly took it into account. It was there for a rainy day and the fact that the gas bill was a month overdue he didn't consider was even a shower.

Anyway, she had said that she had actually bought one. In which case there was nothing more to be said. He gave a little shrug and cut into the beef more vigorously.

She knew that buying a spare bed wouldn't be seen by him as

sensible. 'It was my mother's money,' she said. 'I reckon she would wholly approve of me shelling out for a bed for her daughter, my sister, to sleep on.'

Angel sniffed and said, 'Do you think she will approve next year when we have to buy more beds for her daughters and maybe for a brand new husband when they all descend on us?'

THREE

Angel picked up the phone and tapped in a number.
'Intensive Care,' a woman's voice said.

'Bromersley Police,' Angel said. 'I am enquiring about Harry Weston. Would it be possible to see him briefly this morning? It is extremely important.'

'I'm sorry. Harry Weston passed away in the night.'

Angel swallowed. He took a deep breath then said, 'Right, dear. Thank you.' He sighed as he replaced the phone. He wasn't that surprised. He had lived in improbable hope that Harry Weston might have survived, recovered his health *and* identified the gunman. It was not to be. The young man was dead. It didn't matter how many times he saw or heard about somebody dying, he always felt sad. They say that policemen get hardened to it. Angel never had nor ever expected to be. Death was particularly difficult to deal with when the deceased was young, and Harry Weston was only in his twenties.

Angel rubbed his chin. There was a change in the circumstances. He was now investigating a case of murder. The muscles round his mouth and chin tightened. He reached out for the phone and tapped in a number. He was ringing Crisp on his mobile. It rang out and rang out. As it was still ringing, there was a knock at the door. 'Come in,' Angel called.

It was Ahmed.

Angel looked up at him and said, 'Is Trevor Crisp in CID?'

'No, sir.'

He banged down the phone and said, 'I can never get hold of that lad. I never know what the hell he's up to.'

Ahmed turned to the door. 'I'll try and find him, sir.'

'Hang on. There are one or two more things. Got your notebook?'

Ahmed turned back, his eyebrows raised. He reached into his top pocket.

'That lad, Harry Weston, died in the night. I want you to phone the hospital to check that his body has gone or will go straight to the mortuary. Then phone the mortuary and have them point out to Dr Mac that Weston is a murder case of mine and that I want to know the calibre of the gun that shot him, ASAP, please. Also anything else that might be useful.'

'Right, sir.'

'Then I want you to get Harry Weston's home address. You can get that from the stationmaster, Mr Evans. The key for the place will presumably be among the dead man's clothes. It would be in his pocket when he was taken into hospital yesterday afternoon. Get hold of it and let DS Taylor have it PDQ.'

'Right, sir. Is that it?'

'No. I want you to get an artist from NCOF at Wakefield and set up a meeting, this morning, if possible, with Zoe Costello. She's the only witness who saw the murderer.'

'What's NCOF, sir?'

'National Crime Operations Faculty. You should know that by now. It's a specialist police unit on all sorts of specialist subjects. Chemicals, drugs, engines, gases, et cetera. The point is they have an artist on tap. I'm hoping he can come this morning and that she can remember what the murderer looks like. With a bit of luck, he'll draw him for us.'

Ahmed's face looked bright at that prospect.

'Right, sir,' he said and turned to go.

Angel called after him again. 'By the way, did anybody from Leeds force collect Peter King?'

'No, sir. He's not in a cell. I think I heard in the canteen that the super gave him a caution and released him, when you were out yesterday.'

Angel thought about it for a moment and seemed content with the news.

Ahmed turned to go.

Angel called after him. 'What did you come in for?'

Ahmed frowned, then turned back a page of his notebook and tried to decipher his own handwriting. His face suddenly brightened. 'Ah yes, sir,' he said. 'Yesterday, you asked me to find out if anybody had had any dynamite stolen recently. And I found out that in North Derbyshire, at the South Creekman quarry, overnight November 5th to the 6th, their site offices were broken into and a part box of thirty-two sticks were stolen.'

Angel's eyebrows shot up. 'They should have been in a safe.'

'They were, sir.'

'The safe registered with the local authority and approved by them.'

'It was, sir.'

'And checked every twelve months by the local police.'

'Ah. I don't know about *that*, sir.'

Angel smiled. 'I knew I'd catch you out on something,' he said.

Ahmed grinned.

Angel made a note of the relevant facts on the back of an old envelope taken from his inside jacket pocket. 'Right, lad. Now off you go. Chop, chop.'

Ahmed closed the door.

Angel reached out for the phone and tapped in a number. He was soon speaking to the manager of the Sheffield branch of the First Security Delivery Services.

'It seems to me, Mr Earnshaw,' Angel said, 'that the robbers were expecting your van to take that particular route yesterday.'

'Impossible,' Earnshaw said.

'The two men,' Angel said, 'have they been working for you long?'

'Both impeccable records, Inspector. First thing I thought of when I knew the van was under attack. Both served the company longer than I have. Both come from excellent backgrounds. Both have been double-bonded by our insurance company.'

'They were not harmed at all, Mr Earnshaw.'

'Put that down to their excellent training and discipline while under pressure.'

'Well, it was not a coincidence that a thumping great van was slewed across the road thereby bringing your van to a stop and at the same time a mammoth crane was conveniently hovering over-head ready to pick your van up and drop it so that a team of villains could blast their way into it.'

'I don't see how they could have known, Inspector. The routes of all our vans are changed every day, on a two-week cycle.'

Angel frowned. 'A two-week cycle?'

'I mean we change the route of every van every day for two weeks. For ten working days our drivers call on our clients by a different route and in a different order.'

'Highly commendable,' Angel said with one eye half closed then, drawing the man further, added, 'Then I suppose you start on the same cycle again?'

'Of course. Believe me, the timetable took some working out.'

'And how long have you been using that system?'

'Since I came here, twelve months ago.'

Angel ran his hand through his hair. 'Don't you realize, Mr Earnshaw, that you have established a pattern? And a very distinct and easy pattern indeed. And there is nothing random about it at all.'

'Not random! Nobody could possibly work out the route our drivers take. Every day for two weeks is completely random.'

'It may well be *different*, Mr Earnshaw, but it is not *random*. What about the third and fourth weeks? And the fifth and sixth weeks? I tell you this, Mr Earnshaw, robbers intending stealing four million pounds from FSDS would be more than willing to monitor the route the van took for four or five or six weeks if necessary.'

There was silence for a few seconds, then Earnshaw said, 'Oh. Do you really think that's what happened?'

'At the moment, I cannot think of any other explanation. If I were you, I'd instigate a system *today*, and make the route entirely random. Let it depend on the toss of a coin, the throwing of dice or the cutting of cards. And I'd arrange to have every van driver do that daily. And make it the last job just before he leaves the yard.'

'In that case,' Earnshaw said slowly, 'the driver wouldn't know the route until the very last minute.'

'That's right. There's no harm in that, is there?'

Earnshaw hesitated. 'No. No, I don't suppose there is.'

'It would add another degree of security to the operation.'

'Very well, Inspector,' Earnshaw said. 'It will mean a lot of changes. I will get on to it straightaway.'

Angel replaced the phone.

There was a knock at the door. It was DS Flora Carter.

'Come in, lass. I need eye witnesses. What have you got?'

'Apparently most of the upper rooms on Almsgate are store-rooms, but there was a cleaning lady who saw the whole thing from a window on the second floor.'

'Can she describe the villains?'

'Would you like to speak to her yourself, sir? She's in interview room one?'

Angel's head came up. 'Oh? Yes. *Yes*, I would.' He stood up and dashed out of his office, followed by Flora Carter, along the green corridor, past CID to the interview room. He pushed through the open door and saw a lady seated at the table.

'It's Mrs Vincent, sir,' Carter said as she closed the door.

Mrs Vincent looked up at Angel's face warily.

He smiled at her as he pulled out a chair and sat down.

'I'm Detective Inspector Angel,' he said. 'I know that you've already told DS Carter what you saw this morning. Would you mind repeating it to me, and telling me what you saw?'

'I don't mind,' she said, sitting up in the chair and sticking out her chest. 'Well, as I said, four men appeared from nowhere, three dressed in jeans and jackets and trainers, one looking much smarter in a dark suit and tie. When I realized that it was an FSDS van, that they were all wearing black woollen balaclavas and had guns, I dialled 999.'

Mrs Vincent stopped and looked from Angel to Carter and then back to Angel.

'You did exactly the right thing, Mrs Vincent,' he said. 'Please go on.'

'Well,' she said. 'One man held a gun over the driver and his mate almost all the time. Another of the men had a small bag, like a valise, and another had a suitcase. Anyway, they opened the van door with a crowbar then disappeared into the back of the van with the valise. Half a minute later they rushed out and hid round the front of the van. Then there was a loud bang and a small cloud of grey smoke covered the van. When it cleared, I could see that the back doors were off, there was a big black hole in the van and packets of what looked like paper money thrown around. The men quickly stuffed all the money into the suitcase, then pulled off their balaclavas and ran off in different directions. The man in the suit took the suitcase down Almsgate. He passed the big black van slewed across the street. Very soon after that a police car arrived and then two more ... and that's about it.'

'What did they do with their balaclavas?' Angel said.

'They stuffed them in their pockets, I think.'

'The four men. When they removed their balaclavas, you would see their bare heads. Can you tell us the hair colouring of any of them?'

She frowned then said, 'Oooh yes. I never thought of it. One of them was bald or almost bald. The others were ... well, I don't know.'

'Anything striking? Such as ginger or sporting a strange haircut, or dyed an unusual colour?'

'No. Nothing like that.'

'Thank you. Did you see any of their faces?'

'No. I was two floors up above them.'

'Of course you were,' he said. 'Mmm. And what was the suitcase like, Mrs Vincent?'

'Big, sir. Stone coloured with a sort of pattern on it.'

It would have needed to be big with four million pounds in it, he thought.

'I need a full description of the case, Mrs Vincent,' he said, then he turned to Carter. 'Flora, get a full description and see if you can buy one like it.'

'Right, sir,' she said.

He turned back to Mrs Vincent and said, 'That description of what you saw yesterday will be very useful, Mrs Vincent. We are most grateful.'

She beamed.

'Thank you very much,' Angel added.

He returned to his office.

A few minutes later, after Carter had seen Mrs Vincent out of the station, she made her way to Angel's office.

He wasn't in a bright mood. He was chasing a noisy winter blue-

41

bottle round his office with a rolled-up copy of *Police Review*. It suddenly stopped buzzing and disappeared, back into hibernation. He didn't see where it had landed. He returned to his desk, dropped the magazine on to it and sat down.

'Who would want to murder a ticket clerk, Flora?' he said. Before she could reply, he said, 'It couldn't simply be for a ticket to Sheffield, Land's End or London or somewhere. And it wasn't for the contents of the till. There was only peanuts in it. And it was intact anyway. Miss Costello said she had heard the gunman *shout* at the ticket clerk: "Where was he going? That's what I want to know."'

'Must have been referring to someone they both knew, sir?'

'Mmm. But he was *shouting* it, Flora. Not asking it. Must have been important to him.'

'He wasn't getting an answer, sir.'

'Or he wasn't getting the answer he wanted to hear.'

'Or Harry Weston simply didn't know the answer.'

'It might be that their relationship was more than a ticket sales clerk and rail traveller.'

'Yes indeed, sir.'

'I've met some bent priests and queer vicars in my time,' Angel said, 'but I have never met a reverend who was a murderer, or carried a handgun. The bogus ones that I have had dealings with were pathetic, inadequate men whose crimes were limited to stealing female underwear from clothes lines and manipulating young people to talk freely about their sex lives.'

She nodded, knowingly. 'I had a boyfriend who was a bit like that.'

Angel frowned.

'Only joking, sir. Seriously, do you think that the murder was personal, then? Not really anything to do with travelling on the railway but to do with Harry Weston, the man?'

He shook his head. 'I really don't know.'

There was a knock at the door. It opened. It was Crisp. He peered round the door, smiling.

Angel's eyes flashed. His hands gripped the ends of the arms of his chair until his knuckles went white.

'Am I intruding, sir?' Crisp said.

'Of course you're intruding!' Angel roared. 'But come in anyway. Shut the door. Wait there and keep your mouth shut a minute.'

He turned back to Carter and said, 'Now what were you saying, Flora?'

'I was wondering if the relationship between the murderer and the murdered man had some history to it.'

'I don't know, lass. I want *you* to find that out. SOCO are going over his pad now. They should be finished by lunchtime. They have done the ticket office. I want to know if Harry Weston had a man friend who fits the description of the murderer ... or any sort of a friend of either sex. Find out who he mixed with. What he does – what he *did* – for kicks. What jobs he had before, if any. And in particular, if he had anything to do with the church, or a genuine priest or a man who parades round in a dog collar.'

'Right, sir.'

She nodded at Crisp, who smiled, and went out.

Crisp took a tentative step towards Angel's desk.

Angel glared across at him. 'Where the hell have you been? I give you an important job and then you disappear into outer space.'

'That van, sir,' Crisp said. 'You asked me to—'

'I know what I asked you to do. Right. What have you got?'

'The van was stolen from a removals firm parking lot in Sheffield, Sunday night, Monday morning, sir. Nobody noticed it had been taken until nine o'clock yesterday morning. It was reported stolen by the owners to Sheffield force. It wasn't loaded. An hour later, at ten o'clock exactly, the van was found parked awkwardly across Almsgate with two tyres slashed. I couldn't find anyone who actually saw it being driven into position.'

Angel rubbed his chin. So the removals van had been in position only seconds before the security van arrived and indeed before the assault on the van with the overhead crane. It was pretty close timing. The tyre slashing sounded to be excessively heavy-handed just to make sure the van was kept in position for several minutes.

'Any prints? DNA? Clues? Anything left behind?'

'Just the screwdrivers used to slash the tyres.'

'Unusual. They wouldn't be sharp enough, would they?'

'They were ground to points, sir. Fine points.'

Angel's eyes narrowed. 'Get them. I want to see them.'

'SOCO will have them.'

'Well, you know where their office is,' Angel said. 'If they have finished with them, get them. Bring them here. *Now*.'

Crisp, surprised at Angel's sudden outburst, jumped up, mouth open, said, 'Yes, er, right, sir,' and dashed out of the office.

Angel reached over to the phone. He picked it up and tapped in a number. 'Ahmed, how are you making out with that NCOF artist and Miss Costello?'

'This afternoon, sir. Two o'clock. Here. I thought they'd be all right in the CID briefing room or an interview room if it's busy.'

'Sounds good, lad,' he said and replaced the phone.

It rang as soon as it landed in its cradle. The caller was Don Taylor.

'We've just arrived at Harry Weston's place, sir, 82 Shaw Street. It's a scruffy two-room flat, Victorian house split into eight flats.'

'Well, you'll have to give it the full treatment, Don. Harry Weston died overnight.'

'Oh,' Taylor said. There was an awkward moment while he took in the sad news and the significance, then he said, 'Well, it still won't take long, sir. The bathroom's out for a start. Three other parties share it.'

'Oh no,' Angel said. He raised his eyes heavenward and breathed out. That was more bad news. Private bathrooms were usually a good source for DNA. Shared bathrooms would provide all sorts of irrelevant and therefore unreliable samples.

'What did you get from the scene?'

'There was nothing we could get the murderer's DNA from. There were no fingerprints or footprints. Harry Weston was shot in the chest with one round from a .32 handgun. We found the shell case under the ticket-office window. It had been wiped clean of prints before loading. That's all.'

Angel grunted. 'About as clean a job as a murderer would wish for.'

'I'm afraid so, sir,' Taylor said.

'Right. What about that crane?'

'*That* crane,' Taylor said. 'Phew! I'm still getting my breath. It wasn't safe. It swayed in the wind.'

'You're getting soft. What did you find up there?'

'There were no prints, nor DNA, sir. The control box had been jemmied open and a screwdriver jammed between terminals to bypass the power switch. Crude, but effective.'

'He must have known what he was doing. Let me have the screwdriver when you've finished checking it out.'

'Right, sir.'

Angel replaced the phone and leaned back in the chair. He rubbed his hand slowly over his chin. It was becoming apparent that forensic science was not going to help him solve this case. He was going to have to depend on old-fashioned legwork, intuitive questions and experienced observation.

He suddenly became aware that the bluebottle had started up its monotonous buzzing again. It zigzagged across his desk and made for the closed window. He stood up, reached out for the *Police Review*, rolled it up and was about to lunge into attack when the phone rang.

He turned back and picked up the handset. The caller coughed. Angel recognized the noisy breathing. It was Superintendent Harker.

'Yes, sir?' he said, lowering the magazine.

'It's a triple nine, lad. A priest found in a bad way in St Mary's Church vicarage, by his housekeeper, died a few minutes ago. She said a wound to the chest.'

Angel's head came up. His heart began to pound.

That was the Anglican church closest to the station and regarded as the town church of Bromersley. Angel knew the priest there – Sam Smart, a pleasant, elderly gentleman who wouldn't harm a fly.

'Police and ambulance summoned,' Harker said. 'Man was pronounced dead in situ at 1006 hours.'

'Did the housekeeper give the name of the victim, sir?' he said.

'Reverend Samuel Smart.'

It hit Angel right in the chest. A gentle man, much loved and respected.

'There is a uniformed officer from foot patrol in attendance,' Harker said.

'Right, sir,' Angel managed to say then he replaced the phone.

There was a knock at the door. It was Crisp. He came in brightly. He was brandishing the two screwdrivers recovered from the tyres of the stolen removals van. When he saw Angel, his expression changed.

'What's the matter, sir?'

Angel breathed in deeply, then exhaled. He told Crisp about the triple nine, instructed him to inform SOCO and the uniform branch, and then to join him at the scene.

Angel dashed out of the station, crossed the road, stepped lively along the flagstone footpath towards town for twenty yards or so, then turned left down to the church gates. Beyond the church and gravestones, he could see the bright yellow coat of PC John Weightman. The big man was stamping his feet and rubbing his hands outside the black door of the stone vicarage in the grounds of St Mary's Church. Angel made his way through a gate and along a path towards him.

Weightman threw up a salute as Angel came up to him.

'Anybody in there, John?'

'No, sir,' Weightman said. 'Except the body of the vicar, Samuel Smart, of course.'

'Where's the housekeeper?'

He pointed across the graveyard. 'She *was* in the church.' He shook his head. 'She's taken it bad, sir. Real bad.'

Angel couldn't avoid the slightest sigh. 'Did you get her name?'

'Norma Ives, sir.'

Angel took the short walk along a narrow path through the gravestones towards the church door. As he reached out for the handle, the door opened and a young woman came out. She looked at Angel momentarily then looked away. Her face was white and her hands were shaking in the cold.

'Are you Miss Norma Ives?' he said.

'Yes. You will be the police?'

'I am Detective Inspector Angel. I need to ask you some questions, miss. Shall we walk up to the police station? It's only a couple of minutes away. It'll be warm in there too.'

She nodded, and they set off towards the main gate.

Crisp was on his way down from the station when he saw Angel and Norma Ives crossing the churchyard, approaching him. He made for the gate, opened it and stood back to let them through. 'SOCO and uniform on their way, sir,' he said.

'Right, lad,' Angel said. 'Run on ahead and organize some tea in my office. We're perished.'

Crisp dashed off.

When the three were settled with cups of hot tea, Angel took note of her address then said, 'Now then, Miss Ives, please tell me exactly what happened.'

'Well, I do the cleaning, shopping and sometimes a bit of cooking for the vicar, Mr Smart. Call me Norma, by the way. Everybody does. I start at nine o'clock. I have a key, so I let myself in. The vicar has usually had his breakfast, but not always. He might be in the kitchen, finishing off. Anyway, there are pots from the previous night's supper, so I always wash up and tidy round the kitchen first of all. Then I make him a coffee and take it to him. He could be anywhere ... usually the study. Then he tells me what he wants me to do – what to shop for, what to prepare for his evening meal and so on. Well, this morning, I went in. At first I didn't notice anything unusual, although the sliding wardrobe doors in the entrance hall were not completely closed, and the vicar never used them. He had used them in the past, but they made his clothes damp. So I thought it was unusual. Anyway, I closed the wardrobe doors and went into the kitchen. Again, most of those cupboard doors were open and the stuff inside disturbed. Again I didn't think anything of it. I thought maybe he'd been looking for something and couldn't find it. So I straightened them up and closed the doors. Then I washed the pots, dried them and put them away.'

'Nothing unusual about the dirty pots?' Angel said. 'No signs that the vicar had had a visitor? No extra cups or glasses?'

'No. Just the usual. Then I made his coffee and went to his study. It's only across the hall. The door was open so I tapped on the door and went straight in. And there he was on the floor, his shirt and coat and the carpet covered in blood. His eyes were closed. His face was grey. I knew he was dead. Oh, it was awful. Awful. I immediately dialled 999. Then I noticed the mess the study was in. All drawers opened and stuff thrown about, cupboards opened and papers thrown on to the floor, all the pictures on the walls removed and dumped in a pile, corners of the carpets lifted. I couldn't stay in there. I rushed out. Went upstairs. The scene was the same. All his clothes taken out of the wardrobe and thrown on the floor. Drawers had been pulled out and the contents tipped on to the floor. Pictures thrown in a pile.'

Angel rubbed his chin. 'Sounds as if the intruder was looking for something, Norma. Had the vicar anything of value?'

Her eyes grew big. 'In a vicarage?' She shook her head. 'If he had, I never saw it.'

'To your knowledge, did the vicar have anybody call on him over the past few days? I am thinking in particular of anybody unsavoury, who might wish to harm him?'

'All sorts of people called there, Inspector. Mostly by appointment, so they'll be in his diary, on his desk. But he also had a steady flow of men on hard times. Sometimes women, who came for a handout.'

'Do you remember any particularly difficult person calling, or anyone who you might think would want to do him any harm?'

'Oh no. Mr Smart was the nicest and most gentle of men. But of course there were the down and outs,' she said. 'Hardly a day went by without a knock on the door. It was usually a man who looked a bit grubby, needed a shave, sometimes smelled of beer or something worse. Couldn't look me in the face. He would look down or to one side and say, "I want to see the vicar." If the vicar was in, I'd ask him to wait a moment. Then I would tell the vicar there's a "man of the road" to see him. The vicar would always come out in good humour. Sometimes he would deal with the man at the door. Chat with him several minutes, then put his hand in his pocket, give him something and then he would leave. Other times, the vicar would lead him into his study. And they might be together twenty minutes or more.'

'And would the "man of the road" leave happily?'

She hesitated. 'I think so. I didn't always see them go. Depended what I was doing.'

'The vicar gave them money?'

'Oh yes. And probably said a prayer and gave them a blessing. And in some cases, probably counselling. Not that they necessarily took any notice of him.'

Angel nodded. He squeezed the lobe of his ear between finger and thumb. He was looking for a murderer. Casual callers had been known to be guilty of murder and robbery. He needed to be sensitive to the possibility that the murder might have been spontaneous, committed by a man who saw something he wanted and the vicar was an obstacle in his way, preventing him from getting it.

'Can you recall the "men of the road" who called during the past week or so, Norma?'

'I don't know any actual names.'

'Tell me what you know.'

'Well, there is a big, ugly Irishman in a navy blue duffle coat. The vicar used to refer to him simply as "Irish John". He came only yesterday morning. The vicar took him into his study. They were there twenty minutes or so.'

'Did the vicar keep a record of such a visit?'

'I don't know.'

'And where did he keep the money he handed out?'

'In his pocket, I believe. We are not talking big sums, Inspector.'

Angel understood that and nodded in agreement. 'Anybody else who called during the past week or so?'

'There was a young man who had a crutch. He came last Friday morning. He's been many times before. He used to limp up the path. He also had bandages on one hand. I think the crutch and bandages were just for show. He had very fair hair and for a man, a lot of it. I recall the vicar once referring to him as "Blondie".'

'Blondie,' Angel said, nodding several times. 'And you'd recognize him if you saw him again?'

'Certainly would.'

'Anybody else?'

'There's a man who used to say that he wanted to see the priest to make a confession. Now he comes almost every week. I have heard the vicar call him Peter.'

'Peter,' Angel said thoughtfully and leaned back in his chair. 'Do you think you'd be able to pick out these characters, and indeed any others, from video pictures in our rogues' gallery?'

'Yes. I suppose so,' she said.

He turned to Crisp. 'Set that up, Trevor. See if Miss Ives can find us a suspect.'

Crisp and Norma Ives stood up to leave.

The phone rang. Angel reached out for it.

It was Harker. His voice was stark and emotionless. 'There's another triple nine,' he said. 'Looks like murder and it's another vicar.'

The half-brick in Angel's chest bounced on to his stomach and then back up.

'The Reverend Raymond Gulli,' Harker said. 'St Barnabas Church on Rotherham Road. Found by his wife in the last few minutes.'

Angel breathed in and then out, deeply, and said, 'Right, sir. I'll get straight on to it.' He replaced the phone.

Crisp stared at him. He knew Angel well enough to know that the call must have been significant.

Angel looked up at Crisp and said, 'Crack on with that job, Trevor. Use an interview room. And send Ahmed into me urgently.'

'Will do, sir.'

Angel then turned to Norma Ives and said, 'Thank you, Norma. We appreciate your help. Now if you will excuse me, something else important has cropped up.'

She smiled and went out, followed by Crisp.

As the door closed, Angel tapped Don Taylor's number into the phone and told him the news.

'Two priests within a few hours of each other?' Taylor said. 'Whatever is happening, sir?'

'Who knows?' Angel said. 'How long are you going to be at St Mary's?'

'We've just finished the crime scene routine, sir. We need Dr Mac to examine the body in situ and then have it moved. We need a couple of days to complete the house search.'

'I'll chase Dr Mac up, Don. In the meantime, I want you to scoot over to St Barnabas Church on Rotherham Road and examine the crime scene and the body of the Reverend Raymond Gulli. See if there's anything there we need to jump on immediately. I'll get DI Asquith to provide officers to secure both buildings overnight.'

'What? *Now*, sir?'

'Yes, Don. It means that you'll be at the crime scene of the murder of Raymond Gulli while it is still hot.'

'Yes, sir, but what about searching these premises?'

'Don't argue, lad. You can do that afterwards.'

Angel knew that Don Taylor didn't like working under pressure, or being broken off a job halfway through, but there were times when it was necessary. Over the years, Angel had found a foolproof way to speed him up.

'You can finish St Barnabas, check the immediate crime scene there, then come back to St Mary's tomorrow or as soon as you can fit it in. Or if that is too much for you and your team, we can ask West Yorkshire to help out.'

'No, sir. No, sir,' Taylor said. 'Don't do that. We'll manage.'

Angel nodded with sly satisfaction. It worked every time.

FOUR

Angel knocked and entered Harker's office. His face creased when his nose detected the distinctive smell of TCP.

'You wanted to see me, sir?'

'Oh, yes,' Harker said. 'Come in. Sit down.'

Angel sat down on a chair opposite his desk and peered at the ugly, bald man between two pillars comprising piles of papers, reports, circulars and boxes of Kleenex.

Harker coughed then said, 'I've just had a valuable and very disturbing phone call from a high-ranking officer in the Met. Known him twenty years or more. We trained together in the eighties. He went to London and I came here.'

He paused, briefly screwing up his face as if he had been transported to the cookhouse at Strangeways in a supernatural way and had caught a whiff of the gravy. After a moment, he breathed out, shook his head as if to get rid of the smell and said, 'He told me that a consignment of 250 boxes of pure cocaine in boxes purporting to be biscuits will be delivered to somebody in Bromersley by the end of the week. It is part of a consignment originating in the Caribbean but heading here via Spain.'

Angel was all ears. Information of this sort was often worth more than a judge's pension.

'He assures me,' Harker said, 'that the source is reliable but unofficial and therefore cannot be attributed. I suspect that it has come from a villain taken into custody down there who has exchanged this information for some concession. They're more lax down there about deals with defendants than we are up here. Typical of a big urban force.'

Angel blew out a yard of breath. 'That's a lot of cocaine, sir.'

Harker nodded. 'Make somebody in Bromersley very wealthy.'

Angel slowly shook his head. 'I don't like it, sir. I really do not like it. Is there anything else known? Such as method of transport?'

'Nothing, lad. I've told you all that he told me.'

'What sort of biscuits?'

Harker shook his head.

Angel wrinkled his nose and said, 'What retail or wholesale food businesses in Bromersley could take delivery of 250 boxes of biscuits at a single drop?'

'I would have thought only supermarkets and wholesalers.'

Angel nodded. 'It would be difficult getting a fake delivery into a national supermarket system and then immediately out, sir. They have their own vans, drivers, warehousemen, checkers and shelf fillers. They would all have to be fixed. And there are cameras and computerized checking systems all over the place. They are very concerned with their own security. But independent wholesalers are different. They are much smaller, and there are only two in Bromersley, privately owned. Both seem respectable, but you never know.'

'Nevertheless,' Harker said, 'have officers positioned clandestinely outside their premises tomorrow and Friday to monitor deliveries.'

'Right, sir. Is that all we can do?'

'I think so,' Harker said, looking down at the pile of letters and documents in front of him. 'Well, carry on, lad. I've a lot on.'

'There's something else, sir,' Angel said. 'It's important.'

Harker wasn't pleased. He shook his head rapidly several times then looked up and said, 'Oh? Whatever is it? Spit it out, then.'

'I'm concerned for the safety of the priests, vicars and ministers in the town, sir,' Angel said. 'As you know, two priests have been murdered today. Also, yesterday, strangely, a man wearing a dog collar murdered the ticket clerk, Harry Weston.'

Harker frowned as he wiped his purple nose. 'Mmm. Yes. It has not gone past me unnoticed. What is happening? Is it a rogue priest who has a vendetta against his fellow priests?'

'I don't know, sir. It's too early to say.'

'Or an atheist who thinks he is justified in murdering priests?'

Angel shook his head. 'It would be hard to believe that the man in the dog collar was actually the genuine article. But there are eighteen priests, ministers or vicars in the town. Six of them are women. And I was thinking that we should be providing them with personal protection.'

Harker screwed up his face, breathed in deeply, rubbed his chin then breathed out noisily. Eventually he said, 'That would require fifty-four officers, lad. Three shifts at eight hours a day. Can't afford that.'

Angel's jaw hardened. He wanted to ask how many people he could afford to have murdered, but he didn't. 'We need to do *something*, sir. If another priest is murdered, the force would certainly be heavily criticized.'

'You need to catch the murderer, lad,' Harker said. 'That's the thing to do.'

'SOCO haven't finished their examination of the first crime scene yet. So I can't get in there, and until I have a verbal report, I can't sensibly develop any lines of inquiry.'

'Well, you need to get your finger out, lad.'

Angel's heart began to thump. The knuckles of his fists whitened. He didn't like being criticized when he was doing all that was possible. 'I've men out on door-to-door around St Barnabas vicarage as we speak. St Mary's vicarage is screened from neighbours so there's no point in organizing a door-to-door round there. Also, I have an officer looking up all the characters who like to dress up as priests. I can't initiate any other inquiries until I have a report from SOCO and find out exactly what's happened.'

Harker lifted his hand and made a waving gesture. 'Well, I'll think about it, lad. Can't promise anything. I'll think about it. Carry on with your investigation. Now push off, I have a lot to do.'

Angel's face muscles tightened. He stood up. 'Right, sir,' he said. 'I've made my recommendation. I will now go and put it in writing and I'll send a copy to the chief constable.'

Harker looked up at Angel. He didn't like his last comment. 'You don't have to get smart with me, Angel.'

'Wouldn't dream of it, sir.'

'The chief constable knows about all my decisions, and as I have said before, is always one hundred per cent behind them. You understand?'

'I am sure he is, sir,' Angel said. He didn't necessarily believe that it was true but he thought it was diplomatic to say so. 'Perhaps you and the chief constable would like to reconsider the situation, sir?'

The muscles round Harker's chin tightened, his tiny black eyes stared hard into Angel's and the corners of his mouth turned down.

Harker then held up his hand and waggled his forefinger. 'Sit down, lad,' he said. After a few moments he spoke again, 'Perhaps we can advise the eighteen clergymen and women of the possible danger they might be in.'

'That's the *minimum* we must do. We must also provide some high-profile protection for each one.'

'Yes,' Harker said. 'They must be accompanied whenever they go outside.'

'No, sir,' Angel said, shaking his head. 'They are not in danger when they are *outside* among people. The two victims were in their homes, *inside*, alone, when they were murdered.'

'Oh? Well, yes. Anyway, let DI Asquith have a list of the eighteen,' Harker said, 'and I will see that they are all visited by patrolmen in the next hour. I will instruct Asquith to advise them, for the time being, not to stay in their houses at any time alone. They must always be with somebody. Also, all those who live on their own should move out immediately and stay with family or friends, or have friends in to stay with them. Also I will instruct Asquith to instigate a programme of visits to each house by patrol cars, at irregular times, say three times a day, for the next three days. And that will have to do.'

Harker looked at Angel for approval. Angel just looked back at him. He didn't think Harker's plan was anywhere near adequate but he sensibly reasoned that it would be a waste of time to press him further.

'I'll get that list to DI Asquith straightaway, sir,' Angel said.

He stormed down the corridor back to his office and slammed the door. He yanked open a drawer in his desk and took out a cream file. It was a list of the clergy in the town. He was perusing it when there was a knock at the door.

'Come in,' he said.

It was Crisp. He stood at the door, holding the handle. 'Are you free, sir?'

Angel looked up. 'Come in.' He closed the file, handed it to him and said, 'Find Ahmed. Give that to him. Tell him to take it to DI Asquith straightaway. It's urgent and he's expecting it. Well, he will be by the time Ahmed gets there.'

Crisp stared at him and then at the file.

'Go on, then, lad. Chop chop. Then come back.'

'Right, sir,' Crisp said. He rushed out and closed the door.

Angel reached out for the phone to speak to DI Asquith. He told him that a current list of local clergy was on the way to him. He also conveyed his fears for the surviving clergy, outlined Harker's plan in advance and enrolled Asquith's support in implementing it. Asquith promised to instigate the plan promptly and maintain his close, personal supervision of its execution.

Angel was a little cheered as he came to the end of the call. He then tapped in DC Scrivens' mobile number.

'Yes, sir,' Scrivens said promptly.

'Come to my office ASAP, lad. I've a job for you.'

'Right, sir.'

Angel was replacing the phone as Crisp returned.

'Come in, lad. Sit down. So Norma Ives didn't find anybody in the rogues' gallery?'

Crisp's eyebrows shot upwards. 'I'm afraid that's right, sir. How did you know?'

'If she had picked anybody out, you would have blurted it out, lad, just as soon as you had seen me. But you never said a word.'

Crisp's mouth dropped open. Angel knew him too well.

'Pity, that,' Angel said. 'Never mind. I have another job for you.'

'Yes, sir?' Crisp said.

'There are "gentlemen of the road" who regularly called at St Mary's vicarage for handouts from the vicar there, Sam Smart. Norma Ives said that a big, ugly Irishman in a navy blue duffle coat, known as "Irish John", called only yesterday morning. I expect he also called and some or all of them also called on Raymond Gulli at St Barnabas. Maybe the Irishman also called on the rest of the clergy in the town. Anyway, see what you can find out about him. Also see if you can find him on your travels, in which case, of course, bring him in. But be careful. He could be a murderer, the one we are looking for. All right?'

'Right, sir,' Crisp said as he got to his feet.

'And make sure your mobile is switched on.'

'Yes, sir,' he said.

He reached the door. Somebody outside knocked on it. Crisp frowned and opened it. It was Scrivens.

'Come in,' Angel said.

Scrivens came in as Crisp went out.

Angel told Scrivens that a consignment of cocaine packed as biscuits was destined to be delivered to one of the two food whole-salers in the town in the next few days, and instructed him to mount a covert surveillance of the premises of the two distributors.

'You'll need two cars and three men besides yourself,' Angel said. 'Don't do anything rash. There's a lot of money involved in this trans-action, several million pounds, so some big-time crooks, who could be armed, may be personally involved. So I don't want you to be visible. I want your teams just to act as eyes and ears. Monitor all vehicles as they call at the warehouses. Check them out with Swansea as they arrive. If they don't give them a clean bill of health, or if anything looks at all suspicious, report to me on my mobile. Photograph every vehicle, driver and crew, if you can. All right?'

Scrivens was young, full of enthusiasm and pleased to be given the responsibility to run such an important operation on his own. 'Right, sir,' he said brightly.

It was four o'clock when Angel drove the BMW up to SOCO's van outside St Barnabas Church. Two police Range Rovers, blue lights rotating, were standing in the taped-off churchyard. In the fading daylight, he saw a group of four uniformed police patrolmen in a huddle. One of them, PC Sean Donohue, car patrolman, who saw Angel's car arrive and stop at the kerbside, left the others, lifted up the tape and came up the path and through the church gates to meet him.

Angel lowered the car window, nodded towards the group and said, 'Having a mothers' meeting?'

'Just finished, sir,' Donohue said. 'Reporting in now.'

'Anybody see or hear anything?'

'Nobody *heard* anything, sir, but I spoke to a man who got a sighting of a man who could have been the murderer.'

Angel's heart began to beat out a Sousa march under his shirt.

Another possible eyewitness? It was the best news he'd had all day.

'Where is he, Sean?' he said as he got out of the car.

Donohue pointed up the road. 'It was the man in number eight, sir. Said he saw a man in a white gown, knocking on St Barnabas's vicarage door.'

Angel frowned. 'A white gown? What time was this?'

'He said about ten o'clock, sir.'

Angel's eyes steadied. The time fitted perfectly. Things were getting better. 'I want to speak to him,' he said.

Donohue nodded then led Angel along the pavement. Ahead on both sides of the street were long lengths of terraced houses.

As they walked, Angel said, 'What sort of a chap is this witness, Sean?'

'Elderly, sir, retired, used to work at the glassworks. Name of Cyril Wade.'

Angel nodded.

Donohue stopped at the fourth house on the left, which had a white plastic number eight screwed on to a creosoted paling gate. He knocked on the door.

The door opened. A small man looked up at the two policemen.

Donohue said, 'Mr Wade, sorry to bother you again. This is my boss, Detective Inspector Angel. Would you mind telling him what you saw outside the vicarage door this morning?'

Wade hesitated. 'Aye,' he said. 'You'd better come inside. It's cold with this door open.'

When the three men were seated in the tiny front room of the little house, the man began. 'I was a bit late getting up this morning. Well, I live on my own, I can do what I like, I reckon. When I got downstairs I remembered that I hadn't any milk, so I threw on some clothes and went out to the corner shop. I got a bottle and was coming back past the church gate when I thought that out of my eye corner I saw a strange figure at the vicarage door. Being a bit nosey, I stepped back and saw a man in a long bright shiny white coat knocking on the door. I thought it was odd. I gawped at him for a second, I suppose, then walked on.'

'You didn't see his face?'

'No. He had his back to me.'

'What else was he wearing?'

'I don't know. The white coat almost covered him.'

'Was it white towelling?'

'I don't think so.'

'Was it the sort of coat a surgeon or a scientist might wear?'

'No. Nothing like that.'

'You said it was a long bright shiny white coat.'

'That's right.'

'It wasn't a woman's dress, was it? It wasn't a man in a woman's dress? You get all sorts these days.'

Wade's expression answered the question.

'Not the sort of coat, or garment, you'd wear in the street?' Angel said.

'Oh no. Not round here anyway. They'd laugh you to scorn. It were white and shiny. Like a silk dressing gown, but better.'

'Did the man have a car or any means of transport?'

'I didn't see any.'

'Was the man short or tall?'

'Average.' Cyril Wade said.

Angel and Donohue exchanged glances. Angel rubbed his chin.

Cyril Wade suddenly shook his head irritably. 'Now look, I've told you all I know. Can't we leave it at that?'

Angel said, 'Mr Wade, you may have heard that the vicar of St Barnabas's has been murdered in the vicarage this morning. Well, it seems that you were passing the vicarage shortly before he was murdered and the man in the white gown may well have been the murderer.'

Wade's eyes shone. His mouth dropped open. 'I didn't know,' he said.

'So you will understand that we need to know every possible scrap of information that there is to know about that man. You see why every detail is so important to us?'

'Oh yes. Yes. But I think I've told you all I know.'

'And we are grateful, Mr Wade,' Angel said. 'Very grateful.' He looked at him, then said, 'And there is nothing else you can add to the description of the man in the white gown then?'

'No,' Wade said. 'Did I say he had very dark hair? Black probably?'

'Black hair,' Angel said, writing it on his notes. 'Anything else?'

'No. I don't think so.'

'Thank you, Mr Wade. Thank you very much. Now, I want to ask you about the poor victim. What do you know about the vicar and his wife?'

'I don't know nothing about them, really. Them and the church was more the wife's province, you know. I've not been to church since her funeral. I used to go regular when she was alive but somehow I lost interest since … and I drifted away.'

'What about the vicar, Raymond Gulli? What sort of a man was he?'

'Well, everybody round here spoke well of him. He does – he did – his share of visiting and his wife was always the first round if you were in any sort of trouble, you know.'

Angel rubbed his chin. 'Would you describe them as being well off?'

'They're better off than me, I suppose. I only have my pension. This place is tiny. Look at the size of the place they live in.'

'I wondered if Mr and Mrs Gulli might have had anything valuable around the house.'

'Valuable? You mean gold statues or oil paintings …'

'I mean money, jewellery, anything worth stealing.'

'Shouldn't think so. I never saw anything, anyway.'

'Well, thank you very much, Mr Wade. If you remember anything else you consider might be helpful, please contact me at the station.'

The man nodded, stood up and opened the door. It was getting dark.

The two policemen came out of the little house and Cyril Wade quickly closed his front door behind them.

As they walked the short distance along the pavement towards the church, Angel said, 'Thank you, Sean. That was a good piece of work.'

Donohue smiled. 'Do you think the man in the white coat is the murderer, sir?'

'Yes, lad. I do. The timing fits perfectly.'

'Well, what's the white coat all about then, sir? Doesn't it make him highly conspicuous?'

'It certainly does,' Angel said. 'I don't know what it's all about. I wish I did.'

He looked at his watch. It was too dark to read the dial. 'Have you got the time, Sean?'

'Ten to five, sir.'

'Your shift's almost over. It's time you were on your way to the station.'

'It is, sir. Unless you want me to stay on for anything?'

'No. No. You go. Good night, lad.'

'Good night, sir,' Donohue said, then rushed ahead of Angel along the pavement to the Range Rover.

Angel walked on slowly behind him. He was excited that he had a witness who had probably seen the back of Raymond Gulli's murderer. It wasn't much but it all helped to build a picture, and had come at a time when there was so little evidence arriving from SOCO or anywhere else.

He reached the church gate as the headlights of Donohue's Range Rover swept across the front of the church and the vehicle hurried away.

The night sky had become darker and the corner of the street quieter. The only vehicles outside the church were his BMW and SOCO's van. He turned to go through the church gate when unexpectedly from behind he heard footsteps and a breathless Irish voice say, 'You must be Inspector Angel. I'm Father Hugo Riley, the vicar of All Saints and Martyrs on Sebastopol Terrace.'

Angel stopped and turned round. 'Good evening, Father.'

'This is a dreadful state of affairs, young man, that priests are being cut down in this way. How is Mrs Gulli? Poor, dear woman that she is. I hope that somebody is with her. Have you found out yet who is responsible?'

'No, Father. The investigation has only just started. Mrs Gulli and her daughter are being comforted at a friend's house tonight. Perhaps you can assist us in our inquiries. Is there anybody you know who has a grudge against the clergy?'

'No, why would they? Are we not here to help the poor, the needy and the disadvantaged?' Riley said.

'I hope so, Father, but yesterday a man in a dog collar shot dead a ticket collector.'

'So I heard. It could not possibly have been a priest, Inspector. A man of the true God simply could not deliberately kill another man.'

'Is there any person, group, sect or organization that would want to murder the clergy of Bromersley?'

'I can't think of any, and I certainly hope not. I must say to you that my life as a priest is wholly committed to God. I am unmarried and live on my own. I had one of your officers there today, and because of these two murders, he gave me certain advice. But I told him, there was no way that I could leave the presbytery unattended. A parishioner may have need of me in the night. Nor could I bring in another priest as your superintendent has suggested. There is simply nobody available. Clergy are in very short supply, you know?'

'I'm sorry about that, Father. Police officers are also short on the ground. I strongly recommend you to compromise ... perhaps stay in a hotel for the next few days and nights.'

'*What?*' he said. 'Stay in the luxury of a hotel when so many of my parishioners are struggling to pay their bills and I am trying to preach the virtue of being frugal? I *don't* think so.'

'There is a murderer out there, Father Riley. He seems to be targeting priests. If you think you could still be useful to your flock dead then you *could* take the risk, I suppose. If not, then out of consideration for them, you should take all the steps necessary to stay alive. You do not have to stay at The Feathers. You don't even have to stay in Bromersley. There are probably several very comfortable guesthouses in Barnsley, Rotherham or Sheffield that might not be seen as excessive. We are hopeful that these measures are temporary and will take only a few days.'

'Mmm,' he said. 'Inspector, you may have a point. I must pray about it.'

'Well, don't be long about it, Father.'

Angel heard a door open behind him. He turned and saw a light shine through the open vicarage door and the silhouetted figure of DS Taylor in his disposable paper overalls coming out with a white box on a strap slung over his shoulder.

Angel turned back. 'If you'll excuse me, Father,' he said, 'I need to press on. Nice to have met you. Careful how you go, and remember what I told you.'

Angel reached out in the dark to shake the priest's hand. The man had an earnest grip but his hand was as cold as prison milk.

'Indeed I will,' Riley said. 'God bless you, Inspector Angel. May you find the murderer soon and may he be condemned to a life in purgatory. Good night.' Then the man in black turned swiftly away into the night, his cloak flowing behind him.

'Good night,' Angel said, then he went up to the SOCO's van.

Taylor heard him approach and flashed a torch in his face. 'It's you, sir,' he said. 'We've completed the scene of crime.'

'I'll take a look, then,' Angel said.

'The body's gone,' Taylor said as he held the door open for him. 'Dr Mac saw it in situ. The murder took place in the little office in the vestry. One shot in the chest, through a cushion to deaden the noise. Same as Samuel Smart, sir.'

Angel nodded and said, 'The same man murdered both priests. Through a cushion? It's a long time since anyone used that old trick. Shell case?'

'One, sir. .32. No prints.'

Angel sniffed then nodded knowingly.

Taylor led Angel into a tiny room with only a desk, a chair and a filing cabinet in it. 'The body was found on the floor, squashed between the chair and the desk.'

Angel peered at the space. He saw dried blood on the desk drawer and the carpet. He quickly looked over the front of the desk drawers, the chair, the cushion on the chair, and the floor. His eyes took in everything. He didn't linger over the scene. There would be a hundred or more pics available to him from the SOC photographer in the morning.

'There was more room in Samuel Smart's office, sir,' Taylor said. 'His body was full length on the carpet. Otherwise this seems to be the same layout and MO.'

'Any sign that Raymond Gulli or Samuel Smart had retaliated or had any actual physical contact at all with the murderer?'

'No, sir. But we have a small sample of white thread lifted from Raymond Gulli's left coat sleeve that I think must have come from the murderer. There is no other source of that fabric in the room from which it could have originated. I will send it off to Wetherby – see what the lab boys can tell us.'

Angel's face brightened. 'A man was seen in a white gown, dress or garment of some sort outside the door at ten o'clock this morning.'

Taylor looked up. 'I was going to say the time of death of Raymond Gulli was between 0930 and 1100 hours this morning.'

Angel nodded. A few pieces were fitting into the jigsaw.

'There's something else, Don,' Angel said. 'The calibre of bullet used to kill Harry Weston, Samuel Smart *and* Raymond Gulli is a .32. Check and see if the *same* gun was used in all three murders.'

'Right, sir.'

FIVE

Angel arrived in his office as usual at 8.28 a.m. the following morning, Wednesday 13 January, and was followed in by Ahmed, who had been watching out for him. He was carrying a large brown envelope.

'Got that artist's impression of the murderer of Harry Weston, sir,' Ahmed said.

'Right, let's have a look,' Angel said. He quickly took off his coat and sat down at his desk.

Ahmed carefully pushed to one side the pile of post and reports that always seemed to be there, withdrew the large card out of the envelope and placed it on the desk.

Angel looked at the pencil drawing. He licked his bottom lip with the tip of his tongue as he did so.

The drawing showed a very ordinary-looking man of about forty, wearing a dog collar. It simply looked like a good, wholesome, respectable priest.

Angel considered it to be an excellent portrait, and at the back of his mind he thought he might have seen such a man very recently. He scratched his head and hoped that it was a fair representation of what the murderer really looked like.

'Make six copies and try this picture on the Automatic Criminal Recognition site. See if it throws anybody up. You never know.'

'Right, sir,' Ahmed said and went out.

Angel leaned forward and reluctantly pulled the pile of post towards him. He began fingering through the envelopes, trying to determine what might be urgent and what might be inconsequential. He didn't get far. His fingers gradually stopped moving. His mind wasn't on it; instead it was on the portrait of the murderer. He was back to wondering if he had ever seen the face before when the phone rang. It broke the spell. He reached out for it.

It was Taylor. 'The markings on the shell cases *are* identical, sir,' he said.

Angel's head went up. The obvious implication was that the same person had murdered all three victims. And that was probably exactly what had happened, but it might not be so. It could have been three different killers using the same gun. Or maybe two. You learn in the detection of crime never to take anything for granted. You need to prove the situation step by step. But for the moment, he intended to assume that the same killer murdered all three victims.

'Thanks, Don,' Angel said. 'That's great. Where are you now?'

'Back at St Mary's vicarage. We're trying to catch up.'

'Yes, of course. In your searching there, see if you come across a book or notes or any reference at all to a "Discretionary Fund". It's a note of what the vicar might have handed out to tramps, needy cases or scroungers who knock on his door.'

'Right, sir. Will do.'

He replaced the phone and returned to fingering through the envelopes in the post. He managed to filter out circular letters with literature selling police uniforms, hard-wearing boots, union pensions, savings schemes, and insurance against everything such as being trampled on by a herd of elephants, stung by a swarm of bees, injured by a meteorite falling out of the sky or death from contracting beri beri. He promptly shredded the pages that included any station officers' names in the address or text. He had just returned to the pile when there was a knock at the door. It was DS Carter.

'Is it convenient to report on Harry Weston, sir?'

'Yes, Flora. Come in. Sit down.'

He had been thinking that it was about time she checked in. 'What you got?'

'It's not been easy, sir.'

He pulled a face. 'Come on, lass,' he said. 'If it had been easy, I would have given the job to a schoolboy for a bag of toffees.'

'Well, Harry Weston lived on his own. He was a bit of a loner. He went to the pub across the road from where he lived. He used to go in there and take a girl with him for a drink, regularly. Sometimes, he'd buy a bottle of sherry and they'd go back to his place for an hour or two. He'd been doing that Friday and Saturday nights for a year or so. Then suddenly he stopped. I found out the girl's name. It was Madeleine Rossi.'

Angel pursed his lips.

'She lived in the next street,' Carter said. 'I went round there to speak to her. A man I took to be her father answered the door. When he heard that I was from the police, he told me I had the wrong address and slammed the door in my face.'

'That would be Angus Rossi, a loud-mouthed Scot,' Angel said.

'That's him, sir.'

'Used to be a regular customer here,' Angel said. 'Done time for robbery and handling, but he's kept his nose clean these past few years. I wonder who's been treading on his corns?' Angel considered the matter a few moments then added, 'Wonder what he's got to hide?'

Carter shrugged. 'Anyway, I eventually caught up with Madeleine Rossi. She works part-time behind the grille at the bookies on Dunscroft Street. She seemed straightforward enough. She said that Harry had been her steady boyfriend for about six months, but that he wasn't exactly a firecracker. That was *her* word. Nevertheless, she said she was devastated when she heard on the news that he had been murdered. She said that she had not been aware that he had any other friends, either male or female. He would only take her out on Saturday and Sunday nights, he had said, because he didn't like clubbing, and the other nights he liked to stay in his flat to practise on his guitar. Then about a fortnight ago, a friend of Madeleine told her she'd seen Harry Weston out with another girl in the *Scheherazade.*'

Angel nodded. 'She wouldn't like that.'

'She was furious,' Carter said. 'She had it out with Harry and the end result was that a fortnight ago they packed it in. Now, she said, she already has a better-looking bloke twice as good as Harry Weston.'

Angel nodded. 'Was Harry Weston ever seen with a man about forty wearing a dog collar?'

'No, sir. Nobody I spoke to ever saw him in the company of anybody except Madeleine Rossi and then, latterly, this woman from the *Scheherazade.*'

Angel nodded, leaned back in his chair and said, 'And was Harry Weston a member of a church?'

'No, sir. I checked with the vicars of the two nearest churches to where he lived at the junction of Shaw Street and Sheffield Road, and the Roman Catholic church in town, and he was not known to any of them.'

Angel rubbed his chin.

'The stationmaster, Deri Evans,' she added, 'told me that he came to work at the railway station straight from school as a junior clerk. He had never worked anywhere else. Also he said he didn't know of any friends that he had. He'd never seen him with anybody.'

Angel continued rubbing his chin and looking across the desk at the bare wall, his eyes unfocussed. Something was on his mind.

Carter looked at him and wondered if he had listened to the last part of her report.

'Do you think, sir,' she said, 'it is worthwhile chasing up the girl Harry Weston is supposed to have taken to the *Scheherazade*?'

'Yes I do, lass,' he said, suddenly rising to his feet. 'I most certainly do. Crack on with it,' he said as he reached out for his coat. 'What number Mount Street did you say Angus Rossi lives at?'

Seven minutes later, Angel was knocking on the front door of 12 Mount Street. It was answered by a big Scotsman who glared at him and said, 'What do *you* want?'

'Aren't you going to ask me in, Angus?'

'Have you got a warrant?' Rossi said.

'Do I need a warrant just to *talk* to you?'

'That means you havna. Take a friggin' hike,' Rossi said and stepped back into the house.

'I can just do that, Angus. But with your past record, I might just think you had something to hide. In which case, I could be back here in about half an hour with a warrant and a dozen officers, and we might just have to take this house to pieces brick by brick.'

Rossi hesitated then stepped forward. 'Do I look stupid, Angel? I got the hint you were getting on my back when one of your lackeys called yesterday to see Madeleine. Don't you think that if I had had anything to hide from the police, I would have had it buried some-where by now?'

Angel shrugged. 'Does that mean I get to come in? Or must we both stand here like this until we get pneumonia?'

Angus Rossi stared at him for a moment, then grunted something unintelligible, released his grip of the door handle, turned round and went into the house. Angel followed him in and closed the door. They arrived in the small kitchen, where there was a roaring fire in an old black iron range.

When Angel saw the red-hot coals, his face brightened. He held out his cold hands briefly in their direction and said, 'That's better.'

Rossi sat down, pointed to a chair opposite him and said, 'Well, sit yourself doon, but dunna make yourself too comfortable, Angel, because you're not stopping there long.'

'I never waste time, Angus. You should know me better than that.'

Rossi sniffed then said, 'I know that you think you're somebody these days, Angel. You get mentioned in the papers. They write about you in magazines. They say you've a reputation of always getting your man, like that Canadian Mountie. You must be worried when you get a particularly difficult case and you aren't getting nowhere?'

Angel eyed him for a few seconds then said, 'That's why I'm here. I thought my friend Angus knows what's going on. I'll go down there and maybe he'll tell me.'

Rossi turned the corners of his mouth down. 'I'm no copper's nark,' he said.

'It's like this,' Angel said. 'A young man called Harry Weston was shot dead the day before yesterday.'

'Aye. Well, that's nothing to do with me.'

'I understand that your daughter had been keeping regular company with him.'

'Aye, and she could have done a lot better for herself. He was a pretty useless piece of humanity and a two-timing little bastard as well. While he was taking Madeleine out, sweet-talking her, and who knows whatever else, he had got some other bird up the duff and was parading her round the *Scheherazade.*'

Angel looked up when he heard the news.

Rossi saw that he had made an impression. 'You didn't know about that, eh?' he said. 'Well, anyway, Madeleine gave Harry Weston the old heave-ho two weeks ago. What happened to him after that has nothing to do with her. She's well set up now with another young man who has far more about him. So she doesn't want to know anything more about Harry Weston, thank you.'

Angel nodded. He was prepared to accept that for now.

'Is that it?' Rossi said.

'No,' Angel said. 'A First Security Delivery Services van was stopped and robbed of four million on Monday morning. What do you know about that?'

Rossi's eyes shone. He flashed his uneven, brown teeth and said, 'Not a thing.'

'Where were you at ten o'clock on Monday morning?'

'Here. Right here. And no, I can't prove it. But then again, you can't prove I was anywhere else.'

Angel knew that was true.

He looked carefully at Rossi and said, 'I'm also looking for a man loose on the streets wearing his collar the wrong way round, like a vicar. But he isn't a vicar … and he carries a handgun. I have reason to believe that he has murdered three men. What can you tell me about him?'

'Not a thing,' Rossi said.

Angel looked round the room. He was aware that Rossi was following his eyes. It was a clean, tidy, warm and comfortable little kitchen. The Scotsman didn't seem to be wanting for anything.

'The wife still working, Angus?'

'I have no wife. She buggered off a couple of years back. Good riddance.'

Angel rubbed his chin. He knew that Rossi's daughter, Madeleine, would be bringing in a wage.

'In work, are you, Angus?'

'Aye,' Rossi said. 'As a matter of fact, I am. *Full time.*'

Angel blinked. He was surprised. 'Full time?' he said. 'Well, why aren't you there just now then?'

'Wednesday is my day off.'

Angel thought about it a while then said, 'What do you do?'

'I work at Grogan's. I'm a van salesman.'

Grogan's ice-cream vans were to be seen all round Bromersley. Outside schools, in the market, at the football ground, wherever there were crowds of people.

Angel frowned then he said, 'What, in January?'

'All the year round, if you know where to go. Kids always want ice cream, and so do many grown-ups.'

Angel nodded. He supposed he was right.

'And now,' Rossi said, leaping to his feet, 'Detective Inspector Angel, your time is up.'

'Right, Angus,' he said, also now standing. 'Didn't take long, did it? Thanks for the warm and the information. I can see myself out.'

Rossi was not pleased. He glared at him, his eyes like two fried eggs in a frying pan. 'I didna give you *any* information.'

Angel shrugged. 'Whatever you say, Angus. Whatever you say.'

Angel returned to his office. He slumped down in the chair. He rubbed his hand across his mouth several times. Rossi was certainly involved in some nefarious activity: he was touchy on every crime Angel had mentioned. However the only hard information that he had acquired from him was that the girl associated with Harry Weston was pregnant.

Flora Carter was in the CID office. She saw Angel pass the door and followed him into his office. 'I've just come back from the *Scheherazade*, sir,' she said. 'I spoke to the cellarman. He said that the girl Harry Weston has been seen around with was a Felicity Kellerman. A professional singer. Sings in local pubs, clubs and what have you.'

'She's up the duff, isn't she?' he said.

Carter blinked. 'Yes, sir. How did you know that?'

Angel smiled to himself. 'Seven or eight months gone?' he said.

'That's what I was told, sir. Got her address and phone number from the office. I phoned her there and on her mobile, but there was no reply. Do you want me to follow it up, sir?'

'Oh yes, and find out the identity of Madeleine Rossi's new man. It might not matter at all, but you never know.'

There was a knock at the door.

'Come in,' Angel called.

It was Ahmed. He was carrying a cream paper file. He looked from one to the other. 'Busy, sir?'

'Come in, lad. Sergeant Carter is just leaving.'

'Right, sir,' she said with a smile.

'Keep in touch,' he called after her.

'Right, sir,' she said as she closed the door.

Ahmed produced a sheet of A4 from the file and handed it to Angel.

'Men posing as clergymen, sir,' he said. 'All have served their sentences, believed to be still alive and living in the area.'

Angel blinked and glanced down the sheet. After a few moments he began reading from it aloud: 'Seven persons posing as clergymen in the town who have been charged over the past eight years for various offences. Two with indecent exposure, two stealing under-wear from clothes lines, one attempting to extract money by fraud, one being drunk, disturbing the peace, stealing a bicycle and a pound of plums, and one inciting a minor to perform two acts of lewdness.' He looked up at Ahmed and said, 'Well, thank you, lad.'

'Their full names, last known addresses and telephone numbers are lower down, sir.'

'Yes, Ahmed. Leave it with me. I have taken it in. Mentally ticked off the names. None of them resonate with our present inquiries. I am hopeful that we won't have to start scratching around looking into this lot.'

Before Ahmed could answer, the phone rang. Angel reached out for it. It was the civilian telephone switchboard operator. 'There's an excitable Irishman on the line, Inspector, asking to speak to you,' she said. 'Says he's a priest. Doesn't sound like a priest to me. Calls himself Father Hugo Riley.'

Angel's jaw muscles tightened.

It irritated him to hear the station operator voicing an opinion on the standing of callers to his office as if it was her job to vet them like some upper-class receptionist at a private surgeon's consulting rooms.

He blew out a length of air, then said, 'Put Father Riley through.'

'Yes, sir.'

There was a click and he said, 'Inspector Michael Angel speaking.'

A loud, spirited voice said, 'Father Hugo Riley speaking. I have been out of my house and have just returned, Inspector. In that time, that evil monster has been here. That son of Satan has been in and through my church vestry and presbytery like a plague of locusts.'

'Are *you* all right, Father?'

'Apart from seething with rage, I am very well indeed, my son.'

'What time did you go out?'

'Just past nine. This place has been empty this past three hours. I have been visiting two of my elderly housebound parishioners.'

'Where are you actually speaking from?'

The priest's eyebrows shot up. 'The church vestry as it happens, Inspector.'

Angel had a disturbing thought. 'Are you alone?'

'As I shall be on the day of judgement, Inspector, yes. Why?'

'Well, get out of there, Father. Go to where there are people. There's a pub somewhere round there, isn't there?'

'Next door. But I am not afraid of the fiend, Inspector. I would relish an encounter with the evil one. He would not get past me.'

'He has a gun, Father Hugo. He has already murdered two of your brother priests and possibly another man.'

There was a pause.

'Very well,' Riley said. 'I may wait outside the public house, The Fisherman's Rest. I can keep an eye on the vestry door from there.'

'And don't touch anything. There might be fingerprints. I'll come straightaway. Your church is All Saints and Martyrs, near Canal Road, isn't it?'

'It's on Sebastopol Terrace, parallel to Canal Road, Inspector.'

Angel knew exactly where the church was. It was in the centre of Bromersley's poorest houses, next to Canal Road's red-light district, where the most crime and the most domestic incidents happened.

'We'll be there in five minutes, Father. Now, please, get out of the building.'

'Very well. I will wait on the pub steps.'

Angel ended the call, then tapped in a nine. As it began to ring out, he turned to Ahmed and said, 'Quick. Have you your mobile on you?'

'Yes, sir.'

'Well, ring Don Taylor. Ask him to attend All Saints and Martyrs Church, Sebastopol Terrace, parallel to Canal Road, with a fingerprint man and a photographer urgently.'

Ahmed nodded then began to tap a number into his mobile.

Angel's phone was answered.

'Control room. Duty sergeant.'

'This is DI Angel. Send an armed unit to All Saints and Martyrs church on Sebastopol Terrace, next door to The Fisherman's Rest. The property has been broken into. Intruder may still be on premises and may be armed with a handgun. Also, direct four uniformed officers to rendezvous with me there for house-to-house inquiries.'

'Right, sir. Call timed at 1218 hours.'

Angel banged down the phone, snatched his coat from the hook and put it on.

Ahmed finished delivering his message to SOCO's DS Taylor and closed his mobile.

'Everything all right?'

'On their way, sir.'

'I'm off,' he said and ran out of the office, down the green corridor, past the cells, through the back door to the police park to the BMW. He pointed the car bonnet towards Wakefield Road. A few minutes later, he turned on to Sebastopol Terrace, a cobble-stoned, grimy backstreet. He could see the cross at the top of the church in front of a cold blue sky and below, next door, the front of The Fisherman's Rest. The BMW shook as he progressed rapidly down the road, bouncing through the potholes. As he reached the public house, the tall, dark figure of Father Hugo Riley, with eyes shining like a cat's in headlights, dashed out and waved the car down.

Angel lowered the window.

'Have you seen anybody, Father?' Angel said.

'The evil one must have departed, Inspector,' he said. 'Not a soul has appeared out of the church, the vestry or the vicarage since I arrived.'

A dark-skinned, grey-haired woman in a red dressing gown, thin bare ankles and red slippers was jumping up and down and calling excitedly out from the open door of a terraced house opposite. 'Father Riley! Father Riley!'

The priest heard her, turned away from the car, held up his long arm in acknowledgement and ran across the road. Angel got out of the car and followed him.

'My dear lady,' Riley said. 'Whatever's the matter?'

'A man has been looking for you, Father,' she said, pulling the thin dressing gown across her chest and up to her chin. 'He tried the vestry door and the front door of the church then he went round the back.'

'For me?' Father Riley said. 'Did he ask for me by name?'

'I didn't speak to him, Father. I saw him trying the doors so I assumed he was looking for you.'

'What is your name, ma'am?' Angel said.

'Mrs Injar Patel,' she said. 'I am a widow.'

Riley frowned and said, 'I do not know you. You do not come to my church?'

Her eyes looked at him in a very doting way. 'No. But everybody knows you, Father,' she said.

Angel said, 'I can tell you that Father Riley has recently returned from visiting two of his parishioners and discovered that somebody – almost certainly the man you saw – has illegally entered the church and the vestry and probably the vicarage. And I am a police inspector investigating the case.'

Her jaw dropped.

'Did he actually speak to you, Mrs Patel?' Angel said.

'Oh no. I called out to him but he didn't take any notice. He probably didn't hear me.'

'What time was this?' Angel said.

'Just after nine it was.'

'What did he look like?'

'It was very strange. He was wearing a long white garment that almost covered him.'

Angel pulled a face. He bit his bottom lip. He ran his hand through his hair.

It was frustrating to hear again about a white garment and not know what it was.

'What else can you tell me about him, Mrs Patel?' he said.

The lady shrugged. 'What else is there to say? He had dark hair, I believe. And the way he ran from the church door to the vestry door and then round the back made me think he was not old. I didn't see his face. That's about all I know, Inspector.'

'Did you see what he wore under the white garment?'

'I don't know. Something dark. His suit, I suppose.'

'Did you notice his shoes?'

'No.'

'Did you notice anything else significant about him? Was he big, small, short, tall or fat?'

'He was ... about average, I'd say.'

'Did he come in a car?'

'I didn't see a car, Inspector. I didn't see him arrive. I first saw him when he was trying the church door.'

The sound of motor vehicle engines and the squeal of brakes caused Angel to turn round.

Two Range Rovers in khaki with white on black POLICE signs on the front and back had driven in from Wakefield Road and stopped at the front of the church opposite. It was the Firearms Special Unit. Six men in body armour and helmets piled out of the vehicles. Five of them were carrying G36 Heckler and Koch rifles; the sixth, DI White, had a G17 Glock pistol holstered at his waist.

Coincidentally, at the same time, from the opposite direction, a high-profile police patrol car arrived and four uniformed constables emerged from it.

Angel turned back to Mrs Patel and Father Riley. 'Thank you for your help. Excuse me. I must go,' he said, then he dashed across the road.

It was almost two hours later when Angel received a call on his office phone from Detective Inspector Waldo White, of the FSU.

'We've been all the way through the church, the vestry and the vicarage, Michael, and no signs of the intruder. He must have been and gone before we arrived. The place is in one helluva mess, though. Every cupboard, cabinet and wardrobe door is wide open. The intruder apparently forced entry through a kitchen window at the rear. The place is a tip.'

'Right. Thank you, Waldo. Sorry to have called you out.'

'Not at all. Gives us something to do and keeps my team on their toes.'

'Did you see anything of a SOCO team?'

'Don Taylor and his lads? They went in as we came out,' White said.

'Thank you, Waldo. Goodbye,' he said and replaced the phone.

Angel went straightaway down to Sebastopol Terrace to All Saints and Martyrs Church, eager to see what SOCO may have found. He stopped the car on the road in front of the church. As he got out of the BMW, Father Hugo Riley came out of Mrs Patel's front door opposite and ran across the street towards him.

'Inspector Angel!' he called. 'I've been watching out through Mrs Patel's front window. She has generously provided me with warm shelter, a cup of tea and incessant chatter. And I can positively report that nobody has come out of any of my church building doors except your armed commandos. I presume the evil one has fled. Am I allowed back in my own church and home yet?'

'Only briefly,' Angel said, 'to see how things are, and if you stay close to me and keep your hands in your pockets.'

Father Riley blinked, lifted up his head and said, 'I hope that I will be permitted to talk?'

'I have never yet found a way of stopping a priest talking,' Angel said.

Riley's face straightened. 'Speaking God's truth from the pulpit to a captive congregation on a Sunday is the only luxury a poor priest has. Would you take that away from him?'

'I suppose not,' Angel said with a smile.

They reached the vestry door. The priest reached out to open the door by the handle but Angel quickly pushed him gently to one side and promptly called out, 'Hands in pockets, Father! There might be prints on there.'

Riley shook his head several times quickly and said, 'Oh dear. Oh dear. Sorry.' His hands disappeared under his cloak.

Angel clenched his fist and banged on the door.

There was the sound of the turn of a key and the door was opened by DS Taylor.

Angel quickly introduced the priest to the SOCO man then said, 'Found anything, lad?'

'Not yet, sir. Intruder or intruders wore woollen navy blue gloves, so far. Back window glass and frame damaged to gain entry and exit.'

Father Riley peered over Angel's shoulder through the open door into the vestry and saw the wardrobe and cupboard doors open and all the vestments and contents thrown around the floor in disordered heaps. 'Great heavens above,' he said. 'Looks like it's been hit by the storms of hell.'

'Is there any damage?' Angel said.

'Only the kitchen window, sir, I believe,' Taylor said. 'The vestry, the vicarage and the church have obviously been vigorously searched and left in the same state as St Mary's and St Barnabas's.'

'Right, Don,' Angel said. 'Let me know when you are through.'

'Sir,' Taylor said and he closed the door and locked it.

As Angel and Riley turned away, Riley said, 'Why did the evil monster have to make such a mess in my vestry like that? There is nothing in there he would want – only vestments, candles, my books and service papers. Why make such a mess? May the monster be turned into a pillar of salt.'

Angel's eyes twinkled as he heard the priest's comment. 'I thought good Christians forgave their enemies?' he said.

'So they do. So they do. Who said I was a *good* Christian, Inspector? If I was a good Christian, I wouldn't need the church to discipline me, now would I? And I know that before the day is out, I will have to retract all the bad things I have wished upon this wretched sinner, and ask forgiveness, and that will not be easy.'

Angel reflected on what Riley had said and acknowledged the priest's predicament with a nod.

As they reached the pavement, Angel said, 'Are you sure there's nothing in there that a thief would find valuable? Anything he could sell, perhaps to buy drugs?'

'If there was anything in there *that* valuable, Inspector, I would have taken it myself, sold it and used the money for more pressing things like food, heating and shelter. This is a poor parish. Many of my parishioners have a hard time, I can tell you.'

'Three churches, vestries and vicarages ... all three where the incumbent was a man ... broken into ... Do you realize that if you had not been out visiting this morning, you would probably have been murdered?'

Riley's expression did not change. 'The Good Lord, apparently, does not require my soul just yet,' he said.

Angel nodded and rubbed his chin. 'Somebody wants something – or has found and taken something – from these three churches. But what is it? The intruder wants it so badly that in two of the break-ins, he murdered the priests.'

'Yes. Bless their souls and comfort their loved ones. And two more worthy men you couldn't wish to break bread with. I notice that the evil one has not approached churches where there are *women* priests, and there are six in this town, Inspector. Now I wonder why that would be.'

Angel shook his head. 'Could be coincidence.'

Riley frowned.

Angel looked straight into his face. 'I'm looking for a motive, Father, and you're not helping. In some jammy churches sometimes there is a treasure by some famous artist ... a painting, a triptych, or a silver chalice or paten, Georgian or older.'

'There's nothing like that in All Saints, Inspector. If there had been, the church wardens and I would have sold it to pay for a new boiler and eight radiators. The other churches would have done the same thing, I am thinking.'

A vehicle rattled past them. It was an ice-cream van, bouncing here and there in the potholes left by the heavy snow. Angel looked round and noticed it was one of Grogan's. He stared at the number plate.

Riley noticed his interest. 'Is that poor ice-cream man in trouble, then?'

'No,' Angel said, frowning. 'But would you buy ice cream on a freezing cold day like this, Father?'

'I wouldn't, but children will eat ice cream regardless of the weather. There's an ice-cream van up and down here all the time. I believe it does a roaring trade.'

SIX

Angel took his leave of Father Riley and returned to his office. He hung up his coat and turned back to his desk, when there was a knock at the door.

It was Ahmed. 'I've had one result with that artist's picture on the Automatic Criminal Recognition site, sir.'

Angel's head shot up.

'Peter King,' Ahmed said.

Angel blinked, then pulled a face like a man who had overdone the Colman's on his ham. 'Peter King?'

'Isn't he the man who is always confessing, sir?'

He was, and it made Angel furious. King had taken to confessing to almost every serious crime that came along.

Angel leaned forward, picked up the phone and tapped in a six.

'Control room,' a voice said.

'Angel here. I want you to bring a Peter King in ... for questioning. He lives at – or hangs around – the bottom end of Sebastopol Terrace.'

'Peter King, sir? We know where he can usually be found.'

Angel replaced the phone and then rubbed his mouth and jaw roughly. He looked up at Ahmed. 'Did you want anything else, lad?'

'Yes, sir. I'm ready to print off that artist's drawing, sir. You'll want to add a caption?'

'Yes,' he said. He thought about it for a second, then said, 'This man wanted for the murder of Harry Weston, railway ticket clerk, Bromersley, the Reverend Samuel Smart of St Mary's Church, Bromersley, and the Reverend Raymond Gulli of St Barnabas Church, Bromersley, on January 11 and 12, 2010. Any information to DI Angel, Bromersley Police Station. Got it?'

'Yes sir. How many do you want, sir?'

'You'd better make it seventy, lad. One for everybody in the station and a few left over. See that every constable gets one. And see that it is *put into his hand*, not left around in a pile to be picked up or left there as his fancy takes him, and then what's not been taken, used as betting slips for Brian the bookie.'

Ahmed couldn't prevent a tiny smile developing. He didn't realize that Angel knew that some of the lads sneaked out and placed bets with the bookie in the next street.

There was a knock at the door.

'Come in,' he called.

It was DS Carter.

He pointed to her to come in and sit down.

He looked back at Ahmed. 'Take a copy down to the *Bromersley Chronicle*. I'll have a word with the editor. I'm sure he'll run it.'

'Right, sir,' Ahmed said.

'Is that it, lad?'

Ahmed nodded. He rushed out and closed the door.

Angel turned to Flora Carter. 'Now then, lass, did you catch up with Felicity Kellerman?'

Carter smiled. 'I've brought her in, sir. To see you. She's outside. I thought you might like to interview her yourself?'

'Felicity Kellerman?' Angel said as he scratched his head. 'Yes. All right. Bring her in.'

Flora Carter went to the door and returned half a minute later with a small woman who waddled into the office. She stuck out her huge stomach proudly though she looked uncomfortable. She was dressed in black, with lots of strings of beads round her neck, big rings on her fingers and dangly earrings longer than a hangman's rope in her delicate ears. Shiny bits of black fringe, decorating her dress, flashed here and there at the slightest movement.

Angel blinked when he saw her. He stood up. 'Pleased to meet you, Miss Kellerman,' he said. 'Please sit down.'

'Sure thing,' she said.

They looked at each other very closely.

Flora Carter said, 'I'll go and see to that other job, sir. If that's all right?'

Angel nodded.

Flora Carter went out and closed the door.

Felicity Kellerman said: 'You that big-time Inspector Angel that always gets his man? Wow! I heard of you. Now I seen you. That's real great,' she said with a smile as she eased herself gently into the chair. 'Ever thought of going on tour?' she continued. 'You could get second top billing after Johnny Cash if you didn't mind travelling, you know. Make a mint of money. Do you mind me asking, Inspector, can you sing? Or dance? Can you handle a rope?'

Angel shook his head. He had noticed that sometimes, but not always, she spoke like Dolly Parton.

'You could learn fire eating, or plate spinning,' Felicity Kellerman said.

He shook his head again. 'I'm very happy here, miss, doing what I do, thank you.'

She nodded.

He could see that she had a pretty face when she smiled and a beautiful figure, even when pregnant.

'You may know that I am looking into the shooting of young Harry Weston,' Angel said.

'Terrible,' she said. 'Oh my God. Terrible. Poor Harry. I told him he needed some crystal near him. In his pocket would have been ideal. I guess he didn't have any. I told him many times. It would have been his protection against the evil one.'

The use of the words 'evil one' made Angel blink. 'Who do you mean? Who is the evil one?'

'Ah well, a person or spirit who wishes anyone evil,' she said. 'In Harry's case the man with the shooter. Do you have any crystal on you, Inspector?'

'I don't go along with that, Miss Kellerman.'

'I see a light around your head, the colour of amethyst. I guess amethyst is your colour and I guess your stone. I expect your birthday is in February, Inspector?'

Angel gasped. It was. He was surprised that she knew, and a little uneasy. He had no intention of confirming what she said. She probably knew the date as well. Looked it up on a biography on the internet or something like that. He didn't want to encourage this line of talk.

'I'll send you a piece of amethyst. It will protect you. No charge. My treat.'

'Please don't, Miss Kellerman. I want to talk to you about Harry.'

'Poor Harry. Yes.'

'Tell me all you know about Harry.'

'He was a Sagittarian. Fourteenth. Born on the cusp. Lovely young man. But nothing was ever going to be straightforward for him.'

Angel ran his hand through his hair. With voice slightly raised he said, 'How did you first meet him?'

'I used to work all over, you know, with my partner, Ben Wizard. We covered the States, the southern parts of Canada, Ireland and most of the UK together. Then last March, we split up. He went back to the States and I worked my way around on my own wherever my agent booked me a gig. I came to Bromersley on the 28 March to do a gig at the *Scheherazade*. After I had done my second spot I went into the bar and standing next to me was Harry Weston. I knew straightaway that he was a Sagittarian. We got chatting and enjoyed a glass or two of real ale. He told me about his interest in the music business and the guitar. Later I heard him play. He was pretty darned good too. He said he wanted coaching to bring him up to professional standard. He was fed up with the railway job. He wanted to leave it and make a career in music. Tell the truth, Inspector, I needed a friend and I needed some company. I had intended working until my baby was born, but I'm just too big. Can't sling a guitar around in front of this any more, so I thought I would put down some roots here in Bromersley. Rented a nice apartment. The rent's a bit high, but it faces south and has the right aura. I have a couple of gigs then I have it in mind to rest my voice and hang up my guitar in Bromersley at least until after baby is born. Then I'll see how I go.'

'But what about Harry Weston? Did you have a relationship with him?'

'If you mean did I sleep with him ... I'll not answer that. Damn it, I'm ten years older than he is. Anyway, he never asked me. I think he saw me as an elder sister.'

'So who is the father of the baby you are carrying?'

Her eyes flashed. 'My partner, Ben Wizard. What sort of a woman do you think I am?'

Angel sighed.

'That blue aura round your head has gone, Inspector,' she said.

'It's more of a bright red colour now. It tells me you are thinking bad thoughts, Inspector.'

'I thought you said you had split up with this man, Ben Wizard?'

'To tell the truth, Inspector, I don't quite know where I stand with Ben. We parted friendly, like. I still love him but I can't keep dragging myself round the world after him, toting a guitar. I want to put down roots and have a family. He wants to wander round like a wandering minstrel. I'm hoping when I have this baby that he'll change, or at least find a compromise, and not be constantly on the road. He's a lovely man, Inspector Angel. Have you ever seen Ben Wizard?'

She opened her large, brown leather handbag and fished through some cards.

'No. I can't say that I have,' Angel said.

She handed him a card about as big as a postcard. It had a coloured photograph of an outdoor man wearing a cowboy hat and a leather coat. He had long hair, a beard and sideburns. On the reverse side was a potted history of him, and his agent's address in the US and the UK.

Angel looked at it and offered it back to her. 'Thank you.'

'Naw. Keep it. We got thousands.'

Angel put it on the desk and rubbed his chin. 'So where did Harry Weston fit in then?' he said.

'As I said, we were just friendly. I was telling him how to look good on the stage. How to take a bow. How to milk the applause. I was advising him how to get a good agent, and how to get gigs. Stuff like that.'

'That all?'

'Just about. Hey. There's a lot to being a country and western artist, Inspector, especially when you're well down the bill, working solo, doing a seven-minute spot at a big venue like The Arena. You ain't got much time to get the audience to like you, before you're on your second number, you've finished and you're off.'

'So how far did this friendship with him go? Did you go to his flat?'

'I went once. It was a miserable hole. Faced north-east. The furniture was set all wrong. There was no aura. He came to my place lots of times. He brought his guitar and his music. We played together. We had a lot of fun.'

'You know he broke up with his regular young lady about two weeks ago?'

'He told me. Madeleine Rossi, a young girl who works behind the grille at a bookies. Apparently somebody told her that he was seeing me, and she misunderstood.'

'Perhaps he didn't tell her.'

She shrugged, causing a span of shiny black fringe across her chest to reflect the light.

'Was he very upset?' Angel said.

'At first he was. But after it had sunk in, I don't think he was. I think he was more upset that Madeleine had found out by somebody sneakily telling her, and that she had so promptly taken the initiative without talking it out with him, but I don't think he was madly in love with her.'

Angel considered what she had said and nodded. 'There were no threats, big scenes, that sort of thing?'

She shook her head. The earrings swished down her neck and across the black shoulder straps of her dress. 'Not in front of me, Inspector,' she said. 'No. It seemed to make him more determined than ever to concentrate on his music. He practised his guitar harder and longer. Anyway, it didn't take Madeleine Rossi long to find a new beau. She soon got her claws into somebody called Grogan, Clive Grogan. His father apparently is in the ice-cream business.'

Angel's head came up. Angus Rossi would be delighted that his only daughter Madeleine was courting the boss's son.

'When was the last time you saw Harry Weston, Miss Kellerman?'

She half closed her eyes as she thought. 'It must have been Sunday night, about ten o'clock. Yes, it was. He came about six o'clock, brought his guitar and a bottle of something. We played around, trying out different songs. I had a pizza delivered at about nine o'clock and he left around ten.'

'He never spoke to you about his family or friends?'

'No. Not really. Didn't seem to have any.'

'Did he mention a man about forty, Miss Kellerman? Could have been a priest. The man who shot him was seen wearing a dog collar and a black shirt front.'

Felicity Kellerman stared at him and said, 'Inspector, your aura is going all red again.'

Angel's lips tightened back against his teeth. 'He never mentioned anybody who would fit that description?'

'No. No.'

'Did you ever see anybody like that in company with Harry Weston?' he said.

'No.'

'One last question, then I'll let you go on home. Do you know of anybody who would have wished Harry Weston dead?'

'No. Certainly not, Inspector. He was a nice young man ... wouldn't hurt a fly. Just lived for his music.'

'Thanks very much, Miss Kellerman.'

The phone rang.

Angel looked up at the clock. It was straight up five o'clock. Time for home.

He stood up, glared at the phone, hoping it would stop ringing. It didn't. He wrinkled his nose then reached out for it.

'Angel,' he said.

It was a civilian telephonist from the station reception desk. 'Sorry to bother you, Inspector,' she said. 'I know it's late, but there's a Mr Fiske, the headteacher of Curzon Street School, at the front desk. He says that he has something very important to report, and he will only speak to somebody senior. He has asked to see the chief constable, whose secretary said that he was out, and the superintendent, who, as you may know, left early to go to the doctor's. That left you and Inspector Asquith, and I know that Inspector Asquith is out dealing with a multi-vehicle road accident. That left you. Will you see him? I hope you will. I wouldn't like to have to go back to him again and tell him he'll now have to be seen by a sergeant.'

Angel groaned. Problems with kids and teachers and schools were tiresome, time wasting and not his forte, and he yearned to go home. He had some wide-ranging orderly thinking to do. He solved many of his cases seated in the presence of boring reality television programmes. However, he was there to serve.

'All right,' he heard himself say. 'Yes. I suppose so.'

He heard the receptionist sigh.

'Get somebody to bring him down to my office straightaway, will you?'

Two minutes later, a uniformed constable duly delivered the teacher. He stormed into the little office with a red face and a lot on his mind.

'A disruption of some sort happens every four or five months, Inspector,' Mr Fiske said. 'As you may know, a mutual arrangement has been made whereby the children at my school are protected while they are buying ice cream from Grogan's ice-cream van. From time to time, it parks at four o'clock at the front of the school in a place agreed with Health and Safety. The driver serves from the near side of the van only and passing traffic can see the children and the van clearly enough. I don't like it. I don't agree with it but Health and Safety have sanctioned it, so I live with it.'

'So what's the problem?' Angel said.

'The problem, my dear inspector, is that, in addition, a Grogan's van has now started parking up the side street, on Moon Street, at noon some days, so that when the children are out of the classrooms for their lunch break, instead of going out of the front gate, which anyway is against school rules unless they are going home or have special permission, they scale the wall which is nearly six feet high. This is obviously extremely dangerous. In addition, after they have bought their ice creams from the van, they play around on the verge, sometimes meandering on to the road, before scaling the high wall to come back. Now while the majority of miscreants are boys, there have been seen some girls, which is very unseemly in their uniform of chocolate brown skirts and chocolate-brown socks, tights or stockings.'

Angel took the point. He rubbed his chin.

'Where exactly does the van park? Is it on the road or does it straddle the road and the pavement?'

'Neither. It is on a piece of the verge, which has become packed down by cars and vehicles waiting there, so that it is now quite hard. It is only a few yards from the school wall.'

'What do Health and Safety say about it?'

Fiske's face went redder. 'I haven't been there. If I go there, they will only put me on to you.'

Angel knew that what he said was almost certainly true. 'Well, Mr Fiske, what do you want me to do?'

'Stop the ice-cream van parking on Moon Street at lunchtimes or at any time for that matter. The driver will know he shouldn't park there, enticing the children over the wall ...'

'I don't know if I can do that,' Angel said.

'Why ever not?'

'There is a limit as to how much we can and should interfere with a man who is simply plying his trade. The owner of the van might justifiably argue that his driver is there to sell ice cream to the people in the flats close by and the employees at the glassworks and the cardboard box factory on the other side of the road. And that it is *your* responsibility – not theirs – to keep your children inside the playground and not scaling high walls.'

'Huh. I see that it would have been better for me to have gone to Health and Safety. I see you are not the slightest bit interested in the safety of the children at my school.'

'Of course I am. I am only trying to be fair. This ice-cream manufacturer pays his rates to this council and gives employment to the people of the town so he is entitled to some consideration. Now I don't know all the facts of the case, Mr Fiske. I will look into it tomorrow and get back to you. In the meantime, you should direct your pupils not to scale that wall to take a short cut to the ice-cream van or for any other reason.'

Fiske slowly blew out a yard of breath while shaking his head. 'I thought it would be a simple matter of warning the driver off.'

Angel pursed his lips. Nothing was simple any more. He only wished that it was.

Fiske said: 'I hope you are not going to be a long time getting back to me.'

'Give me your phone number,' Angel said, 'and I will get back to you as soon as I can.'

'Good morning, sir,' Flora Carter said. 'Got a message you wanted me.'

'Yes. Come in, lass,' Angel said. 'Sit down. You were looking up Madeleine Rossi and her wonderful new boyfriend.'

'It's a Clive Grogan, son of Raphael Grogan, the ice-cream manufacturer,' she said.

'Yes, I know. Felicity Kellerman told me.'

'Strange woman, Felicity Kellerman. Do you think she's for real, sir?'

'I don't know.'

'I was thinking ... She could have had a strange influence on Harry Weston.'

He shook his head impatiently. 'Well, she could have, but she isn't the murderer. It was a man of about forty wearing a dog collar.'

'She gives me the creeps.'

'You're a copper, for God's sake. That aura and crystals is just so much tripe. The world is full of it. Now, never mind about her, did you meet this ... Clive Grogan?'

'Yes sir,' she said. 'He works for his father. Good-looking, well-turned-out young man. Says he didn't know Harry Weston, though.'

Angel nodded. 'Did you interview Madeleine Rossi?'

'Yes, sir. I caught her coming out of the bookies on Dunscroft Street, where she works. She said she knew nothing about Harry Weston's murder. She admitted to shedding a tear or two when she heard about it. But she was still vindictive about his relationship with Felicity Kellerman, which she described as an affair, and she insisted that it was going on at the same time that he was regularly courting her. She said that he was lying.'

Angel smiled. 'In those words, Flora?'

'Well, all right, sir. Her language was a little more colourful.'

'I bet it was. I know her father.'

'And she said that she still believes that Harry is responsible for Kellerman being pregnant.'

'Kellerman insists it is her partner, a man with the unlikely name of Ben Wizard, who she says is currently in the States.'

'That's what she told me, sir.'

Angel licked his bottom lip for several seconds, then said, 'Well, however spiteful Madeleine Rossi felt towards Harry Weston, our witness has said that the murderer was a man, so *she* couldn't have murdered him.'

'Anyway, there's no link at all between her and the two murdered priests, sir.'

'The only link we have between them and Weston at this time is the gun. We know that the same gun was used to murder all three, but we don't know that the trigger was necessarily pulled by the same person each time.'

'You mean the gun used to murder Harry Weston could subsequently have been stolen or sold on?'

'Or discarded then found. Yes. Could have been.'

Flora Carter nodded. 'Well, sir, do you want me to see if I can contact this Ben Wizard character, sir?'

'Of course. Got to keep it tidy. But something else has cropped up, Flora. *That* will have to wait.'

Angel then told Flora Carter in detail about the conversation he had had with headteacher Fiske the previous afternoon. Then he said, 'So I want you to drive up Moon Street shortly after twelve noon today, and observe. See if there's one of Grogan's vans parked up there, and see if there are any school kids coming over the wall. Note where the van is parked. Also take a discreet look at their behaviour. Are they a danger to themselves or anyone else? All right?'

'Right, sir.'

She went out.

SEVEN

A few minutes later, the phone rang. Angel reached out for it. It was the desk sergeant. 'You asked uniform to bring Peter King in, sir.'

'Yes, sergeant. That was yesterday. Have you got him?'

'Yes, sir. Is he to be charged?'

'Not yet. Put him in an interview room but don't leave him unattended. There's no telling what he might nick or damage. I'll be along in a minute.'

'Right, sir.'

Angel replaced the phone then set off up and went up the green corridor, past the men's locker room to the interview rooms. He glanced through the small glass window at eye level in the door of interview room number one and saw a man in a shiny dark suit sitting in a chair by a table. That was Peter King. A uniformed constable was sitting opposite him. Angel opened the door and went in.

The constable jumped to his feet. 'Sir,' he said.

'Thank you, lad,' Angel said as he cocked a thumb towards the door.

The officer nodded, went out and closed the door.

Peter King looked up at Angel and, through his unwashed and unshaven features, smiled like a baby at its mother's wedding. 'Hello there, Mr Angel,' King said.

Angel didn't smile back. He didn't reply. He pulled out the chair and sat down opposite him.

King said: 'They said you wanted to see me. They brought me here in a car.'

Angel looked at King and said, 'I suppose that, now you're here, you want to make a confession?'

King blinked. Angel had clearly caught him offguard. He thought a moment then said, 'What about?'

'You tell me.'

He licked his lips and said, 'Well, I raped and murdered a girl in Leeds before Christmas.'

'You didn't.'

'I did. They haven't got anybody else for it, either.' His eyes took on a glow. 'Her name was Sharon. She was very slim. I did it under the railway arches that Saturday night before Christmas. She was willing at first, but when I began to—'

'Don't bother lying, Peter. Leeds tell me that it couldn't possibly have been you. Now what else do you want to confess to?'

King's eyes flitted to the left, the right and then downwards. After a few moments he said, 'Can't think of anything.'

Angel thought that it was a good start and said, 'Well, where were you on Monday afternoon?'

King peered at him briefly then said, 'Don't know.'

'All right,' Angel said. 'Where were you on Monday evening, Tuesday morning and Wednesday morning?'

Again, he didn't answer immediately. He looked round the room, eventually arriving back to look into Angel's face. 'Don't know.'

'Have you no idea? Were you at home? In the pub? With your friends?'

'I don't have any friends, and I don't have any money to go to the pub with, until Friday when I get my money from the post office, and anyway Joe Morrison, the landlord, won't let me in The Fisherman's Rest unless I buy a drink.'

'Would you have been at home then?'

'Might have been.'

'Anybody with you?'

'No.'

Angel wasn't pleased. He looked as if he'd been to the Police Dog Awards ceremony and trodden in something.

He continued. 'So you can't prove where you were on Monday afternoon, Monday evening, Tuesday morning and Wednesday morning?'

'No. Why? Has somebody done something? Has it taken them *all* that time?'

'Have you got a gun?'

King's eyes glowed like traffic lights. 'No. Yes. Well, not now. I threw it away.'

'What sort of a gun?'

'A handgun. I don't know what sort it was, Mr Angel.'

'How many bullets did the cartridge hold? And what was the calibre?'

'I dunno for sure. At least six. It was a .32.'

Angel wrinkled his nose. King could guess a minimum of six. That was the smallest number of rounds a handgun cartridge might hold. .32 *was* the calibre of the bullets that killed Harry Weston, Samuel Smart and Raymond Gulli but he could possibly have gleaned that info from the newspapers.

'You get an automatic sentence of five years for possession of a deadly weapon such as a gun,' Angel said. 'Did you know that?'

'Yes. Of course I knew that, Mr Angel. That's why I threw it away. I'm not daft. Huh.' He grinned.

Angel frowned. 'Where did you throw it?'

'I threw it where you can't get at it. And I wiped off my finger-prints. You'd never be able to trace it back to me.'

'If you threw it where I can't get at it, it doesn't matter if you tell me where you threw it, does it?'

King put his fingertips to his mouth. He chomped briefly on his fingernails. His eyes flitted in different directions. Eventually he said, 'I threw it into Woolley Dam.'

This was a big stretch of water between Barnsley and Wakefield with a busy road bridge by it.

Angel thought a moment. The answer to his next question could possibly eliminate King from suspicion. 'When?'

'Some time ago. You'll never find it.'

'When exactly, and was anybody with you?'

'No, I was on my own. And it was after dark about six o'clock on Tuesday evening. That's almost thirty-nine hours ago. By now it will be swallowed in tons and tons of mud, about a mile down now, I should think. You'll never find it. Water sucks stuff down, you know, and the dam is ever so deep. There's a whole village under that water.'

Angel shook his head slowly. 'You'd be surprised, Peter. We could have Woolley Dam completely drained. We wouldn't have need to search for it with handtools using our naked eyes. These days, we have giant electromagnets powerful enough to work through rock six feet thick, and we can utilize powerful X-rays to pinpoint its exact position. Believe me,' Angel said, 'if it was there, we would find it.'

He looked closely into King's eyes. There was very little truth in what Angel had just said. The cost would run into millions. Superintendent Harker would probably have a terminal heart attack at the thought of it.

Angel noticed that instead of getting King worried, which had been his intention, the young man was sitting there still smiling. His face was glowing, and his eyes shone like traffic lights. He must be visualizing such a scene and enjoying the chaos that he would have caused.

'Why did you throw the gun away on Tuesday night? Why not Monday night or Wednesday night?'

'I didn't want it any more. I had finished with it. It wouldn't have been safe for me to hang on to the gun a moment longer than necessary. Your cops might have been round and found it in my pocket.'

There was coincidence or logic there. The third murder, Raymond Gulli, took place on Tuesday morning. Tuesday night would possibly have been the earliest the murderer could have disposed of it using the cover of darkness.

'If you had a gun, what did you want it for?'

King's nails went back up to his teeth again. His eyes narrowed. The pupils travelled to the left, to the right, then back again several times. Eventually he said, 'No comment.'

Angel's eyebrows shot up. 'No comment?' he said. He frowned and added, 'Why no comment, Peter?'

'No comment,' he repeated.

Angel rubbed his chin. 'You mean you don't know what you wanted the gun for?'

'Naw,' he said, screwing up his face impatiently. 'I mean, no comment. I'm allowed to say no comment, if I want to.'

Angel pursed his lips. Of course he was. Experienced crooks do it all the time. Some don't even admit their name.

'How did you get the gun?' Angel said.

'Found it.'

'Where?'

'In the park. In Jubilee Park. In the rubbish bin at the entrance, by the iron gates.'

'Anybody with you or saw you, when you found it?'

'Naw. I was just walking through and happened to see it,' he said with a grin.

Angel shook his head. 'On top of the empty ice-cream tubs, the lager tins, the cigarette packets and the sweet wrappers, a loaded gun happened to be there. People walking past all day and don't see it. You come along and happen to see it.' He shook his head again. 'Where do you get these tales from, Peter? I wish you would give it a rest and start living in the real world.'

The smile left King's face. 'It's true, Mr Angel, every word.'

'You wouldn't know the truth if it jumped up and bit you,' he said, rubbing his hand across his face. 'You know, Peter, I like the one about the three bears better.'

'That's where it was. It's absolutely true, Mr Angel. Honestly.'

Angel's jaw muscles tightened. 'Don't tell such lies! You've always been a liar. One of these days, lad, you're going to finish up doing life – and I mean life – in Wakefield. Don't you realize that?' Angel then stood up. 'This interview is over,' he said, then he fastened the middle button of his jacket and made for the door.

King reached out and grabbed the cuff of his sleeve. 'Well, all right, Mr Angel,' he said. 'Maybe it wasn't *exactly* like that.'

Angel stopped and looked at him.

'Well, maybe the gun wasn't on top like that,' King said. 'Actually, I had to rummage around a bit. Sometimes somebody throws away a sweet bag with one left in the bottom. Or a ciggie packet with a dog end in it. I once found an envelope with a photograph and a five pound note in it. Anyway, I was hungry.'

Angel wasn't sure whether he believed him or not, but he sat down again.

King smiled. 'I actually found a sort of badly packed parcel, right underneath, near the bottom … a small sheet of brown paper and a short knotted-up piece of string wrapped loosely round it. As I picked it up, the gun slipped out. I saw it and put it into my pocket and went out of the park to the bus stop. As I stood in the bus shelter I took it out and looked at it again. It was the real thing. Fabulozo!'

'What did you intend to do with it?'

King thought a second and said, 'Turn it into cash. Sell it. Yes.'

'Would you be able to identify the gun if you saw it again?'

He smiled. 'If you can get it out of Woolley Dam, I'd know it for certain, yes.'

Angel sighed. 'If I showed you photographs of different guns, would you be able to pick it out?'

'I dunno. No, I don't think so. They all look alike.'

'They usually have a maker's name stamped on it, sometimes a number. Did you notice anything like that on the gun?'

'It might have. I didn't notice.'

'What do you mean, "I didn't notice"? If it was there, you couldn't *miss it*!'

'You know I am dyslexic, Mr Angel. I'm not good with letters and numbers and reading. I wanted to be a history teacher but I couldn't read, and besides you've got to remember stuff … like dates.'

Angel sighed again. 'Can you remember any of the letters?'

King brought his fingers up to his mouth again. He closed his eyes briefly then said, 'There might have been an "m", or it might have been a "p". I am not sure.' Then the smile returned.

Angel brushed his hand through his hair. He licked his lips. His patience was deserting him. He really wanted to charge King with something or else get him out of his sight. But the interview had to go on.

'Did you know Harry Weston?'

King frowned then said, 'No comment.'

'What do you mean, no comment? He's that ticket clerk who was shot dead in the ticket office at the railway station.'

'Oh, him?'

'Yes, him. Do you know him? *Did* you know him?'

'I saw him around. I didn't know him. He used to go with Madeleine Rossi but chucked her to go with that singer, Felicity Kellerman,' he said, then with a snigger added, 'Did you know she's pregnant?'

'Yes, I know she's pregnant,' he said quickly. 'What do you know about that?'

He grinned again, dirtily, almost obscenely. 'Nothin'.'

'So you knew Harry Weston?'

'Well, yes.'

'How did you come to know him? Was he a friend of yours?'

'No, Mr Angel. I didn't know him to talk to. He had been dancing with Felicity Kellerman at the *Scheherazade*. I had been watching her. She looks ... very nice. I was just interested.'

'But how did you know the man she had been dancing with was Harry Weston?'

'I asked the barman.'

Angel rubbed his chin. 'But why would you want to know who he was?'

King frowned. 'I dunno.'

'When was this?'

'Ages and ages ago.'

Angel's neck went red. He dragged down on his collar to loosen it. 'What do you mean, ages and ages ago? Do you mean two years ago? Ten years ago? 1939? 1066? At The Flood? When?'

King looked shocked at Angel's reaction. It took him several seconds to answer. 'Seven or eight months ago, I suppose, Mr Angel,' he said.

Angel reckoned that King's answer was in accord with the facts. At least the maths were correct. Felicity Kellerman had been in Bromersley since late March, and her pregnancy would not have been showing at that time.

Angel sighed. King had not said anything that he could check on, which would have enabled Angel to charge him. Nor had he appeared to be so scrupulously snow white that Angel could have sent him back home. Angel had had times like this with King before, and invariably finished up without finding a single offence he could make stick.

Angel wondered if he should stick a priest's collar round King's neck and have Zoe Costello look at him in a line-up with nine other men dressed the same. The trouble was, she might artlessly pick King out. That wouldn't help at all if he was innocent. That was the way things seemed to go. The case against him might then zip along out of Angel's control. Meanwhile the real murderer would get away scot free.

There had been too many cases of wrongful arrest and imprisonment because the accused simply couldn't tell the truth, and there was no system in place to protect the man against his own ignorance or stupidity. Angel didn't want this to happen if King was innocent. He shook his head and turned back to King, who was still smiling. Even though his intellect was limited, King knew the chaos he was capable of creating in his interviewer's thought processes.

Angel must continue the questioning. Something irrefutable might come out of it.

'Did you know the Reverend Samuel Smart and the Reverend Raymond Gulli?'

'Yes, Mr Angel. Used to call to see them. Regularly. They gave me money. They used to give me money when I had nothing. Nothing to buy for my tea. My giro would run out on Tuesday for certain. I used to call on them. They gave me enough to buy a sandwich or some chips. When you have nothing, it's a lifesaver, particularly in the winter. There's no St James's Crypt in Bromersley, you know.'

'Let's take one man at a time. The Reverend Samuel Smart. When did you last see him?'

King took a deep breath. He screwed up his eyes. Eventually he said, 'It must have been last Monday morning.'

'What time?'

'I don't know. In the morning. Not too early. His cleaner was there. The sexy one.' He sniggered.

Angel frowned. He thought about King's description of Norma Ives. When Angel had interviewed her, he saw her as a small, slim, shapeless young woman, pleasant enough but in no way overtly sexy. He considered it a frivolous comment for King to make in view of the horror of Sam Smart's death.

'You *knew* her, did you?' Angel said.

'I'd seen her before but I didn't *know* her, Mr Angel. I could have done her a bit of good, if you know what I mean,' he said with a snort and a titter.

Angel turned away. His patience was oozing away.

King said, 'You can tell when somebody don't dislike you, Mr Angel.'

'What happened then?' he said.

'The usual. I asked to see the vicar. He came along to the door. He looked at me and I told him the tale. He invited me into the office. It was the same stuff. He asked me if I had got a job yet. I told him that I had this back problem, two disintegrating discs, and that I am dyslexic. I've told him that a hundred times before. He told me I must get a job of some sort. He gave me a blessing, a five pound note and I'm on my way.'

Angel rubbed his chin. 'This conversation took place in his office?'

'Yes.'

'Where did he get the five pound note from?'

King's fingernails went up to his mouth again. His eyes flitted to the left and to the right. He didn't say anything.

Angel said, 'Well, did he get it out of his pocket or out of a cash box or a safe ... or somewhere else?'

Eventually King blinked and said, 'Out of a wallet in his pocket.'

'Were there any other notes in there?'

'I didn't notice.'

Angel's face muscles tightened. He ran his hand through his hair. 'Of course you noticed. You were anxious to get some money for some food, weren't you? Money was the reason for calling on him, wasn't it? You would be naturally curious.'

'I won't answer you if you shout at me,' King said, his bottom lip quivering.

Angel sighed heavily. He pulled out an empty drawer in the table between them and slammed it shut with a loud bang. Then he sat back in the chair, closed his eyes, took control of his breathing and relaxed until it became normal.

King meanwhile looked round the room as if he was a painter and decorator thinking about preparing a quote.

Angel said, 'You sure it was out of a wallet in his pocket?'

'I think so.'

'You *think* so? What was the wallet like?'

'I don't know,' King said quickly, then he added, 'No comment.'

'Is it no comment because maybe there wasn't a wallet and you're therefore stuck for what to say next, or because you think I want you to say that he got the money out of a drawer or a cash box or a safe or some other place?'

'No comment.'

Angel clenched his fists and shook them momentarily. He blew out a balloon's worth of breath, then rubbed his chin hard.

'This is getting us nowhere, lad,' he said. Then suddenly he said, 'And all this time, did you have that gun in your pocket?'

'Yes.'

Angel's patience was exhausted.

'There *never* was a gun, was there?'

'I told you.'

'So you pulled it out and shot him?'

'I might have.'

'What for?'

King's face went scarlet. 'No comment.'

Angel stared into his eyes. 'You didn't shoot him because his housekeeper, Norma Ives, was there. You would have had to shoot her as well.'

His eyes rolled round his head. Then he smiled and sniggered. 'No. You don't know what she's like ... she's lovely.'

Angel turned away, his face registering disgust. After a few moments, he turned back and said, 'I feel sorry for you, lad.'

King looked at him and smiled like a baby.

Angel shook his head. He couldn't stand any more. He stood up and dashed out of the interview room. He collared a PC on the corridor, and told him to go in and stay with King while he arranged relief. Then he returned to his office, phoned Transport and instructed them to convey the man back to Canal Street as soon as they had a vehicle going in that direction.

'Excuse me, sir. Can I have a word?'

It was Constable John Weightman at the door.

Angel looked up from his desk. 'Of course, John. Come in, lad. What is it?'

He closed the door.

PC Weightman was a policeman of the old school, in his fifties and on the verge of retiring. Angel had known him more than fifteen years and always found him rock-solid and reliable.

'Funny thing, sir,' Weightman began. 'I was doing a routine check on the display of gambling licences this morning, and I called in on

Brian Glogowski's shop round the back of the station. Trades as Big Brian, the bookie.'

'I know it, John. Know it well.'

'I was behind a young woman, waiting to see Brian. I thought I knew her but I wasn't sure at first. She passed Brian a list of bets she wanted putting on at Kempton *and* Doncaster this afternoon. Then she gave him a plastic bag. I could see it was stashed with paper money. When Brian read the betting slip, he leaned through the grille and whispered, "I can't take all this, Elaine. It's far too much. I would need to lay some off and there isn't enough time. The first race is in ten minutes. Give my apologies to Miss Wilkinson, will you? And explain. I can't take the first race. I'll deduct that. So I'll give you that five thousand back now. All right. I'll take on the others. To tell the truth, she's getting too expensive for me, Elaine".'

Angel frowned.

'Aye,' Weightman continued. 'Now that was Elaine Jubb, sir. She's housekeeper to Father Tom Wilkinson at St Joseph's Catholic Church. Phoebe Wilkinson is his sister. She's quite a bit older than him, disabled and, they say, a bit simple. Now Brian whispered all that to her but I could still hear him. He knows me, of course. The uniform didn't worry him, so I don't think *he* was up to anything shady. About Elaine Jubb or Miss Wilkinson, well, I don't know.'

Angel rubbed his chin.

'But I wondered where the money had come from,' Weightman said. 'It was a lot of cash. I wondered if everything was all right.'

'Right, John. Sounds odd. I can't think that the Reverend Tom Wilkinson would do anything dishonest.'

'Oh no, sir. Lovely man. Lovely man.'

'It would need handling with kid gloves,' Angel said.

'That's why I came straight to you, quiet like.'

'Leave it with me, John. I'm glad you did.'

Weightman nodded, smiled and went out.

Angel's face creased as the door closed. Another inquiry – as if he didn't have enough on. He thought about St Joseph's Catholic Church, a beautiful building in the centre of Bromersley, and Father Tom Wilkinson, a much respected priest as straight as the icicles that hang down from Strangeways' loos. He couldn't visualize him hawking the church treasures then putting the loot on a horse to raise the air fare to abscond to Rio de Janeiro. Anyway, he also understood that the Wilkinsons were rather well off in their own right. He must call there to see what was happening. There would no doubt be some sensible explanation. However, he had heard that Tom had a sister, who had not got a full row of beads.

He stood up and reached for his coat.

He would need to think of a reason to call.

There was a knock at the door.

'Come in,' he called as he pushed his arm into a sleeve.

It was DS Carter.

'What is it, lass? I am just going out.' Then he remembered. 'You've come back from Moon Street, checking on Grogan's ice-cream van,' he said, before she could reply.

She smiled. 'That's it, sir.'

'Sit down,' he said. 'Tell me.'

He peeled off the coat, tossed it on the chair in the corner, returned to the swivel chair and sat down.

'Well, sir, I drove up Moon Street at five minutes past twelve noon exactly as you said. There *was* one of Grogan's ice-cream vans parked on the grass verge, and a few boys and the occasional girl were climbing over the wall, which I agree was not to be recommended. It could be dangerous if one fell or there was any larking around. I think their ages would be around twelve to sixteen. There was a short queue at the ice-cream van. The driver seemed to be doing good business.'

'Were all his customers kids from the school? Were there any people from the cardboard factory, the glassworks or passers by?'

'I only saw schoolchildren there, sir.'

Angel nodded.

'Well, I drove up to the top of the street, sir, parked there and sauntered back down on the opposite side of the road.'

Angel nodded. 'Is that it?'

'Not quite, sir. No. Strange thing. After having a good look round, I walked back up to the top of Moon Street to my car. Then I drove back down. I suppose it was then about half past twelve. Grogan's van had gone and I noticed some ice-cream cornets thrown down on the grass verge, near where the van had been. I counted fifteen actual cones in a big splodge of ice cream. I didn't understand it.'

Angel stood up. He wanted to get away. 'I don't understand it, either, Flora. Maybe the ice cream was off, or it was too rich. I have much more to worry about than the quality of Grogan's ice cream. I am hunting down a triple murderer.'

'Yes, sir, but I have never known kids throw ice cream away.'

'Nor have I. But it is the middle of winter. Maybe they should have been served hot chocolate.'

'I am serious, sir.'

'So am I. Anyway, I hope to see Raphael Grogan this afternoon. If there's time, I'll ask him about it. I intend to stop any of his vans exceeding their presence near the school over and above that already agreed with the headteacher and confirmed by Health and Safety. Also, I need to phone headteacher Fiske and settle him down, but I also have another call to make first.'

EIGHT

It was 2 p.m. when Angel pressed the doorbell to the presbytery of St Joseph's Catholic Church. The door was eventually opened an inch at a time by Elaine Jubb in her blue overall. Angel heard a television or radio blaring out behind her. It sounded like crowds of people shouting excitedly.

Angel held up his ID card and badge. 'Sorry to bother you, miss, I am Detective Inspector Angel from Bromersley Police. Could I see Father Tom Wilkinson? He may remember me. We have met several times.'

'Oh' she said. 'I am afraid Father Tom is in Rome, Inspector. He's there for two weeks. His duties have been taken over by Father Roebuck. Miss Wilkinson has a telephone number for him somewhere. I will ask her for it, if you like.'

Angel frowned. He was surprised to hear that Tom was away.

'Who is it, Elaine?' a voice called from the inside of the house.

'It's a policeman, Miss Wilkinson,' she called. 'A Detective Inspector Angel.'

'A policeman?' the voice said.

Elaine Jubb said: 'That's Miss Wilkinson, Inspector. Father Tom's sister.'

'Well, kindly show him in, Elaine,' she called.

Angel stepped into the hall. He wondered what the potty Miss Wilkinson was like.

'Please go straight ahead,' Elaine Jubb said, pointing to the sitting-room door behind her. She then closed the front door, locked it and ran along the hall and down a staircase at the far end.

Angel crossed the hall through the open door facing him into the sitting room. His eyebrows edged higher as he entered. It looked very different from the way he remembered it the last time he was there. In the middle was Miss Wilkinson in her electric lounger chair with the foot rest up; a bed-table was across her lap, littered with newspapers, writing pads covered in notes and figures, pens, three remote controls, a calculator, a mobile phone and a cup in a saucer. Two very large slim-line television screens were set facing her. Both showed different pictures. On one screen, horses were being walked round a paddock and on the other a jockey was being interviewed by Clare Balding.

The rest of the furniture had been pushed to one side, except for an occasional table and two chairs placed strategically next to Miss Wilkinson's big chair.

She looked up at Angel, smiled sweetly, picked up a remote, pressed a button and the televisions were silenced. She then looked back at him and said, 'Good afternoon. A policeman? An inspector? That's very interesting. Come in, Inspector. Excuse the disorder. Please sit down,' she said, pointing to the chair next to her.

'Good afternoon. Thank you, Miss Wilkinson,' he said.

There was a heavy red book on the seat of the chair. Angel picked it up, looked at the spine and read Tootal's Horse And Jockey Form Book 2008/2009. He sat down on the chair and put the volume on the floor.

'Sorry to intrude while you are so very busy,' he said, smiling.

She noticed the smile and beamed back at him. 'My brother Tom is away so I am enjoying myself at the races, and having a rollicking good time. I haven't enjoyed myself as much since I was a girl. And that's more years than I am willing to admit to, I can tell you.'

He smiled at the old lady and nodded.

'Now what can I do for you?' she said.

'It was really a matter for your brother Tom, Miss Wilkinson. But as he's away I am afraid I will have to mention it to you.'

'Yes. Yes,' she said, occasionally glancing at the television screens.

'You will be having regular visits from our patrol cars?' Angel said.

'Yes. Yes. Oh yes. Goodness me. I see what this is all about. I know about the murders, Inspector. Ghastly business. God bless those poor, dear Anglican priests. Nice men, I heard. I have tried to keep up with it all from the newspapers. Have you come to tell me you have caught the wretched murderer?'

'I am here to make a few checks. I didn't know that your brother was away. Are you presently here in the presbytery alone?'

'No. Elaine is here most of the day.'

'And at night?'

'Quentin, our driver and gardener, checks the doors and locks up for me at seven o'clock.'

'But you are on your own after that?'

'Yes, of course. Oh, don't worry about me, Inspector. It's only a few more days and Tom will be back. And I have been on my own many times in my life. I have my personal alarm phone. I wear it all the time,' she said, pointing down the front of her dress. 'Besides, your murderer is obviously only interested in male Anglican priests. I fit none of those categories.'

Angel thought about that for a moment. 'That might only be a coincidence, Miss Wilkinson. It would be safer if you could arrange not to be here alone.'

There was a knock on the open door and Elaine came in with a tray laden with pots.

'Ah, tea,' Miss Wilkinson said, pleased to be interrupted.

Elaine said, 'I brought a cup for the inspector.'

Angel's face brightened.

The picture on both televisions had changed. One of them showed horses being directed into the starting gates.

'Excuse me,' Miss Wilkinson said as she pressed the button on the remote.

The sound of the racecourse and a commentator came up.

'They're off!' the man's voice said and continued verbosely, faster than a television weathergirl.

Miss Wilkinson's eyes were on the screen and stayed there, hardly blinking.

Elaine poured the tea, silently handed Angel a cup, put a cup on Miss Wilkinson's bed-table and then sat back to enjoy her own.

For the next one minute and forty seconds the commentator's voice reigned supreme. His last few words were, 'So first is Rat Trap at ten to one, second Widow's Weeds at twenty to one and third Archie Pelago at four to one.'

Miss Wilkinson beamed. She turned off the sound, did some quick calculations on the calculator and wrote a figure on the writing pad.

'Highly satisfactory, thanks to Widow's Weeds,' she said, banging the pen down on the bed-table. 'I always said outsiders were the best.'

Elaine smiled. 'Good going, Miss Wilkinson,' she said.

Angel strained to make out what the figure was but all he could see was a series of squiggles.

'There's a fresh cup of tea, Miss Wilkinson,' Elaine said, pointing towards the table.

'Thank you, dear,' she said and reached out for the cup.

Angel said, 'I was saying, it would be better if you could arrange never to be here alone, Miss Wilkinson.'

'So you were, Inspector. But I don't think the murderer would bother with an old lady like me.'

'Murderers are not normal people. You can't know what this man might do.'

She put a forefinger to her mouth. 'On the other hand, he might be interested in stealing the money. Tell me, Inspector, what would you do with it to keep it safe? It's my inheritance, you know. It's my half share of the sale price of The Grange, my late father and mother's house.'

Angel frowned. It would be quite a sum. 'You have all that here, in cash?' he said.

'Yes. It's well hidden, of course.'

He pursed his lips. Thieves, like policemen, are good at finding hidden treasure of any kind, but he couldn't get heavy-handed about it. It was the Wilkinsons' money and nothing to do with him. And the old lady seemed compos mentis, a little eccentric maybe. He hoped she wasn't gambling it all away on the horses.

'My advice would be to put the money in a bank, Miss Wilkinson.'

'Would you really?' she said. 'That's what Tom would have said, I'm sure. I must give that some thought.'

'Pay it in there today,' Angel said. 'And please don't stay here on your own tonight. I shouldn't think The Feathers will be booked up at this time of the year. Have you got transport?' he said.

'Oh, Inspector, Elaine can soon organize a taxi for me, thank you.'

The picture on one of the televisions changed again to show horses being lined up for a race. Miss Wilkinson said, 'If you will excuse me, I don't want to miss this.' Then she reached out for the remote, pressed a button and the voice of the race commentator began again.

Angel quickly finished the tea, thanked Miss Wilkinson for her courtesy, and Elaine for the tea, and made a quick exit.

He pointed the bonnet of the BMW back towards town, turned on to the ring road then on to the Fitzallan Trading Estate to one of the modern units situated at the end of a lane which had a big sign on the roof that read, 'Grogan's Ice Cream'. It was a large brick-built single-storey building with two delivery vans waiting to be unloaded at one side, and Grogan's vans at the other being loaded up with ice cream, boxes of cornets and wafers and so on, ready for release on to the streets. He drove to a car space marked off for visitors only, parked up and walked through an automatic door to a busy reception desk. Unusually, it had a large plate-glass window directly behind it through which visitors could see right into the factory.

He had to wait at the desk until the young lady who was on the phone had finished taking an order from a customer and then dealt with a man in a brown overall standing in front of him waving a piece of paper around, who needed to know where to deliver a consignment of cones and wafers.

Angel spent the time he had to wait looking through the big window into the factory. At the forefront was a huge, enclosed, ribbed refrigerated structure with steaming cream-coloured liquid mix dribbling down it from the height of the building into a giant funnel which was directed over a cold holding vat at the bottom. He watched the process and assumed it was to cool the hot mix rapidly to complete the important pasteurizing process. He was impressed with being able to see part of the ice-cream-making process in a factory that illustrated its cleanliness and modernity.

He eventually reached the receptionist and introduced himself. She made a phone call, then promptly showed him into a small office close by where a pleasant, middle-aged man in shirt sleeves stood up from behind a big desk, hand outstretched.

'Good afternoon, Inspector. I am Raphael Grogan. Very pleased to meet you. Please sit down. What can I do for you?'

Angel relayed details of the phone call he had had from the head-teacher of Curzon Street School, Mr Fiske, and the subsequent findings of DS Carter about the positioning of one of Grogan's vans by the school yard wall.

Grogan listened attentively then said, 'And what do you want me to do, Inspector? My drivers are paid on commission. Of course, I would not have them break the law or park anywhere where they would be a nuisance or be dangerous, but my driver stops on Moon Street hoping to sell ice cream to the workers from the glassworks and the cardboard factory during their lunch break, and of course any other passers by. He certainly does not expect pupils from the school to scale a six-foot-high wall to reach him. If they are that eager to be served, then they could come round the outside perimeter of the school to reach the van.'

'Apparently they are not allowed out of the school gates at that time unless they are going home. It's a school rule. Matter of road safety. Keeps them off the roads away from traffic.'

'Oh? I understand that, but surely it is the responsibility of the school to stop their pupils scaling the wall to get to the van then,' he said. 'Anyway, one of my vans serves them most days after school at the main gate. We have an arrangement with Health and Safety which I believe is working all right.'

'I believe that arrangement is satisfactory. By the way, my sergeant reports that while she was observing on Moon Street, nobody from the factories at the other side of the road, nor any passers by, bought anything. Indeed, children from Curzon Street School appeared to be your driver's only customers.'

Grogan looked thoughtful.

'Don't you think, Mr Grogan,' Angel said, 'that under the circumstances, you could instruct your drivers not to park on that spot or indeed anywhere else where the children can actually *see* the van from the school grounds, except of course at the agreed place at four o'clock each day?'

Grogan rubbed his chin then said, 'I don't like making an arrangement that I might later regret, Inspector. After all, in the summer, on a hot sunny day, the workers in those hot factories there on Moon Street might be eager to buy a nice cool ice-cream, lollipop or cornet. Now if I had made an arrangement not to trade there, I would have simply lost out, wouldn't I? And worse than that, my competitors from out of town could come along, park there and clean up.'

Angel pursed his lips. Taking everything into consideration, he didn't think that what Grogan had said was unreasonable.

'I'll tell you what I'll do,' Grogan said. 'I'll instruct my vans not to park anywhere on Moon Street for the next three months provided that no other ice-cream vendor parks up there, and provided that the headteacher at Curzon Street School institutes another school rule, that no children should attempt to climb over school playground walls, especially when they are over six feet high. Does that fill the bill, Inspector?'

Angel smiled. 'I'll have a word with him and see what I can do. Thank you very much for your cooperation.'

'It's a pleasure.'

Angel stood up. 'By the way, Mr Grogan, would it be possible for me to see your son, Clive, on an entirely unrelated matter?'

Grogan frowned.

'It's a confidential matter,' Angel said.

Grogan pursed his lips. 'He's not being getting up to anything he shouldn't have, I hope,' he said, picking up the phone and pressing a button.

'I shouldn't think it's anything for you to worry about,' Angel said. 'I assure you.'

'There's an Inspector Angel of the police to see you, Clive,' Grogan said into the phone. 'I'm sending him down. And I shall want to see you as soon as he's gone.'

'Thank you for your cooperation,' Angel said.

Grogan replaced the phone, followed him to the door, where they shook hands, then he directed Angel down a long corridor. At the far end of it, a door opened and a smartly dressed young man came out. He saw Angel, acknowledged him with a wave and took a few paces towards him. As soon as they were in speaking distance, the man said, 'Inspector Angel? I'm Clive Grogan. I'm very pleased to meet you. I've heard a lot about you. Please come into my office.'

They walked back together into a tiny private office.

When they were seated, Angel said, 'I have to speak to you about the death of Harry Weston.'

Clive blinked several times then said, 'I never met him, Inspector. I know who you mean, of course. A nasty piece of work.'

'Why do you say that?'

'I thought you would know all about it. You know he was going steady with Madeleine Rossi?'

'So I am given to believe.'

'They had had an understanding, Inspector. They were planning to get married next year. Well, while he told Madeleine he was in his flat at nights, on his own, studying and practising the guitar, he was actually in the backroom of that sleazy club, the *Scheherazade*, bedding a woman considerably older than he was, a Felicity Kellerman, who he eventually managed to get pregnant.'

'Felicity Kellerman says the father is her long-term partner or ex-partner, Ben Wizard.'

'Ben Wizard is supposed to be touring the States, Inspector,' Clive Grogan said. 'If he were the father do you think he'd be three thousand miles away from her so near to the time he expects his child to be born?'

'I don't know,' Angel said. 'I really don't know. Some fathers just don't want to be fathers. I'm asking questions of you and all the parties involved to try to get answers.'

'You are investigating the murder of Harry Weston, Inspector. Well, I didn't like what I heard about him but I wouldn't want to kill him. I wouldn't want to kill anybody. I hope you don't suspect that I had anything to do with it?'

'If you are innocent, you have nothing to fear,' Angel said. 'I understand that you are now seeing Madeleine Rossi?'

'Yes. I am. A lovely girl.'

'Her father works here?'

'Yes, he's a van salesman, and very good at it, he is, even in this weather. And we know all about his record. He's turned over a new leaf. We have absolutely no complaints at all about him.'

Angel was surprised but he didn't show it. 'Good. Good,' he said. 'Well now, all I need to know, Mr Grogan, is where you were at three o'clock on Monday afternoon.'

'I was here, of course, Inspector,' Clive Grogan said. 'Huh, my father wouldn't let me out of this building during working hours, I can tell you. You can ask him.'

'I will,' Angel said. 'I will.'

Then he courteously took his leave, walked along the corridor to Raphael Grogan's office, knocked on the door and briefly spoke to

Grogan Senior, who confirmed that his son Clive was in the factory all Monday afternoon.

Angel thanked Grogan for his cooperation, came out of the factory and returned to the BMW on the car park. It was cold and dark. He started the car engine, switched on the lights and checked the dashboard clock. It was five minutes to five. He nodded. He reckoned he had just enough time to make one more call if he was quick.

He touched a button on the car radio. A lively orchestra was vigorously playing the Radetzky March. He steered the BMW out off the industrial estate on to Park Road. Then it was a straight run for about a mile, so Angel lightly hummed the Strauss and banged out the beat on the steering wheel until he reached the street he was looking for on the left, a short street called Dunscroft Street that led to Wakefield Road. He looked along it for a bookies. On the right, he saw a brightly illuminated window amid a row of terraced houses in darkness. That was it. He saw a small illuminated sign informing him that he was outside Felton's the bookies. He pulled the BMW across to the wrong side of the road into the grey slush in the gutter against the kerb, right outside the shop door. He heard six pips on the radio. It was five o'clock exactly. He turned the radio off but kept the car engine running. Warm air circulated round his face, ears and fingers.

Three men came out of Felton's with their heads down and their hands in their pockets. They shuffled quickly away through the snow in different directions. Then, a big tall lump of man in a dark overcoat came out and looked round. He saw Angel's car and came down the two steps. He walked over to the driver's window, leaned down and peered at him through the window. He had a big nose, big ears and a mouthful of big teeth.

Angel looked back at him.

The man acted out a circular winding action with his hand.

Angel pressed the button and lowered the window.

'Are you wanting summat or what?' the big man said.

Angel didn't like the approach but he accepted that the man had a job to do. He took out his warrant card, opened it up and held it so that the man could see it in the light from the shop window.

'I am Detective Inspector Angel from Bromersley Police,' he said.

'I understand that Madeleine Rossi works here and I want to see her.'

He blinked. 'Oh. Oh, I see,' he said. He straightened up and returned to the shop doorway.

At that moment a chubby blonde girl in a very short coat came out.

The big man said something to her.

She looked down at the BMW, nodded, pushed her shoulders back and picked her way through the snow to the car window.

'You must be Inspector Angel?' she said. 'I'm Madeleine Rossi.'

'Yes. I want to talk to you about Harry Weston,' he said. 'I know you only live in the next street. I'll take you there and we can talk in the car, if you would like?'

She agreed, and she called across the pavement to the big man at the door. 'This man is giving me a lift home, Jim.'

'Right, Madeleine,' he said. 'Good night.'

She came round to the nearside door and got in.

Angel noticed a lot of leg with an unbecoming rubber boot round the foot. At her other end was a tower of hair supporting what looked like a young aspidistra. When the door closed, a strange smell that he assumed was Madeleine's perfume assaulted his nostrils. It seemed to be of watered-down petrol mixed with a potent cleanser he had noticed Mary used in the bathroom from time to time. It was very clingy and nothing like the sweet-smelling Californian Poppy his mother had used from time to time when he was young. He wrinkled his nose. He hoped that Miss Rossi's overpowering fragrance would not linger, or he might have difficulty in explaining it to Mary.

The shop lights went out and another man stepped briskly outside carrying a shopping bag. The big ugly man took the bag, then stood close to him while he turned to lock the door.

Angel put the BMW in gear and pulled away from the shop as Madeleine Rossi struggled with the seatbelt.

'So you're Michael Angel, the wonder cop,' she said in an aggressive manner. 'You're the man that put my dad in prison, aren't you?'

'That has, unfortunately, been my lot,' he said. 'Several times, I believe,' he added. 'And on each occasion he was tried fair and square by twelve ordinary men and women, who heard what he had to say, and what his barrister had to say, but still found him guilty.

That is history. It is behind us, you, me and him. This is today, and I want to talk to you about the late Harry Weston.'

The BMW was soon in Mount Street. There was a streetlight on the pavement opposite the front door of number twelve. Angel drove up to it, stopped, extinguished the car lights, but kept the engine running. The light wasn't good but he could see her profile in silhouette.

'I've already told that woman copper all I know.'

'I'd like to hear it for myself, if you don't mind.'

'Huh. You think my father shot him?' she said.

'I don't know *who* shot him. I want to know about your relationship with Harry. Tell me about that. And tell me exactly how it was, the truth.'

He heard her breathe in, then sigh. He could see her shaking her head several times. There was a pause. He thought her attitude might have changed.

'It isn't easy going back over all that, Mr Angel,' she said.

'Go on,' he said.

She sighed again, then said, 'Harry was my first real love. I loved him, *all* of him. He wasn't much to look at but he was all mine. Exclusively, all mine. Looking back, those Saturday and Sunday evenings we spent together was like waking up in a different world, as if my life until that moment had been in black and white and was now in glorious Technicolor. That'll sound silly to you.'

'No, no,' he said.

'We didn't do anything extravagant or spectacular. We would go to the pub, have something to eat, have a few glasses of vino, talk about music, new discs, new people, the music scene, he was mad about all that. Then we'd come back to the flat, talk some more, listen to music, watch films on the telly, make love, snooze for a couple of hours or so ... It'll never happen to me again. It was a once-in-a-lifetime experience. I was mad about him.'

She stopped. She turned her head away from Angel briefly, then turned back. A tear caught the light as it trickled down her cheek.

He didn't say anything. He waited.

She brushed it away with the back of her hand.

'I was a fool,' she said. 'I thought he thought as much about me. I was stupid. I wanted to meet him in the week sometime but he always said that he wanted to practise on his guitar. We only met at weekends. Spoke a lot on the phone, though. I used to ring him every lunchtime … I always made the running … I should have known.'

She stopped again.

Angel waited and waited.

'What happened then?'

'We had had wonderful times together that Christmas. Then on the Monday evening, three days after Christmas, I got a phone call at home from somebody I didn't know to say that he'd seen Harry with Felicity Kellerman at the *Scheherazade*, and that he knew that we were going steady and that he thought I'd want to know.' She swallowed. 'I was almost sick,' she said. 'My heart was in my mouth. Deep down inside me I knew that it was too good to last. Anyway, I phoned for a taxi and smartened myself up. I couldn't do much in the few minutes the taxi took to come. The taxi arrived at the *Scheherazade* at five minutes to eight. I went in. They were at the bar drinking. He was holding her hand. He didn't see me. Then he leaned over and … he kissed her. Just a peck on the cheek, but I knew. I knew then. For me, it was over. It was eight o'clock and it was all over.'

'What did you do then?'

'I dashed outside. I was in a flood of tears. I had asked the taxi to wait. I went straight home. I cried all night. Dragged myself to work on the Tuesday morning. As wonderful as it had been, there was no way I could take him back. He phoned me … at home and at work three times. He came round here. Dad sent him off with a flea in his ear. That was it.'

'Your father told me you were dating Clive Grogan.'

'Yes. That's right,' she said. 'He's perfectly charming.' Her voice had changed. It was lighter. 'I met him at Grogan's staff Christmas party,' she added. 'Dad took me. I've been out with Clive four times now. He's very different from … him, you know.'

Angel was certain that he was, but he was thinking of other matters. He rubbed his chin. 'Did you find out who phoned you that Monday evening to tell you about Harry and Felicity Kellerman?'

'No. I never did.'

'Have you any *idea* who it might have been?'

'No.'

'Have you any idea who shot Harry Weston?'

'No,' she said. There was anger in her voice. She didn't like that last question. 'I think I've told you all I know, Mr Angel,' she said, fumbling for the door handle. 'I must go in now. Dad will wonder where I am.'

'All right, Miss Rossi. Thank you very much.'

'Good night,' she said.

'Good night.'

She slammed the car door.

Even though it was ten minutes past five, Angel returned to his office and phoned headteacher Fiske to tell him the content of his meeting with Raphael Grogan. At first, Fiske wasn't at all satisfied but Angel reasoned with him and argued with him and eventually seemed to settle him down. Angel thought it would keep him out of his hair, at least until the three months were up.

He replaced the phone and looked at his watch. It was 5.30 p.m. He yawned. He was ready for home. He looked through his office window at the night sky. It was blacker than fingerprint ink. He pushed all the papers and stuff on the desk into a drawer, grabbed his coat, switched off the light and closed the office door.

NINE

Angel turned the BMW into his drive and up to his garage door. He unlocked the garage and raised the up-and-over door. In the car headlights, he saw a very long object wrapped in brown paper, leaning against the wall. He frowned. It was longer than he was. He wondered what it could be. Anyway, it was in the way. He couldn't get the car into the garage. It would have to be moved. It was not as heavy as he had expected. He wondered what on earth it could be. He looked round it for a label, found one and turned it towards the car headlights. He read it. It was addressed to 'Mrs M Angel', and was from the 'Sleep Sweeta Bed Company, Hangchow, China'. It was then that he realized it was the bed Mary had bought for her sister. He nodded knowingly, then pulled a wry face.

He drove the car in, locked the garage and went in the house.

In the kitchen, Mary was hovering over something bubbling on the gas ring. She looked up, smiled, leaned over towards him and gave him a kiss on the cheek.

Angel considered a kiss while she was busy at the oven was a bit unusual. He thought about it a moment, then said, 'What's that for?'

'Can't I give my husband a welcome home kiss?'

He pursed his lips briefly, then turned back, pulled her gently away from the oven, put his arms round her and gave her a bigger, longer, more tender kiss on the lips. She put her free arm round his neck and held the wooden spoon she had been using up in the air, so that gravy would not drip on to either of them.

As they pulled away, she smiled and said, 'And what's that for?'

He blinked. 'It's called a show of spontaneous affection, sweetheart.'

She smiled. 'Oh?' she said as she unravelled her arm from round his neck. 'And did Superintendent Harker teach you that, or was it the chief constable?'

'Huh,' he said.

He walked to the hall and took off his coat.

'Any post?' he called.

'One from Lolly. Got it here, in my pocket.'

He pulled a face.

'Will you set the table, sweetheart?' she said. 'This is about ready to serve out.'

'All right,' he said from the sitting room.

'She's ever so excited at coming over ...'

Angel wrinkled his nose.

They finished the meal and Mary arrived with the coffee. She sat down and then eagerly produced the letter from her sister, Lolly. She took it out of the envelope. Angel asked to be given it, to read it for himself, but Mary insisted on reading it to him.

'I'll just read the relevant bits, then. She's ever so excited.' She opened the letter and glanced through the first page, reading bits and commenting on them. Then she read: '"The decorator is very experienced and works at great speed. So he is a few days ahead of schedule. He tells me that he expects to be finished by Tuesday the 19th, so I would be free to come on Wednesday the 20th, if that's OK."'

Angel sighed.

Mary continued reading: '"Can't wait to see you both. It will be great to give you a big hug. And Michael, of course. Lots of kisses. Love you. Lolly."'

Angel sighed again. He didn't say anything for a moment and then said, 'What's on the telly?'

Mary banged her cup down in the saucer. 'I hope you are going to bring that bed in and set it up for her.'

He frowned. 'What bed?' he said.

'Don't tell me you didn't see it in the garage.'

'Oh. *That's* what it was.'

'Huh. And you supposed to be a detective.'

He shuffled uncomfortably. 'What, tonight?'

'Yes, tonight. I've been round the room. Washed all the paint. Cleaned out that bedside cabinet. Washed the curtains and put them up. You know, Michael, I didn't realize what a nice outlook that room has.'

The corners of his mouth turned down. 'What's on the telly?'

Mary glared at him. 'Nothing you like. I've looked.'

Angel wrinkled his nose. He knew he had lost the battle. 'Just let me have five minutes to let my tea go down,' he said, moving from the table to his favourite easy chair.

Mary stood up and began to clear the table.

Angel reached out for the *Radio Times* and glanced down a page, and then another, and another. After several minutes he tossed it to one side with a grunt of dissatisfaction.

Mary looked across at him. 'I'm right, aren't I?'

With a lazy flamboyant wave of the arm, he said, 'Darling, you are always right.'

'Come on, Michael. You've had a good twenty minutes. Bring that bed in for me. *Please.*'

He stretched his arms and looked out of the window. 'It's freezing out there.'

'Put your coat on.'

It was another ten minutes before Angel put on his coat, went out to the garage and returned with the bed. It wasn't heavy, but it was big.

With Mary's assistance, Angel managed to angle the bulky parcel through the back door into the kitchen, over the top of the gas oven, the table, then into the hall, across the banisters, up the stairs, and round the turn at the top ultimately into what had now inevitably become known as Lolly's room.

He leaned it against the bedroom wall. Then together they tore off the strong outer waterproof wrapping paper. There were Chinese symbols in red paint over the inner brown paper wrapping, under that was a polythene cover that entirely enrobed a mattress and bed base, and strapped to that was a long, narrow cardboard box. Angel opened the cardboard box to find that there were many wood parts, some in the form of decorated wooden rings that apparently, when assembled in the correct way, would form the legs. Other shapes made up the complementary pattern which would make up the bedhead. Angel looked at the parts and counted them. There were 128, including steel screws of three different sizes.

He pursed his lips. 'We need daylight really to be playing about with this,' he said.

Then the phone rang.

Angel and Mary looked at each other. Neither was expecting a call.

Mary's face hardened. 'It'll be the station,' she said.

Angel thought it would more likely be somebody selling wheel-chairs at thirty-five per cent off, or inviting him to enter into a survey for some dubious opinion poll. He went out on to the landing, into their room, crossed to the bedside cabinet and picked up the phone. 'Hello, yes?'

'DS Clifton here. Sorry to bother you, sir, but one of the patrol cars was doing the round of the vicarages and was making a call on St Joseph's presbytery on King Street. The driver, PC Sean Donohue, observed a prowler, who ran off. Donohue and his partner gave chase on foot, caught him and brought him in. It turned out to be Peter King.'

Angel sighed.

'Now, I knew you'd seen King earlier today ... I can charge him with trespassing but—'

'Is he armed?'

'No, sir.'

'Have you checked the presbytery? I have reason to believe that there's a disabled old lady, Miss Wilkinson, in there ... possibly on her own.'

'Oh,' the sergeant said promptly, alarm in his voice. 'I'll get someone round there straightaway.'

'Yes. And I'll go straight there myself. I'm nearer.'

'Right, sir. In the meantime, what shall I do with King?'

'Charge him with trespassing, then process him and, for once, *take your time about it*, understand?'

'Oh *yes*, sir, I understand,' he said. 'I take it you're coming in then?'

'Yes, Sergeant. But I'll go to St Joseph's first.'

Angel replaced the phone, rubbed his chin, turned off the light and came out of the room.

Mary had been in the bedroom next door, on her knees sorting through the small parts of the new bed, and had heard every word of his side of the conversation. She stood up. They met on the landing.

She was not pleased.

'You're going back out then?' she said, hands on hips.

'Got to. There's an old lady possibly in danger. A patrolman has arrested a man, a prowler. He's known to us.'

'Is he your murder suspect?'

He knew she worried about guns and knives, the dangers of the job and his safety in particular. He would have to tailor his replies accordingly.

'Erm, no. I don't think so,' he said.

'Don't you know? You said something about somebody being armed.'

'No. I asked *if* he was armed and he wasn't. The old lady is probably perfectly safe. Look, Mary, I have to go.'

'You said you were going to St Joseph's Church.' There was a tremor in her voice.

He began to put on his coat. The business gave him time to think what to say.

'There's a man with a gun on the run,' she said. 'He's murdered a railway worker and two priests. It's in all the papers, even on TV. And you're not telling me about it. That's the case you're working on, isn't it?'

Angel realized she knew more than he'd thought. 'Yes, but this lady isn't a priest. It's a lady who is old, disabled and has won a lot of money, so she's a prime target for thieves. That's what this is all about. So stop worrying. There's nothing to worry about.'

'Oh Michael.'

'It's all right. I won't be long. Look, it's 10.30. If I'm not back by midnight—'

'I'll wait up for you.'

Angel didn't like telling Mary half-truths and misleading her in that way, but he had a job to do and he felt that it was justified.

He was seriously worried about Miss Wilkinson. She was on her own, her brother was away and her life was potentially in danger. He didn't believe the old lady had had any intention of leaving the presbytery and checking into a hotel as he had urged her to do earlier that day. She was far too involved in her racing project.

As he made his way along the path to his garage, he noticed a white mist in the air. A hard frost had settled on top of the earlier fall of three inches of snow and had frozen harder than the crust on a Strangeways' meat and potato pie.

He drove the BMW carefully towards town then along Park Road, cut through several side streets until he was soon on Birdwell Street, where he stopped and parked up by the cemetery wall, sixty yards away from St Joseph's Church. He switched off the lights, took a torch out of the glove compartment, got out of the car, quietly closed the door and moved silently across the snow, making less noise than a villain slipping a tenner into a screw's pocket. He passed the dark stone walls of the graveyard, on to the small presbytery forecourt next to the church, then stopped and listened. Apart from the humming sound of the M1 two miles away, all was quiet.

Firstly, he searched around the outside of the presbytery, the garden, the bushes and the trees. There were many footprints in the snow, indicating that somebody had been snooping around. He sighed. He found it disturbing. He looked closely at the prints. They certainly seemed to be those of a man. There was a cluster of prints under the sitting-room window that suggested that the man may have been trying to glimpse into that room.

Angel also identified the footprints of two other men, presumably PC Sean Donohue and his colleague. There were a lot of those, clearly on the chase of the other man through the evergreen bushes, apparently round the house and terminating in a scuffle near the front door. There were also fresh tyre tracks there, which would be those of the patrol car. Angel was satisfied that there were only the three men's footprints there.

He then stepped smartly up to the front door of the presbytery, put his hand round the cold copper doorknob, turned it and pushed. It didn't open. It was securely locked. That was a relief. He nodded accordingly. Then he turned round, stepped back to the entrance to the presbytery forecourt, pointed the torch up at the front elevation of the house and methodically scanned every pane of glass in each window. He found that all the glass was sound and all the windows were closed. He had the same result for the left and right sides. He was pleased about that. However, when he scanned the glass on the rear elevation, he found a broken window on the ground floor. He ran up close to it. There was a hole in a glass pane the size of a slop-bin lid, easily big enough to let an average man gain access. He flashed the torch on the ground. Directly beneath it in the snow were more footprints and a few shards of broken glass. His pulse began to race. He was worried for Miss Wilkinson. He shone his torch inside. It revealed a small room such as a storeroom or a pantry. He hoped that Miss Wilkinson had taken his advice and moved out of the house. The murderer could be inside at that moment: Angel reckoned that he might be only yards away from him. He decided not to wait for any support from the station. He put the torch between his teeth, reached under the bottom of the window with the broken pane in it, and with both fingertips managed to lift it up. It slid up easily and he was inside the pantry in seconds. He stopped and listened. All was quiet. He hoped nobody had heard him. He quietly found his way out of the pantry. He made his way quickly through the kitchen into the hall and up the stairs, pushing past the stairlift, which he noted was at the head of the staircase. That position indicated that Miss Wilkinson was probably still in the house and upstairs ... and hopefully alive! He flashed the torch around the landing. There were six doors leading from it. Four were closed. He could see from the white tiles reflecting from his torch that one of the two open doors led to the bathroom, and he assumed that the door ajar next to it was the lavatory. He supposed therefore that the four closed doors were bedroom doors, so he approached the one nearest to him. He gently turned the knob. It rattled with age but he couldn't avoid it. He was as quiet as he could possibly be. The loudest noise was his pulse banging in his ears. The door led into a large bedroom, tidy, clean and unoccupied. He moved to the next room; that was the same. And so were the next two. He therefore had to assume that the last bedroom was Miss Wilkinson's. He subconsciously breathed in, put his hand on the doorknob and turned it. It was at that moment that his mobile phone rang out. It surprised him and he wasn't pleased, but he ignored it and pushed open the door. He flashed the torch around. It was another bedroom, in darkness like all the others, apparently empty but with the bedclothes turned back indicating that someone had been sleeping there. His mobile was still ringing. He switched on the light and walked quickly round the room. There was a dress, some stockings and other women's underclothes over a chair near the bed. But there was no sign of Miss Wilkinson. He put his hand in the bed. It was still warm. Surely she was not far away. He had another quick look round and ran his hand through his hair.

The mobile was still ringing. He took it out of his pocket and looked at the LCD. It was Duty Sergeant Clifton calling.

He pressed the button and said, 'Yes, Sergeant?'

'We've received an urgent call that somebody has broken into the presbytery, and is there now. I've sent another patrol car.'

Angel's eyebrows shot up. 'That's *me*,' he said. 'I'm in the presbytery now, in Miss Wilkinson's bedroom. But she's not here. There's nobody here. Who was the caller?'

'Miss Wilkinson herself, sir. She's patched through to me via a nursing service. They give 24/7 telephone cover to subscribers, particularly those who are disabled and live on their own. I have her on hold now.'

Angel scratched his head. 'Miss Wilkinson? Well, how on earth did she know?'

Sergeant Clifton hesitated, then said, 'Because she's *there*, sir.'

'Here? In the presbytery?' he said, his face creased by the mystery. 'Is she? Well, *where*? Ask her. *Where* is she exactly?'

Through the phone earpiece, he heard Clifton say, 'Inspector Angel says that everything is all right now, Miss Wilkinson. He's in the presbytery looking for you. He wants to know where you are.'

Angel pressed the mobile closer to his ear, intent on hearing her reply. He heard nothing through the earpiece though, but instead was startled by the squeaking sound of the hinge of a wardrobe door directly behind him, followed by the gentle and now familiar voice that said, 'I'm here, dear Inspector Angel. Where did you think I was?'

He turned round, startled to see the dazed but smiling little old lady, swathed in a large red dressing gown, framed in the doorway of the wardrobe, shielding her eyes against the light.

'Oh, Miss Wilkinson,' he said. Then he sighed. He was so relieved to find her.

She stepped tentatively out of the wardrobe.

'Are you all right?' Angel said, putting a hand out to support her.

'Oh yes, thank you, Inspector. But I will be better in my bed.'

He helped her across the room.

She flopped on to the bed, took off her slippers, swivelled round and pulled the bedclothes over her.

'What were you doing in the wardrobe, Miss Wilkinson?'

'Hiding,' she said. 'I heard the sound of breaking glass. I didn't know what it was. I assumed it was an intruder, and I had no wish to be murdered in my bed. So I hid in there. Then I remembered I was wearing my personal radio alarm,' she said, pointing to her chest, 'so I pressed the button.'

Angel nodded. 'And they rang the station.'

'I believe so,' she said, tidying the duvet cover then stroking it.

Angel suddenly heard a sound along the landing through the open bedroom door.

Miss Wilkinson heard it too. She looked at Angel, open mouthed.

Angel's pulse raced.

A stern voice called out, 'This is the police! Identify yourself. Come along. Come on now. This is the police.'

He sighed and said, 'This is DI Angel. Who is that?'

'Oh. PCs Donohue and Elders, sir.'

Angel pulled back the bedroom door. There were smiles and sighs all round. The PCs nodded and smiled at Miss Wilkinson, who looked bemused.

'Sergeant Clifton sent us,' Donohue said.

'How did you get in?'

'There's an open window at the back, sir.'

Angel nodded. 'Search downstairs, quickly. Someone could still be around.'

The two PCs ran out of the room and along the landing.

Angel turned back to Miss Wilkinson, scratching his head. 'Now what are we going to do with you?'

'I'm all right, Inspector, thank you. If you switch the room light out, I will probably go back to sleep straightaway.'

'No. No, Miss Wilkinson. We can't just leave it at that. There's the matter of a broken window.'

'I had thought about that. Quentin, our gardener and driver, will see to that in the morning. He's very handy at all those little jobs.'

'We can't leave it until then, Miss Wilkinson. It isn't safe and the hole will rapidly bring down the temperature of the house, which is not healthy for you, could be dangerous. With your permission there is a twenty-four-hour emergency service the police use. They are expensive, but they do a first-class job and turn out straightaway even in this sort of weather.'

'Very well, Inspector. If you think it's the best.'

'And you must realize that somebody has been snooping around outside and may be in the house now. I have two men looking round downstairs now.'

'Well, you're here now, Inspector, so that's all right.'

'No. It isn't all right, Miss Wilkinson. I can't stay here all night. You know that we are looking for a man who has killed two priests and another man. He broke into their vicarages, ransacked them and shot the priests. That could happen to you.'

'I heard he also broke into All Saints and Martyrs on Sebastopol Terrace, but he didn't harm dear Hugo Riley.'

'That's because Father Riley wasn't *there*.'

She blinked. 'Oh dear.'

'He was out visiting some of his parishioners.'

'I didn't know, Inspector.'

Angel shook his head. 'So you see you can't stay here on your own. Not for a few nights anyway, not until we've caught the man. I tried to persuade you of that this afternoon but you were far too taken up with the racing.'

Her face brightened. 'Oh yes. It's such fun, you know.'

Angel considered that it certainly was, if you always won. The regular work of the horses he backed was pulling hearses at Co-op Funerals.

'And did you pay your winnings into the bank, as I suggested?' he said.

She pursed her lips, lowered her head on to her chest and frowned.

Angel understood that to mean that she had not.

'Well, let's hope you've hidden it well,' he said.

Her face suddenly changed. She sat bolt upright in bed. The pupils of her eyes darted in every direction. She was clearly worried about something.

'I take it the money is still in the house?' Angel said.

'I didn't have the time to bank it, Inspector,' she said. 'The banks closed at four o'clock, and the last race was at 3.50. But I really must check that it is safe. It is not *all* mine, you know.'

She whisked back the duvet and reached down for her slippers.

'Will you help me?' she said.

He wasn't pleased. It was nearly midnight. There was nothing he wanted more at that time than to be at home in his own warm bed with Mary snuggled next to him.

'Yes, of course,' he said, holding out his arm.

She took it and they went out of the bedroom, along the landing, on to the stairlift, which took her downstairs. Angel walked slowly behind it.

The lights were on in all the rooms, and Donohue and Elders arrived from opposite directions and met them in the hallway.

'Nothing, sir,' Donohue said.

'There's nobody downstairs, sir,' Elders said.

Angel said: 'Are there any indications that anybody has been in the house?'

'No, sir.'

'Good,' Angel said. He looked at Miss Wilkinson and nodded, and she smiled back. He turned back to Donohue and Elders and said, 'Right. Have a good look round upstairs, and one of you organize that 24/7 joiners to repair that pantry window before Miss Wilkinson turns into a snowman.'

'Right, sir,' Donohue said. 'I'll do it.'

'Right,' Angel said, then he turned back to Miss Wilkinson.

She led the way down to the far end of the hall, through the ice-cold kitchen to the pantry. The door was partly open and freezing cold air was wafting in through the broken window.

She reached up and switched on the pantry light.

There were shelves of tinned foods and groceries in packets all round the little room. Broken glass and a little snow covered the provisions near the window, but most of the glass and snow was on the floor.

On the floor stood six huge, old, green and gold containers with the names of various foodstuffs printed on them: Currants, Raisins, Sugar, Flour, Coffee and Salt.

Miss Wilkinson made a bee-line for the one marked Flour, and put her hand across the lid, which was about as big as a dinner plate. The lid fitted tightly but she eventually managed to remove it.

Angel saw packets of paper money roughly stashed in the container and loose notes, tens and twenties, bursting out of the top. His jaw dropped. He was truly amazed. He rubbed his chin. There was a very great sum of money in there, and that could make Miss Wilkinson very vulnerable to assault and robbery.

She glanced at the container, nodded with satisfaction then replaced the lid.

She turned back to Angel and said, 'It's all right, Inspector. It's all there. Thank you.'

They came out of the freezing pantry and Angel closed the door.

He was deep in thought. The situation could not stay as it was. Miss Wilkinson could not be left in the presbytery on her own, particularly now that he knew that she had such a large stash of money there.

He tried to persuade her to book into The Feathers for several nights without success, but she did agree to have Elaine Jubb sleep in the presbytery, in the room next door to hers, for two nights, if Elaine was willing. This was a tortuous business to arrange over the phone in the middle of the night, but everybody cooperated and PCs Donohue and Elders eventually set off out in the cold to collect the young woman and bring her back to the house.

Angel then brought up another matter.

'Now, Miss Wilkinson, the presence of all that money in the flour bin makes you vulnerable to robbery, you know that.'

Miss Wilkinson yawned.

'That cash really needs to be in a bank,' he said.

'Oh dear. I've heard all that before, Inspector. But I don't see why I should. And look at what a mess the banks are in.'

'Your private account is safe enough, and it doesn't mean that it is out of your control. You can still access it when the bank is open, and you can move it around with a debit card and a cheque book without even physically touching it, you know. And the banks don't charge you for this.'

'I don't like banks, Inspector. Never liked them. I had an account for years, but lost the cheque book so my brother Tom closed the account on me.'

'Even so, having all that cash in your house makes you vulnerable to thieves, and might put you in grave danger.'

'Oh dear.'

'I wouldn't be doing my job if I didn't warn you. That broken pantry window is almost certainly the work of the man who was disturbed by my patrolmen. I am pleased to say that they caught him. He's a well-known villain, and he's in a cell at the station waiting to be interviewed.'

'Really, Inspector? Well, I don't know how he found out about my good fortune. Nobody knew except Elaine Jubb, and I would trust her with my life.'

'Well, *I* for one knew that you were betting big money before I came to see you earlier today.'

She screwed up her eyes to look at him and said, 'How could you possibly have known?'

'Because one of my officers was in the bookies when Elaine Jubb went in yesterday lunchtime with a bag of money and overheard Brian say that he didn't want to take the bet on the first race because it was too much money and he hadn't time to lay it off.'

She straightened up. Her mouth dropped open.

'If my officer overheard her,' he said, 'other men in the bookies could have heard, and there's no saying whom they might have told.'

She rubbed her chin thoughtfully.

'I think, therefore, Miss Wilkinson,' he continued, 'that you should allow me to seal that flour bin of yours here, take it down to the station, put it in a cell and lock it up until tomorrow, when you must take it to the bank and have the money deposited. That will help keep *you* safe and it will ensure that the money isn't stolen from you. Are you agreeable to that?'

'Oh dear. Very well, Inspector. You win.'

TEN

It was 2.30 a.m. when Angel pushed his way through the front door of Bromersley Police Station. He was hugging a large flour bin, its lid secured with strong brown sticky tape. He was admitted through the security door on sight by a PC in reception, and he then made his way to the duty sergeant's counter. There was nobody there. There was a bell to press for attention, but Angel ignored it.

'Anybody there?' he called.

Sergeant Clifton appeared from behind the barrier. He blinked when he saw Angel carrying the flour bin. 'Oh, it's you, sir. Taking up cooking?'

'Very funny,' Angel said, resting the flour bin on the counter. He looked round. 'Are you having a quiet night?'

'Makes a change, sir.'

'Is there anybody who could make a cup of tea?'

Clifton smiled. 'I think we can organize that, sir.'

'Who is in the cells?'

'Just Peter King. Waiting for you, sir. We couldn't make processing him stretch out any longer,' he added, passing three sheets of A4 stapled at one corner over to him. 'He's not a happy bunny.'

Clifton placed a key deliberately on the counter, then produced a clipboard and held it up for Angel. who scribbled his initials on it.

'Nobody on duty down there then, I take it?' Angel said, picking up the key.

Clifton shook his head. 'The super's on one of his economy drives.'

Angel nodded. 'Better make it two cups. And will you let me have a key for an empty cell?'

Clifton frowned, put another key on the counter, then said, 'Number two, sir.'

He scribbled something on the clipboard, passed him a pen and Angel initialled it.

Clifton looked at the flour bin on the counter and said, 'Is it for that, sir?'

'It's more valuable than it looks, Sergeant.'

Clifton scratched his head then said, 'I take it it's a rare Victorian antique, sir.'

Angel picked it up and said, 'Something like that.'

He returned to the green corridor, which was unusually deserted, and went straight down to cell number two. He put the flour bin on the floor, came out and locked it up. The other key was for cell number one. Angel peered through the inspection slot and saw Peter King, laid full length on the bed, hands behind his head, his feet crossed and his eyes closed.

He put the key in that lock and turned it. Before he had time to follow through and push the door open, the loud voice of Peter King said, 'Who is it? Who the frigging hell is it?'

Angel pushed into the cell.

King saw it was Angel. 'About frigging time,' King said.

Angel was in no mood to be messed around. It was almost three o'clock in the morning and he was tired. 'Shut up and listen,' he said. 'You've been arrested for attempting to burgle St Joseph's presbytery.'

'It wasn't me.'

'You were seen by two patrolmen, and your footprints confirm it. Yours are the only prints there on fresh snow.'

'It wasn't me. You coppers do whatever you like. You don't take any notice of me. If I say I done something you don't believe me. If I say I *haven't* done something you lock me up. I can't make you out.'

'Don't talk in riddles, lad. I'm too tired to play games.'

'I told you I raped and murdered that girl in Leeds before Christmas but you don't believe me. Now that's a big case, isn't it? It was front page in the *Yorkshire Post* and the *Mirror*. It was even on TV. Breaking a little window in that church house place is peanuts, and I say it wasn't me, but you don't believe me when I say that either.'

'Had you ever thought it was because you are an inveterate liar, lad? Leeds police say that that rape and murder couldn't have been you, so there's an end to it. And so far as breaking the window is concerned, you know and I know that your boots will be a perfect fit to moulds Forensic will make when they check them later this morning.'

They heard footsteps and there was a knock on the open cell door. A constable brought a tin tray with two beakers of tea on it. He passed it to Angel.

'Thank you, Officer,' Angel said.

The young policeman nodded and went out.

Peter King's face brightened and he sat upright when he saw two beakers on the tray. He looked at Angel and said, 'One of them for me?'

Angel offered him the tray.

King took one of the cups, sipped the tea and nodded approvingly.

Angel also enjoyed the tea, the only refreshment he had had for hours.

After a few moments, King looked over the rim of the beaker and said, 'I suppose you're not bad for a copper, Mr Angel.'

Angel looked at him and shook his head. 'Why don't you tell the truth for a change, Peter? You'd be in less trouble if you did. This offence has two police witnesses and forensic to back them up, so you are certain to be found guilty.'

He sipped the tea thoughtfully then said, 'If I'm found guilty, Mr Angel, how long would I get?'

'You *are* guilty, lad. With your record, you will probably get thirty days, or at worst ninety.'

'All right, and if I *pleaded* guilty, how long?'

'The same, lad. Even if you had O. J. Simpson's brief, I don't see you getting off with less.'

He nodded. 'That's what I thought,' he said and returned to sipping the tea.

Angel looked at him and pursed his lips. He really wanted to know King's motivation. This was the closest emotionally he had ever been to the man. Did King actually know there was a mountain of cash in St Joseph's presbytery, or was he breaking into the place on the off-chance there might be something there worth stealing? Also, was he the murderer of Harry Weston, Samuel Smart and Raymond Gulli, and the man who broke into Hugo Riley's church? He could fit the witness's description. But he wasn't seen wearing a white cloak. Could he really be that man? He supposed he might resemble the drawing executed by the police artist.

Angel warmed his hands briefly round the beaker then finished off the tea. He breathed deeply three times and tried to think friendly thoughts towards King. It wasn't easy.

'So, Peter, tell me,' Angel said, 'why did you try to break into the presbytery, the house where the vicar lives? There's nothing there – is there? – but the usual domestic clobber. You might have found a surfeit of dog collars, Bibles and candles, maybe ... but nothing really worth serving time for, was there?'

King smiled, his mouth puckering up like a baby's. On him it was grotesque. 'I think you are trying to pump me for information, Mr Angel.'

'I think I am. It's what coppers do.'

'It must be very boring.'

'It is sometimes, but not always. Not in your case, Peter.'

'What do you mean exactly?'

'Well, you know you have a very interesting personality.'

'Do I really, Mr Angel? In what way?'

'Oh yes. In many ways. For instance, you try and tell me that you *haven't* tried to break into St Joseph's presbytery when all the evidence indicates that you have.'

'Well, you don't expect me to admit that I have, just like that, Mr Angel. I *have* got standards, you know. In what other ways do you find me interesting?'

'Well, attempting to break into a place where there is virtually nothing useful to take.'

'Ah, well now, that's where you're wrong, Mr Angel. You might think that I don't know what I'm doing. You might think that I think that St Joseph's is a broken-down, poverty-stricken church, whereas I know it's a very wealthy church. I know that the vicar there is well off. His father lived in a big house on Creesforth Road. The old man died recently; now that house must be worth a few bob. Also, Mr Angel, there's more.'

'Oh,' he said.

'Yes. The old lady of the house, his batty sister, is regularly winning big lumps on the ponies.'

'Really? That's extremely clever of you, Peter.'

'I was in Brian's the bookies a couple of days back when her cleaner came in to collect the old lady's winnings. And it was a fair wad, I can tell you. Just about cleaned Brian out.'

'Really?' Angel said, trying to sound impressed. 'I knew there were hidden depths to you, Peter.'

'So you see, if your men had not driven up like lunatics and caught me in their headlights, I would have gotten into the house – there was no burglar alarm – and I might have found the old lady's winnings and come out loaded. There!'

Angel nodded. King's motive appeared to have been simple robbery. He was glad to have cleared that up.

'That was good for us, Peter, but bad luck for you.'

'Yes, Mr Angel. Bad luck, that's all it was. Bad luck.'

King pounced on the words 'bad luck' like Harker spotting a five pence piece on the office floor. Angel knew he would. Villains always believed they'd got a bigger measure of bad luck than anybody else.

'I've been dogged with bad luck all my life,' King said.

Angel wanted to smile. He rubbed his chin to cover his mouth. He still wanted information about the murders. He wondered if King might be persuaded to talk about them. Everything he had said when he had last interviewed him had been annoyingly and deliberately inconclusive. Time had moved on, maybe circumstances had changed. He wondered how he might get round to reintroducing the subject.

'You weren't afraid then?' Angel said.

'Afraid? Me? Nah,' he said, shaking his head then putting his nose into the beaker.

Angel waited. He expected King to say more.

King finished the tea and then half closed his eyes and pursed his lips. After a few moments he said, 'Afraid of what?'

That was what Angel had hoped for.

'The murderer, of course,' he said as casually as he could. 'He could have been ransacking the house. You could have interrupted him.'

King's arms and shoulders twitched. The pupils of his eyes slid to the side and back. The mood had changed. 'I'd better say no comment to that one, Inspector,' he said. Then he leaned back on to the pillow and stretched out his legs. 'I'm answering no more questions. Leave me alone. I'm tired. I want to go to sleep.'

Angel returned the key to cell number one to DS Clifton and went home. It was 3.30 a.m.

Mary was in her nightdress and housecoat and had fallen asleep in an easy chair. She awoke instantly when she heard Angel turn the key in the lock in the back door. She was relieved to see him but angry that he had not phoned. They had a few words but when he explained the situation concerning Miss Wilkinson, she quickly forgave him. She made them a hot drink, which she took to bed on a tray.

Angel got undressed, had a good wash, set the alarm for nine o'clock, finished the drink and went straight to sleep.

Next morning, he was in the office for ten o'clock. He had to attend court with Peter King at eleven. Despite the evidence, King pleaded not guilty, which angered the magistrate's clerk, who gave him a telling off. The upshot of all that was that he was remanded to the Crown Court at a date to be notified, and made the subject of an interim Probation Order.

Angel was tolerably well satisfied with the result and he dashed back to the station. As he made his way up the green corridor to his office, he could hear his phone ringing. He pushed open the door and answered it in time.

It was DC Scrivens. 'I tried to get you earlier, sir, but your mobile was on voicemail.'

'What is it, lad? Something urgent?'

Scrivens hesitated. 'Well, sir, I have still got two unmarked cars in positions observing the two warehouses.'

'I know, lad. Has there been a delivery of phony biscuits, then?'

'No, sir. We've monitored all the deliveries, videoed all the vehicles, drivers and crew, checked the index numbers with Swansea, and everything has been entirely in order.'

'Pity. What are you bothering me for?'

'We have been here since Tuesday afternoon, sir, and I am

concerned that if we stay here much longer, we are going to be sussed.'

Angel's eyebrows went up.

'I wondered what you would want us to do?' Scrivens said.

Angel frowned. The lad had a point. It was a big consignment of cocaine they were on the lookout for, worth a very big lump of money, which would have to be paid for in cash. Drug deals were always cash. Therefore the delivery crew could very well be the principals, and if they were, would very likely be armed.

'What do you want me to do, sir?' Scrivens repeated.

'Well, do you think you can hang on there and stay unobserved until the warehouses close today, lad?'

'I daresay we can, sir.'

'Do that then. Stand down for the weekend, report to me on Monday early doors and I'll make my mind up then whether to continue or not. In the meantime, keep your eyes peeled.'

He replaced the phone. It was always worrying when a large consignment of a Class A drug was reported to be coming into the area.

Angel ran his hand through his hair and looked at his watch. It was 11.30 a.m. and Miss Wilkinson had not yet arranged for the collection of her flour bin. He was still holding the key to cell two. So many things to do. So much detail. He reached out for the phone.

There was a knock at the door. More disturbance. There was no time to think. He looked at it, mouth slightly open and his lips tight back against his teeth. 'Come in,' he bawled.

It was DS Carter. She looked excited. She was carrying a suitcase.

'I've got it, sir,' she said, holding the case up for him to see.

'According to Mrs Vincent, the witness, this is an exact replica of the suitcase she saw the thieves pack the money into, sir,' Carter said.

He replaced the phone and blew out a lungful of air.

The suitcase was mainly stone coloured but had a dozen or more thin brown stripes across the lower half of it.

Angel looked at it thoughtfully, then he said, 'It would hold four million quid, in tens and twenties, I suppose.'

Carter nodded in agreement.

'I have seen that pattern before, but it *is* a bit unusual,' he said.

'That *should* help us,' she said.

He agreed, then silently reckoned he needed all the help he could get.

'It would be worthwhile having a photograph of it in the *Bromersley Chronicle*, Flora,' he said. 'If we could recover it, even if it had been discarded empty, we might get some DNA that could lead us straight to the thieves. Get Ahmed to photograph it.'

'Right, sir. But there's something else.'

He looked up.

'That American, Ben Wizard character, ex-partner of Felicity Kellerman, sir. Got his email address from her.'

'Yes. What about him?' he said.

'I managed to catch up with him, sir. He said that he has a two-week booking at the Cat and the Canary, Washington Avenue, in Seattle. I asked him where he was at three o'clock on Monday afternoon, the time that Harry Weston was shot, and he said on a train travelling down from Liverpool to London, on his way to Heathrow.'

Angel sighed. 'That's not good enough, Flora. He could have shot Harry Weston at the ticket office at three o'clock, taken a later train via Sheffield to Euston, then on to Heathrow.'

She nodded. 'I'll check on the CCTV, sir?'

'It will be too late for that. British Rail won't have kept tapes since then. You could try Heathrow. See what flight he was on, and the time of its departure. That might confirm his story. If he was in the air before, say, seven o'clock, Monday night, he couldn't possibly have murdered Harry Weston, or the two priests, and he couldn't have been the one who turned Father Riley's place upside-down.'

'I'll get straight on to it, sir.'

She went out.

The arrival of Flora Carter with the suitcase reminded Angel that he was in possession of three exhibits that were actually used by the robbers in the security van robbery. He swivelled round in the chair to the small table behind him and picked up two evidence bags. He looked at the labels. In one bag was the screwdriver used to short circuit the key switch on the crane, and in the other bag the two that had been sharpened and used to puncture two of the tyres of the stolen furniture van. SOCO had been unable to find any prints or DNA on any of them and they had been on the table behind him for the past two days.

He took them out of their bags and examined them carefully. The three screwdrivers matched each other. They were ten inches long, the handles were made from a dark burgundy-coloured rubber material and had six sides. On each of the sides was a tiny logo composed of five white rectangles, three black rectangles and the letters MO scrolled over them all.

Angel looked at the logo, trying to work out what it might represent. He pulled open a desk drawer, rummaged around inside it and brought out a jeweller's 8x loupe. He fitted it into his eye and peered closely at the screwdriver handle. He went over to the window for the best light and turned it over for different angles, but he couldn't work out what the logo represented. He looked at it with the loupe again. The phone rang. He returned to his desk and dropped into the swivel chair. He picked up the receiver and got a loud blast of a man coughing loudly into the earpiece. He knew it was Harker. The coughing persisted. Angel held the phone away at arm's length until it stopped.

'Are you there, Angel?' Harker said, clearing his throat. 'I want you in my office, now.'

'Right, sir,' Angel said.

Harker banged down the phone.

The muscles of Angel's face tightened and he rubbed his chin hard. He had no idea what the superintendent wanted to see him about. It was probably to chivvy him up about his lack of progress with the case. He always had a go at him about two or three days into a murder investigation. Whatever it was, it would be annoying, difficult and unhelpful. It always was. He dropped the loupe back into the drawer and closed it, but left the screwdrivers and everything else as it was. He dashed out of his office, up the corridor, knocked on Harker's door and went in.

The superintendent was sitting at his desk behind piles of papers, wiping his purple nose.

'Come in, lad,' Harker said. 'Keep that door shut, and sit down.'

Angel quickly closed the door and turned round into the room. A shaft of warm air hit him in the face. He blinked. The office was hot enough to grow mushrooms. Angel soon found out why.

Harker had a large portable fan heater behind the desk about a yard away from his feet and legs. He grunted and said, 'There's a flour bin occupying a cell. The duty sergeant said that it was yours, and that you're hanging on to the key.'

'Yes. That's right, sir.'

'I presume there's a reason for it. It's not that flour is going to be in short supply and it would interfere with your cake baking, is it?'

Angel wasn't pleased. He quickly told him what was inside the bin, and that it belonged to Miss Wilkinson and that she was due there that morning to take responsibility for it and organize the counting and payment of it into a bank.

'We're not Securicor, you know, lad. Get shot of it.'

'Yes, sir.'

'Now how's the murder case coming along? Who have you got in the frame?'

Angel didn't want to answer him. 'Nobody, actually, sir.'

'*Nobody*?'

'There are several people who might have a motive for murdering Harry Weston, but no *one* suspect stands out.'

'Who, for example?'

He would ask that, Angel thought. 'Well, sir, witnesses have said that Harry Weston had relationships with two girls at the same time. I don't see that as a motive for murdering anybody, but some people do. Matter of pride. So there's Angus Rossi, father of the girl Weston had been seeing on a regular basis until two weeks ago. Angus Rossi is a hot-tempered, uncouth and proud sort of man. Then there's Ben Wizard, partner or ex-partner of the girl Weston had abruptly befriended a few months back. But Ben Wizard has a beard and whiskers, and the murderer is clean shaven. Or there's Clive Grogan, son of Grogan, the ice-cream manufacturer, now courting Madeleine Rossi. He might be under pressure from Madeleine to prove his love for her by shooting the young man who she says was cheating on her, except that he's far too civilized, well brought up and, I think, too young. And there is a man of the road, known as Irish John.'

'Is this Irish John known to us?'

'No, sir. I've got Crisp trying to find him. He hasn't reported back yet. He might be having a difficult time. I thought it might be possible that he might have called for a handout at each of the two vicarages, had the gun and shot each priest, robbed him and then turned their places upside-down looking for more money. Also, there might be other men of the road I may have to find and interview. I'm hopeful of turning up a discretionary payment record at one of the churches that might produce information about other regulars calling at the vicarages, manses and presbyteries.'

Harker's ginger eyebrows floated upwards. 'Is that the extent of your progress?'

Angel wasn't pleased. 'Well, I have been diverted by other cases and security matters,' he said.

Harker sniffed. 'What about the murderer of the other two men?' he said.

'I've nothing new on that, sir.'

'What forensic have you got?'

'Only a white thread found on the body of the priest, Raymond Gulli of St Barnabas's Church. I am waiting for SOCO to report further on it, if there is anything more to say. They confirm that it has definitely come from the murderer's clothes because there aren't any textiles in the vicinity that match it.'

'And what's this about the suspect always seen in a white gown? What sort of a white gown?'

Angel shook his head slowly. 'I don't know, sir. I really don't know.'

'Why would a man walk around in white, in Bromersley?' Harker said. Then he suddenly looked up. 'I suppose it is a man, and not a woman?' he added.

'It's a man, sir,' Angel said.

'A man in a dog collar?'

Angel nodded then said, 'I have a witness. She says she saw a man in a dog collar leaving the scene.'

'Well, have you evidence to show that the murders were committed by one and the same person?'

'No, sir. But I do know that the victims were all killed by the same gun. Last night, Peter King made an attempt to get into St

140

Joseph's presbytery. At first I thought he could have been the murderer but I don't know. He's such a liar. He might even confess to it but it wouldn't necessarily be valid. He confessed to murdering and raping that girl in Leeds just before Christmas but of course he didn't do it.'

'You have an eye witness, a woman, Zoe Costello?'

Angel shrugged. 'Yes.'

'Have you had King in a line-up?'

'I considered it, sir. He'll probably invalidate it by making himself conspicuous. He always looks guilty.'

'Never mind that. Put him in a line-up and go for a confession.'

Angel's jaw muscles tightened. 'I don't want a false arrest,' he said.

'I don't,' Harker said quickly.

Angel didn't believe him.

'Peter King is a bloody nuisance,' Harker continued. 'He's responsible for half the petty crime in this town. If he wants a spell inside again, he can have a spell inside. We've got to get our figures up. There are too many criminals in Bromersley.'

Angel was outraged. He had difficulty remaining seated. His eyes shone like lasers and he had to consciously regulate his breathing to control himself. He'd known Harker eleven years and he knew he couldn't reason with him but he would have to think very carefully indeed about what his boss had just said. He felt uncomfortably hot, and it wasn't entirely caused by the fan heater. He ran his fingers round his shirt collar, pulling it away from his neck. It didn't afford him much relief. He knew he must change the subject, move on and get out of Harker's office.

'About that cocaine intelligence, sir,' Angel said.

Harker's bushy eyebrows shot up. 'Aye. What about it?'

'How long do you want to maintain the surveillance? I have had two teams outside those warehouses for two days now. Could be getting risky.'

'Mmm,' Harker said, nodding. He pursed his thin blue lips.

Angel watched him and waited. Harker wouldn't be pleased if his posh mate in the Met had fed him duff information.

'Call the surveillance off at the end of today's shift, lad,' Harker said.

Angel looked up, his mouth open. He was amazed to find that

there was something they agreed on. It was years since that had happened.

Then Harker started coughing. He quickly took two pills with a sip of water. The coughing continued. Angel waited. Harker went red in the face. As soon as the coughing subsided, it started up again. Eventually, Harker picked up a throat spray, pointed to the door and waved Angel away. He didn't need telling twice.

He came out of the sweatbox and made his way down the green corridor to his office. He slumped down in the swivel chair. His face was a picture: he looked like he'd bitten into a Jaffa and found it was a lemon. He leaned back in the chair, rubbed his face and considered what exactly had happened in those last few minutes. Harker had instructed him to organize an identity parade, and he wanted him to fix it (if it needed fixing) so that Peter King was picked out as the murderer by the witness, Zoe Costello, then to build a case against him to make sure he was convicted. And he wanted him to do that to increase the clear-up rate, because King was a nuisance when he was out of prison and because Harker considered it would be relatively easy to build a case against him as King was so desperate to be a famous criminal, even a multiple murderer.

Angel didn't like it one bit and he knew he couldn't do it. He mulled over the problem a little while then made a decision. He would do all that Harker had said, go through all the motions, but stop before actually charging the man. If King was innocent, there were bound to be big holes in the case. Angel could highlight them to Mr Twelvetrees, the barrister at the CPS, if needs be. He would reject the case and hopefully that would be the end of the matter. Of course, a more certain way of preventing Peter King being charged, tried and imprisoned was for Angel to find and charge the actual murderer.

His thoughts were disturbed by a knock at the door.

'Come in,' he called.

It was Ahmed. He was holding an envelope. 'There's a young lady at reception, sir. She sent this letter down for you. There's a man with her. I think he's her driver.'

Angel tore open the envelope. The letter was handwritten on blue letter-headed notepaper. It read:

St Joseph's Presbytery,
St Joseph's Catholic Church,
King Street,
BROMERSLEY.

Dear Inspector Angel,

Thank you so very much for kindly attending to me and advising me last night. I certainly intend to put most of that money in the bank. However, I need some readies, as they say, on hand because I am going racing again this afternoon. Accordingly, I have arranged for my help and friend, Miss Elaine Jubb, the bearer of this letter, assisted by my brother's driver, Mr Quentin Lamb, to collect the flour bin from you.

Please accept and hold this letter as authority from me for you to give it to them.

They have instructions to take it to the Northern Bank where I have made arrangements with the manager for the money to be counted, in their presence, checked and deposited there in my name.

Many thanks again,
Yours sincerely,
Phoebe Wilkinson (Miss)

Angel looked up at Ahmed. 'Good,' he said and he patted his jacket pocket to check that he had the key to cell two. 'Come with me, lad.'

They trudged up to the reception office and Angel peered through the partially obscured striped glass window to check that it was Elaine Jubb who had brought the letter, and also to clock in Quentin Lamb and make sure that everything was above board. Then Angel gave the key to cell two to Ahmed and instructed him to hand the sealed flour bin over to them, return the key to the duty jailer and report back to him ASAP.

Ahmed rushed off in the direction of the cells, while Angel went back down the green corridor. When he arrived at his office, Angel picked up the phone and tapped out a number. It rang out a long time but was eventually answered by Crisp.

'Where are you, lad?' Angel said. 'The south of France?'

'I'm down Canal Road, sir. Looking for those men of the road.'

'Aye, that's what you're *supposed* to be doing. Haven't heard a peep out of you for days. I thought you'd taken off on your annual holidays.'

'That's not funny, sir. I've put a lot of leg work in, and there's no sight or sound of any men of that sort. I can only think that they must have gone to ground. The one known as Irish John used to be in and out of The Fisherman's Rest on Canal Road all the hours it was open. But he has not been seen since last Monday, the day the murders began.'

'All right, lad,' Angel said. 'Leave that for now and come on in. I've another job for you.'

He cancelled the call and immediately tapped out another number.

'Probation Service,' a voice said. 'Kathy Ellison speaking.'

'Ah, Kathy, Michael Angel here. That chap, Peter King, made the subject of an interim Probation Order this morning. What address have you got for him?'

'Oh yes, Michael. Just a minute.' There was a rustle of papers. 'Yes. We haven't got one yet. He wouldn't tell us.'

'We'll get it. Thank you, Kathy.'

There was a knock at the door.

'Come in,' he said as he replaced the phone.

It was Ahmed. 'You wanted me, sir?'

'Yes, lad. I want the most recent address of Peter King. Check on his past records and somewhere you'll find his National Insurance number. Then phone Social Security, give them his name and that number and they'll give you his address.'

Ahmed's face brightened. 'Is it as easy as that, sir?'

'Yes, lad,' Angel said. 'Where the giro goest, the villain goest.'

Ahmed nodded.

'Then give that address to DS Taylor. He'll need it to be able to search King's pad, all right?'

'Yes, sir,' he said and turned to go.

'Just a minute,' Angel said. 'Before that, I want you to get ten square yards of plain black cloth and ten priest's dog collars, smartish.'

Ahmed's mouth dropped open.

'Well, don't stand there looking like Goldie the goldfish,' Angel said, 'Swim off and get them.'

ELEVEN

The identity parade in this instance had to consist of white men between five foot six and five foot eleven, of proportionate build, dark haired, no beard or moustache, no spectacles, in a dark suit, wearing a black frontal and a traditional priest's dog collar.

It took more than an hour to organize such a line-up. Some of the men were off-duty policemen, some clerks from the insurance company next door and two pedestrians simply accosted while passing the station who had the time to spare and were seemingly persuaded by the token sum of money they would be paid.

The CID briefing room was transformed into the site for the ID parade simply by stacking the chairs and pushing them against the wall. The procedure could be observed through a one-way glass from an observation gallery. All audio communication between the rooms was through mikes and loudspeakers. Observers in the gallery could speak to those in the briefing room when required through a mike which was on a small table next to a telephone.

The shirt fronts were simply made from two lengths of black cloth used as table coverings when ad hoc meetings such as press conferences had been set up in the canteen. Ahmed had cut the cloth into suitably sized pieces, which were attached to the collar and tucked in the trouser top and stuck over the man's own shirt where necessary with Sellotape. He had contrived the priest's collars from white, glossy cardboard retrieved from two boxes which had contained high-profile luminous waistcoats delivered to the station the previous day. He had carefully cut and fitted the cardboard collars round the necks of each of the men and fastened them to size at the back of the neck with the CID office stapler.

Angel arrived and went into the briefing room. He looked down the line of the nine 'vicars' and involuntarily shook his head. Then he looked at Ahmed and winked.

Ahmed smiled and nodded. He knew Angel was pleased with the way the line of men looked.

'Right, gentlemen,' Angel said. 'Are we all ready? Please stand with your backs to the blackboard … That's it. Thank you … Now when the accused is brought in, he is entitled to choose where he stands, so please, allow him that courtesy. All right?'

There was no response.

'Then when the witness comes in,' he said, 'please keep still and look straight ahead. It is possible that she may touch you lightly on the shoulder. Please allow her to do that, and don't worry about it. It simply means she has chosen you and she could be wrong. It happens sometimes. Do not speak to her unless she speaks to you. All right?'

Some muttered 'Yes' but most of them looked at each other and shuffled uneasily.

'Thank you,' he said. He turned and went out of the briefing room, along the corridor a little way then through a side door, up six steps into the gallery where Mr Bloomberg, Peter King's solicitor, was already waiting. He knew him of old and had had many clashes with him over the years in the magistrates' court.

'Good afternoon, Mr Bloomberg,' Angel said. He pointed with his thumb through the one-way glass. 'Is everything all right? Are you satisfied?'

'Good afternoon to you, Inspector. Yes, of course.'

King had not wanted a solicitor to represent him but in an identity parade it was a regulatory requirement. The police needed his presence there as much as the accused, otherwise the line-up – a procedure that can only be undertaken once – might not be regarded as fair and square. In the case of murder, such as this one, an error by a witness at an identification parade could take away an innocent man's freedom for many years.

Angel picked up the phone and tapped in the number of the extension phone on the wall down in the cells. It was promptly answered.

'PC Weightman, sir.'

'We're ready, John. Bring him up.'

'Right, sir.'

Then Angel phoned the superintendent. 'We're ready for you, in the gallery, sir.'

'Right. I'll be straight down,' Harker said.

Ahmed began to go down the line, checking that all the men's cardboard collars and improvised black shirt fronts still looked good. He also tidied up any disorderly pocket flaps and jacket button fastenings.

A few moments later, Peter King strutted into the CID briefing room followed closely by Weightman.

The policeman waited by the door while King looked along at the line-up of the nine men dressed similarly to himself. He seemed to think it amusing.

Ahmed finished titivating them and then stepped back to the door.

Angel picked up the mike and pressed the switch. 'Thank you, John.'

Weightman said, 'Right, sir,' and took up a position by the door next to Ahmed.

'Now then, King,' Angel said.

King looked up and around, not pleased that he couldn't see Angel.

'Decide where you want to be. You can stand in any position you like.'

King looked towards the door, and decided to take the first position nearest to it. He stood there a moment, thinking about it. He looked each side and then decided that he didn't like being there. He came out of the position, turned round and looked at the line-up. He stood there a few moments, then he pushed his way into the second position in the line-up. He looked to his left and his right and still seemed unsure.

Angel switched on the mike. 'Are you satisfied that's where you want to be?'

King looked around the room, then looked along to his left and then his right and eventually said, 'Yes.'

'Are you sure?'

King's face suddenly creased up. He put up both his hands, spread his fingers and shook them very quickly. '*Yes*. I'm frigging sure. I said so, didn't I?' he bawled. 'Frigging hell, let's get on with it.'

Ahmed went up to him to check on his shirt front, collar and so on. King made a fierce face at him and waved him away.

Angel saw it, pressed the button on the mike and said, 'All right, Ahmed. Leave him. Thank you.'

Ahmed turned away and returned to the door.

King maintained the position, but kept looking at the men to his left.

Angel turned to Bloomberg, pointed through the window and said, 'Are you satisfied with that?'

Bloomberg, who Angel thought had been following events, didn't seem very interested. 'That's fine by me, Inspector.'

Angel picked up the phone and tapped out a number.

It was promptly answered by Crisp, who was waiting in Angel's office with Zoe Costello. 'Yes, sir?' he said.

'Right, Trevor,' Angel said, 'bring her up. And don't forget, bring her back to my office after the parade.'

'Right, sir.'

He replaced the phone.

King suddenly yelled out, '*Where the frigging hell is she?*'

Angel heard him, looked through the window and reached out for the mike.

Weightman stepped forward with his hands open and in front of him in an effort to quieten him. The other men in the line stared down at King. They didn't like the disturbance. They pulled faces and began to shuffle their feet.

'Be quiet, King,' Angel said, squeezing the mike. 'You have to keep quiet until the witness has been *and* gone.'

'I can't stand here all day like a monkey up a frigging stick.'

'You have to. The witness is on her way. It is only a matter of seconds now. And then it won't take long.'

The other men in the line muttered between themselves.

'Now everybody, back in position, please,' Angel said.

Superintendent Harker arrived in the gallery in a haze of TCP.

Angel noticed the smell and turned round.

'Is everything all right?' Harker said.

'Yes, sir. King is getting a bit worked up, that's all.'

Harker smiled.

Angel frowned. He couldn't understand what he was smiling at. He hardly ever saw him smile. Angel had heard years ago that the officers in the station said that every time the superintendent smiled a donkey died.

Harker nodded at Bloomberg, who nodded back and said, 'Good afternoon, Superintendent.'

Harker stood next to Angel and surveyed the line-up below. 'I see King is in position number two, Inspector?' he said. 'I've never known a suspect stand *there*.'

'That's where he chose, sir.'

Suddenly, from the briefing room, PC Weightman looked up in the direction of the gallery window and said, 'The witness is here, sir.'

Angel reached out for the mike, pressed the button and said, 'Right, John. Tell DS Crisp to carry on, please.'

Weightman waved an acknowledgement and went out into the corridor.

King looked agitated and kept looking towards the doorway.

Seconds later, Zoe Costello arrived. She stood there and looked round the room. When she saw the line of men in dog collars, her eyes opened wide and she froze on the spot. She couldn't move.

Crisp and Weightman edged close up to her.

'Go on, miss,' Crisp whispered. 'I'm going to be right behind you.'

'It's all right, miss,' Weightman said.

Angel, Harker and Bloomberg looked down at the doorway from the gallery in silence.

Zoe Costello took a tentative step into the room.

King stared hard at her.

'Now then, miss,' Crisp said, 'look carefully at each man. If you see the man who shot the ticket clerk at the railway station last Monday, just touch him on the arm. That's all you have to do. Now take your time.'

Zoe Costello looked back at Crisp, nodded and edged towards the first man. She stopped in front of him, looked at his face and into his eyes. He avoided looking directly back at her. She glanced down his front to the floor then back up to his face, pursed her lips momentarily, relaxed them and then moved on.

Crisp was only a step behind her, and Weightman only a step behind him.

King was next in line and he was staring at her hard.

The three men in the gallery leaned forward so that they would not miss anything.

Zoe Costello was aware that King was staring at her. Her face creased. She found it an embarrassment and wished that he would stop. She had to look at his face, which she did quickly, then glanced down at the front of his jacket, and to the floor. As her head came back up, she noticed out of her eye corner that in addition to staring at her, he was now making small, quick nodding movements.

She pursed her lips and turned to Crisp, her eyebrows raised and her open hands turned upwards with her fingers spread.

Crisp shrugged. He couldn't say anything. Identity parade rules did not allow him to make any comment about any individual person in the line-up until the witness had left the parade.

Zoe Costello frowned.

Harker watched from the gallery, rubbing his bony chin hard and fast, his lips twitching.

Bloomberg simply wondered whether at the end of the parade he would have a man to defend against murder or not.

Angel licked his bottom lip and hoped that Zoe Costello was simply going to pass King by.

She did. She moved on to the third man.

Harker's face dropped. 'What's the matter with the woman? Is she blind?'

Angel sighed but he knew it wasn't over. 'She might pick him out on the way back,' he said.

'No, she won't,' Harker said.

Zoe Costello continued down the line. Crisp and Weightman followed close behind. She was painstakingly thorough and slow.

Angel, Harker and Bloomberg stood patiently, observing in silence.

Then, suddenly, their eyes were averted to King, who had unexpectedly walked over to a stack of chairs that had been moved out of the way. He lifted off the top one, managing to rattle the legs of it on the lower one to produce the maximum amount of noise.

Angel's jaw muscles tightened. 'Just look at that, sir,' he said.

Harker said, 'The silly bugger.'

Angel shook his head.

Their eyes stayed on him.

King then proceeded to take the chair back to where he had been standing, banged it on the floor, pushed it up against the blackboard, sat down on it, crossed his legs, folded his arms and pulled a face like a disinterested bystander.

The other men nearest to him in the parade glared at him.

Zoe Costello suddenly glanced round, followed by Crisp and Weightman, who had only just caught up with the disturbance. They couldn't see King seated in the chair from where they stood. Seeing nothing, they turned back.

Minutes later, Zoe Costello had reached the tenth man.

Angel ran his hand through his hair and paced up and down in the limited area at the back of the gallery. He had never experienced this behaviour in an ID parade before and was glad it was almost over.

He returned to the glass and watched Zoe Costello surveying the last man. She nodded, turned away and seemed to have finished. She turned to Crisp and said, 'Can I just have a quick look down the line again, just to make sure?'

He nodded, and he and Weightman stepped back a few paces to allow her to take the lead.

She retraced her steps away from number ten, and past numbers nine, eight, seven and six. She hovered over number five for a moment or two. It looked as if she might touch him on the arm, but she didn't. She moved on to four. It was then that she noticed King seated in the chair. She turned to Crisp. A word formed on her lips. She decided not to say it. He shrugged. She frowned briefly.

In the gallery, Harker almost exploded. 'This is intolerable,' he said, and he snatched up the mike, switched it on and said, 'Miss er, Miss Costello. Miss Costello. This is Detective Superintendent Harker. If you want the gentleman in the second position to stand up, so that you can see him better, I believe that if DS Crisp asks him, he will.'

Crisp didn't need to do anything. King had heard Harker, and promptly stood up. He wasn't sulking any more either.

Angel thought that the mere fact that Harker, a superintendent, had noticed him and picked him out had greatly improved King's spirits.

Zoe Costello seemed at a loss and, after hesitating, looked towards the body of the room and vaguely said a weak, 'Thank you.'

She looked carefully at King, who now showed himself off as if he was a male model.

The men in the gallery stared down at the pantomime.

Zoe Costello soon turned away from him and moved on to the man in the first position, by the door.

Harker put his hands up to each side of his head and groaned.

It was virtually all over.

Angel sighed but kept his eye on the action in the room below … just in case.

Zoe Costello gave a cursory glance at the first man again, then with a slight shake of the head looked at Crisp and walked out of the room. Crisp followed her.

That really was it.

Angel saw Bloomberg pick up his briefcase. He thought he would want to rush off and tell King that – thanks to his efforts! – he was free to leave, which indeed he was.

Angel didn't quite know what to say to King's solicitor. Bloomberg *might* allege that the identification parade was invalid but Angel didn't think that likely because the witness had not identified his client as the murderer. If Bloomberg *did* claim that the parade was invalid, Harker would know exactly the course of action to be taken. He could leave them to chew the rag about that and decide what to do. Angel had enough trouble. Harker, of course, would not be pleased with the outcome either. He had hoped for the ID parade to have produced a positive result and it hadn't. Harker had hoped to see Peter King put away for a twenty-year stretch at least and it looked like it wasn't going to happen. Angel could not see how they could possibly go through the exercise again.

'Excuse me, gentlemen,' Angel said. 'Must catch up with the witness.'

He dashed down the steps and through the door into the green corridor. He could see Zoe Costello, escorted by Crisp, stepping towards his office as arranged.

By the time he caught up, Crisp was leaving his office and closing the door.

'The witness is in your office, sir,' Crisp said.

Angel nodded.

'What happens to King now?' Crisp said.

'For the time being, we have to accept the witness's judgement that King isn't the murderer. So ring Kathy Ellison at the Probation Office and tell her that he is no longer an official suspect in this case, and then release him.'

'Release him?'

'Yes, lad. *Release him.*'

Crisp looked thoughtful but said, 'Right, sir.'

Angel cocked a thumb at his office door and said, 'How is she? Zoe Costello? How did she take it all?'

Crisp smiled. 'I think she's cooled down now, sir.'

It was eight o'clock on Saturday morning, 16 January, and Michael Angel was still in bed asleep. He was dreaming of a hot sun, a golden beach and a turquoise and aquamarine blue sea. He was dreaming of willowy girls with no hips, in minuscule bikinis, carrying trays of champagne cocktails. There was laughter, gentle string music and the swishing sound of the sea. One of the girls lay next to him. She snuggled into his arms. He kissed her tenderly on the lips. It was a warm kiss. A kiss full of promise. He gently manoeuvred his arms under hers and pulled her to him. She didn't resist. She was soft and compliant. She was totally under his spell.

'Michael,' she said appealingly.

He didn't reply.

'Michael,' she said again. This time there was an urgency about it.

'Be patient, my beautiful one,' he murmured.

Then he felt a strong tugging sensation at his shoulder. 'What did you say, Michael?' she said.

It was a voice he knew well.

He opened his eyes.

Mary was tugging at his shoulder. 'Whatever are you doing with that pillow? It's one of the new ones, you know ... filled with goose feathers. I thought you were going to eat it. And what was it you said?'

He rubbed his eyes, sniffed and said, 'I must have been dreaming.'

He noticed that Mary was fully dressed. He glanced at the clock.

'It's Saturday, isn't it?' he said.

'It *is*,' she said, surprising him with a quick kiss. 'And I want you to get up now. *Your* breakfast's ready. I've had what *I* want.'

Angel frowned.

'Come on, love,' she said. 'Hurry up. Bathroom's free.'

He looked up at her. She didn't look back. She rushed off.

His eyes followed her out of the bedroom.

He sat on the edge of the bed, looking at the anaglypta and scratching his stomach. There was something unusual about Mary's behaviour. Something was afoot ... very definitely afoot. He recognized the scenario. She had some plan, some horrible idea on her mind. Something she knew he wouldn't like and would object to. She wouldn't want to drop it on him all at once. She would have planned to feed titbits out to him as necessary as the plan progressed. In that way, he would be cushioned to the shock when the full scheme became known.

It would be as well if he could have some idea what she was up to. It would almost certainly involve spending money. All Mary's schemes and plans involved spending money. And that always came at a bad time. It certainly was a bad time on this occasion, just after Christmas. Funds were very low indeed. Her last idea was buying that bed for her sister, a bed which they didn't need and couldn't really afford – and which he had not yet assembled due to shortage of time, a certain lack of know-how and because he didn't want to do it.

'Michael! Michael!' she called from the kitchen.

He reached down for his slippers. 'Yes? Yes?'

'Are you moving?'

'Yes, love,' he called. 'I'm coming.'

'Are you in the bathroom?'

'Yes,' he lied.

He took off his pyjama jacket, stood up and crossed the landing to the bathroom. The room seemed brighter. He didn't need the electric light. He looked out of the window; the sun was trying to be seen. The big freeze had taken a breather and most of the snow that had been gripping the fields and hills for the earlier ten days had gone and the rest had turned to grey slush and soaked into the grass or disappeared into the brooks, becks and streams or down the drains.

The sight of the bright sky and the green fields made him wash and shave with enthusiasm. He even found himself humming, 'Oh What A Beautiful Morning'.

He walked into the kitchen wearing a dressing gown.

Mary gawped at him but said nothing. She put the teapot on the table. The muesli was already in a dish. He sat down, poured the milk over it and took a mouthful.

'You're not dressed,' she said.

Without looking up, through the muesli he said, 'It's Saturday.'

It had taken her long enough to state the obvious, he thought. She must be wanting him to get dressed and smarten himself up to go out somewhere. Perhaps take *her* out. He wouldn't mind that, now that the weather had changed and the roads would be clearer. But he wondered where she would be wanting to go.

She poured out two cups of tea and passed one over to him.

'Thank you, love,' he said.

She smiled. 'I thought we might go out somewhere nice.'

He nodded.

She didn't want him to do anything in the garden. That was good. It was far too cold and everything was soaking. He was pleased about that.

'Have lunch in a nice restaurant somewhere?' he said.

'We haven't done that for ages.'

'How about The Feathers?'

'I thought we might have a run out in the car. Make a day of it.'

Angel's face brightened. 'You mean the seaside? Scarborough? Bridlington? Skegness? Blow the cobwebs away?'

'I wasn't thinking of going *that* far,' she said. 'I was thinking that there are some lovely places to eat at Meadowhall.'

'Meadowhall?' Angel looked hard at her. 'That's just shops,' he said. He knew it. That was Mary's game. She wanted to go to one of the biggest shopping centres in the country, to eat.

Mary kept a dead straight face and said, 'There are all kinds of restaurants there.'

'I don't want fish and chips again!' he said. 'We are not going *there.*'

It was half past two.

Michael Angel followed Mary Angel across the busy tarmac of one of the packed car parks in Meadowhall to the BMW. He was carrying a parcel of five rolls of wallpaper. He sighed with relief as he lowered it into the car boot. Mary added two plastic bags containing sachets of paste and other bits and pieces. She hadn't planned on buying anything other than wallpaper and paste, but she had seen all sorts of knick-knacks in eye-catching wrapping on the shelves, had picked them up, decided they could be useful and popped them in the wire basket.

Angel had discovered, of course, as he knew he would, eventually, the con Mary had in her mind to work across him. It was the burning necessity, she reckoned, which hadn't been apparent to him (and probably never would have been), that the bedroom that was to be temporarily occupied by her sister, Lolly, very much needed refreshing and brightening with new wallpaper.

He wasn't pleased about this. He had slapped it on his credit card and had no organized thought-out way in which he was going to repay it without paying the bank's exorbitant interest. The gas bill was still not paid and was about a month overdue. But since the early days of their marriage, he had always said that Mary could have her own way, and without abusing the privilege, she always got it. Naturally, she was delighted and had pledged to do the paper-hanging herself, thereby saving that expense.

Angel slammed down the boot lid and they got into the car. They had had a passably good lunch at an expensive restaurant in and among the myriad of lanes of shops and were on their way home. Angel had nothing much to say in the way of conversation. It had all been exhausted in the earlier abandoned argument about the unnec-essary wallpapering of Lolly's room, as it had become known.

As Angel reached the outskirts of Bromersley, he saw one of Grogan's ice-cream vans parked near the gates of a small park off Sheffield Road. Two girls aged about fourteen suitably dressed in warm boots, overcoats with furry hoods and gloves, were walking away, laughing and licking on ice-cream cones.

He slowed the BMW down, pointed to the van ahead and said, 'Would you like an ice cream, Mary? Never tasted Grogan's ice cream. I wonder what it's like?'

'No, thank you, love,' she said. She pretended to shiver. 'It's too cold.'

He smiled. 'When was the last time you had a cornet?'

'A cornet?' she said, her eyebrows rising upward. She considered the suggestion. 'Are you having one?'

'Why not? Be a devil.'

'All right, love,' she said.

He stopped the BMW just behind the smartly painted ice-cream van and went round on the pavement to the serving window.

The salesman slid open the window. 'Good afternoon, sir. Now what can I get you?'

'Two vanilla cornets, please.'

'That's two pounds, please,' the man said.

As Angel dug into his pocket and fingered through his change, the salesman reached into a box, pulled out two large orange cones then deftly scooped large semi-spheres of ice cream and perched them on top of each one.

Angel put the correct money inside the window.

The salesman handed him the two cornets. As he did so, he quickly turned away as if he didn't want his face to be seen.

'Thank you,' Angel said.

The ice-cream man then picked up the money and said, 'Thank you, sir. Have a nice day.' He closed the window, put the server into a drawer and made his way to the driver's seat.

Angel nodded and wondered where he had seen the face before. He turned away from the van window to find himself facing the gate to the small park, which was wide open. Looking through it and along the path towards the swings was a strange sight he had heard reported before. About ten feet from the entrance, at the side of the path, was a small puddle of melting ice cream with six or seven cones sticking out of it. He went into the park and down the path. He crouched down to have a closer look. The ice-cream cornets appeared simply to have been discarded. Perhaps because they were sour or didn't taste right. He couldn't think of any other explanation. He looked at the two cornets he was holding. They looked identical to the ones thrown away. He straightened up and stood there a few moments, struggling for a reason, but none came.

He returned to the car. He noticed Grogan's van had packed up and gone.

He handed the ice cream to Mary, who took it eagerly. 'I don't think I've had a cornet for ten years or more. Thank you, darling,' she said.

He smiled and the couple began to lick the white stuff.

Mary dived straight in, and after a few preliminary licks made a suitable hole in the dome shape.

Angel didn't know what to expect. He started cautiously, considering each lick, ready to dispatch the cornet to a waste-bin if necessary.

Mary soon licked through the ice cream, reached the biscuit, crunched all the way through that, reached for her handbag for a handkerchief, wiped her lips and fingers with it, and said, 'Thank you, Michael. That was quite the nicest ice cream I have ever had.'

Angel had to agree. It really had tasted remarkably good. He started the car engine and pointed the car bonnet towards home.

However, the identity of the driver salesman in a Grogan's van and the reason for the ice-cream cornets being placed upside-down in the discarded ice cream around the town monopolized his thoughts throughout the weekend and beyond.

TWELVE

Sunday came. It was cold but there was no snow. Angel avoided looking at the clocks because although he was up early enough to go to church, he didn't really want to go. Mary said nothing. He thought that she probably felt the same.

He munched his way through his muesli and drank endless cups of tea, his mind on the upturned cone biscuits stuck in the melting ice cream. At the same time, Mary was wondering where she had put the paper scrapers after decorating the kitchen the previous spring, and how she could talk her husband into helping her to scrape paper off the bedroom walls. There was now less urgency to assemble the bed. That would be a job to do after the decoration had been completed.

They spoke only in monosyllables through breakfast until Mary said, 'Look at the time. Quarter past ten. We can't possibly get to church now.'

'No,' Angel said. He felt a little uncomfortable as he knew he had connived at being too late.

He left the breakfast table, taking his tea cup with him, moved into the sitting room, turned on the gas fire and switched on the TV. Up came the sound of a church organ followed by the picture of stained glass windows, candles and a choir in full voice. He watched it with interest. He could see it was an Anglican church and wondered from what part of the country it was being broadcast. He reasoned that if he watched that, it might mollify his conscience. Halfway through the second hymn, he began making notes about what he had to do the next day, Monday.

*

Angel arrived in the office at 8.28 a.m. as usual that Monday morning and was looking through the pile of envelopes and reports on his desk when there was a knock at the door. It was DC Scrivens.

'Good morning, sir. You said you would tell us whether you still wanted us to continue keeping obbo on those two warehouses.'

'I hadn't forgotten, Ted,' he said. 'Sit down. The super insists that the intelligence was from a very reliable source. Is it possible the delivery in some way got passed you chaps?'

Scrivens blinked. 'I don't see how, sir. We were in position before 8.30 until after five each day. Those were the times both warehouses were advertised to be open. All delivery vehicles were videoed. Every driver and any crew were photographed and were not recognized by the ARS. Every licence plate was logged and checked with Swansea while the vehicle was still at the warehouse. Details of every consignment were checked with the vehicle owners, and none of the vehicles delivered any biscuits.'

'Right, Ted. Well, stand down. We can't afford any more time on that. If a load of cocaine arrived packed as biscuits in Bromersley last Wednesday, Thursday or Friday, I don't know where it was delivered to.'

'Nor do I, sir,' Scrivens said, standing up.

'Sit back down a minute, there's something else,' he said. He reached behind him to the small table on which there were two polythene EVIDENCE bags. He opened the one with only one screwdriver in and passed it over to him.

'This is one of the screwdrivers used in the robbery of the FSDS van, isn't it, sir?' Scrivens said.

Angel nodded. 'If you look carefully on the handle, there is a tiny design or logo constituted from five white rectangles, three black rectangles and the letters MO embossed over the design.'

'Yes. I can see it, sir.'

'Does it mean anything to you?'

'No, sir.'

'Ask around ... try the library. Maybe garages might know. See if you can find out what it means.'

'Right, sir.'

'And don't mess about. Put your mind to it. It's got to mean something.'

Scrivens went out and closed the door.

Angel picked up the phone and tapped in a number. It was soon answered.

'Ahmed,' Angel said. 'I want to speak to the office, department or authority that checks on the purity and quality of dairy food products such as milk and ice cream here in Bromersley. Find out who that is, will you?'

'Yes, sir,' Ahmed said and rang off.

Angel leaned back in the swivel chair and looked up at the ceiling. He had three murders and the robbery of a security van on his plate and he wasn't making any progress with solving any of them. For the first time he noticed a ring of black all the way round the rose directly above the frosted glass globe which illuminated the room. He was thinking it must be ten years since his office was decorated.

There was a knock at the door. He leaned forward in the chair. 'Come in.'

It was DS Taylor waving a sheet of paper.

'I've got a report back from Wetherby, sir, about that thread found on Raymond Gulli's sleeve,' he said.

He offered it to Angel.

'You read it, lad,' Angel said. 'Save time.'

'Report on textile sample submitted 13 January 2010.'

'Yes. Yes. I know that. Get to the meat of it, Don, if there is any.'

'Well, sir, it says sample is 4.2 centimetres long, and is described as a thread of tussore that contains traces of oxidized borate with a peroxide linkage of sodium salt used as bleach.'

Angel's jaw dropped. 'It's a thread of strong silk that has been bleached, at least twice.' He gave a heavy sigh.

There was no hiding his disappointment.

'Why might it have been bleached twice, sir?'

Angel rubbed his chin. 'I suppose because the weaver or thread maker wasn't satisfied with the shade the first time.' Then his face lit up. Something dawned on him. 'The thread must have been needed for something very special.'

Taylor frowned. 'What sort of thing?'

'Well, not some humdrum inconsequential garment or trimming. No. But for something that was going to be used for important ceremonial purposes, such as a garment for a monarch or archbishop at

a coronation, or for special garments for priests to wear when consecrating the bread and wine. The thread needed to be whiter than
white, purer than pure.'

Angel's eyes glowed. He looked at Taylor. 'You know what this
means, Don.'

'That the thread is, after all, from a priest,' Taylor said.

'Yes. Now I believe that the garment the murderer was seen
wearing, variously described by witnesses as a gown, a cloak and a
coat, was in fact a scapular. That's the very special garment a priest
wears over his other attire when he is consecrating the bread and
wine.'

'But this thread is white, sir. I've seen priests in green and purple
and scarlet.'

'They *wear* different colours, but at Christmas and just after, they
always wear white. All three witnesses agree that the colour of the
mysterious garment was white.'

'Do you think that the murderer is a priest, sir?'

Angel's face creased with distaste. 'All three victims were shot
with the same gun, and all three murders were the same MO. We
know that much for certain. The murderer at the railway station was
in a dog collar, and is presumably the same man. I've always fought
against it, but I am sadly coming to the conclusion that all three
murders were committed by a priest who has gone out of his mind.'

'Good morning. This is Detective Inspector Angel at Church Street
Police Station. Have I the right extension number? Is that Mr Jarvis?
Is your office responsible for checking the quality and purity of food
products sold in the town?'

'It is, Inspector, why? Is there an item you want us to look into?'

'No, not specifically. I need some general information.'

'Has there been a complaint?'

'No. This is in the nature of a personal inquiry, but it *could*
become an inquiry in the public interest. I'm not sure that I want to
complain about anything at all, Mr Jarvis. All I really need at this
stage is some information.'

'Ask away, Inspector.'

'My wife and I had an ice-cream cornet from one of Grogan's
mobile vans on Saturday. And I have to say how very nice it was.'

'It's a bit cold for me is ice cream at this time of the year, but I had some in the park with my children several times last summer and we enjoyed it too. So what's the problem?'

'I need to know if you make tests on the ice cream.'

'We certainly do. Being a milk-based item, produced in the town, we take random samples twice a year, which are sent to an independent laboratory for analysis and report.'

'And what do the reports say?'

'Well, I can't remember any details without looking them up, Inspector, but Grogan's reports are and always have been quite excellent. I would have remembered if we had had to submit a warning or take any disciplinary action. And I wouldn't be buying any of *their* ice cream for my children, I can tell you.'

Angel nodded. 'Thank you very much, Mr Jarvis. Goodbye.'

He replaced the phone.

It rang immediately. It was Crisp.

Angel's lips stiffened. He clenched the phone tightly. 'I'm glad you've decided to clock in, lad. I thought you'd emigrated. Where are you? You're supposed to be looking for Irish John and any other tramp-like character who just might be able to give us a lead.'

Crisp's voice was stark. 'I think I've found "Irish John", sir. Fits the description. Behind some rubbish bins at the back of All Saints and Martyrs Church on Sebastopol Terrace. He won't be able to help us much. He's been shot in the chest and he's dead!'

Those last two words echoed in Angel's head.

It was an hour later when Dr Mac, in white disposable overalls, carrying his bag, came out of the canvas marquee which SOCO had erected over part of the back yard of All Saints and Martyrs Church, Sebastopol Terrace. Mac lifted the blue and white DO NOT CROSS tape and passed a small line of women onlookers who were standing shivering on the snow-covered pavement. He was making his way to his car when Angel arrived in the BMW and stopped behind it.

Angel lowered the window and called out, 'Have you finished, Mac?'

Mac took the few steps up to the car and said, 'Aye, I have that, Michael. And do you know, it's as cold as Hogmanay in the Cairngorms.'

'Jump in a minute,' Angel said. 'I'll keep the engine running, warm your little haggis-filled toes.'

Mac opened the car door, put his bag in the footwell, climbed in and quickly closed the door. He peeled off the rubber gloves and briskly rubbed both the palms and backs of his hands.

He looked at Angel. 'You've got me in here under false pretences,' he said with a straight face.

Angel turned the heater blower up to the top setting and put his foot on the accelerator. 'I'm trying to save you from getting pneumonia,' Angel said with a grin.

Mac held his red hands out to the warm vent on the dashboard, and with a sober face, he said, 'I'm afraid it's the same MO, Michael. He was shot, at close range, in the heart. Don Taylor found one bullet case. It's a .32. Same as the other three victims.'

Angel put a hand up to his chin and rubbed it. 'Why?' he said. 'Why murder a tramp?'

'Why murder anybody? Your lad, Crisp, said that his name was Irish John.'

'That's all I know. It was a nickname given to him by Sam Smart from St Mary's. It was told to me by his housekeeper. I've no idea what his real name is.'

'I'll put that on the docket for the time being.'

'But why murder a tramp? The only reason I can think of is because he knew too much. He saw or heard something that jeopardized the murderer's anonymity.'

Mac nodded.

'Well, it certainly wasn't to rob him,' Angel said. 'He had nothing.' He looked at Mac. 'Was he shot in situ?'

'I believe so. Can't be sure until I've got him on the table.'

Angel's eyebrows shot up. 'The sound of the shot? It would waken the universe, wouldn't it?'

'There was a kneeling pad ... a thing you kneel on in church ... cast away on top of him. It has powder burns and a hole through it. It was used to deaden the noise.'

'A kneeling pad? From out of the church? You mean a hassock?'

'All right, posh boy, a hassock. Not being high church and with a free church background, I wasn't brought up to call things by fancy names. It's about fourteen inches long by ten inches wide and about one inch thick. Call it a hassock if you like. I call it a kneeling pad or even a kneeler.'

'Yeah, that's a hassock. I wonder how he came by that?'

'Simple. The murderer saw his prey, nipped into the church, came out with a kneeler and shot him. He would have to be able to get into the church, wouldn't he? I thought churches were locked up when not being used for a service.'

Mac was right. Angel rubbed his chin hard. He was conscious that rubbing his chin was getting to be a habit but it helped him with his thinking. He didn't like what he was thinking.

'The priest here would have access *all* the time,' Angel said. 'What time did the murder take place, Mac?'

'My sums are a bit rough and ready. I need to know what the temperature was at its lowest last night, but it looks like he died between 7 p.m. and midnight.'

'At this church, I spotted on the noticeboard that evensong in the winter is at 4.30. That would last about an hour. Half an hour to tidy up, put the lights out and so on. So the church I expect would be locked up by six o'clock.'

'Sounds as if you've solved it, laddie. I must go.'

'Thank you for the info,' Angel said.

'Thank you for the warm. I feel more human now. I will email my findings tomorrow morning,' he said, and he opened the car door, letting in a blast of Arctic weather, picked up his bag, closed the door and was gone.

Angel switched off the engine and got out of the car as Crisp came running out of the marquee towards him.

'Ah, there you are, sir,' Crisp called. 'Don Taylor wants you to see the scene of crime and OK the removal of the body to the mortuary, if you don't mind.'

'I'm coming, lad. I'm coming,' Angel said. Then when they were up close, he said, 'Find Father Hugo Riley for me urgently. I want to speak to him.'

Crisp blinked. His face went blank. 'What's he look like, sir?' he said.

'He'll be in a dog collar, won't he? And a black coat or a cloak. This is *his* church. We're in his parish. Dammit! Ask around. Ask anybody. You're a detective, aren't you?'

Crisp was taken aback. 'Yes. Right.'

'And have you done the door-to-door?'

Crisp's face went scarlet. 'No, sir,' he said.

Angel's face muscles tightened. 'Well, crack on with it. Let me know what you find out.'

Crisp dashed off towards the presbytery.

Angel strode quickly off to SOCO's marquee. He lifted the flap and went inside.

A powerful light was trained on the dead body of Irish John laid on the snow-covered ground. The top half of the body was covered with dried blood.

DS Taylor and a PC, both in white disposable overalls, looked across at Angel and gave a respectful nod.

'Well,' Angel said, 'what you got?' He peered closely over the corpse's face, then the chest, then the stomach. He worked his way slowly down to the dead man's boots.

'Footprints, sir,' Taylor said. 'The murderer's footprints. They're unfortunately smudged and might not be acceptable to the CPS as evidence but we have taken eight casts, five of the left foot and three of the right. We should be able to get rough composite moulds of each foot, then work out the size.'

Angel's face brightened. That was something. He pursed his lips and nodded. 'Anything else?'

'I'm afraid that's it, sir.'

Angel pulled a face. He needed more direct clues. He had to find a suspect first before he could check on the size of his foot.

The only facts he had were that Irish John was just another body along with three other bodies who had been murdered at point-blank range by a man of average proportions who wore priest's clothes and had dark hair. That's all he knew. He didn't even know the motive.

He turned to Taylor and said, 'And what do you think happened, Don? What's the choreography of the thing?'

'I think that Irish John had been here a little while, sir. There are footprints that suggest he was stamping around between two wheelie bins trying to keep out of the wind, possibly hiding, possibly waiting for somebody. Also, in the snow there were some spent matches. If Dr Mac finds a box in the victim's pockets, we can probably link them to him. If they *are* his, and as no cigarette ends have been found, it suggests that Irish John was smoking a roll-up. People who smoke roll-ups never throw the tab end away. Anyway, it looked as if the murderer had nipped into the church and purloined a kneeling mat. Then he came straight up to Irish John, and holding the kneeling mat over the gun, shot him at close range, dropped the mat and left the scene. Our ability to trace both the victim's and the murderer's footprints began and ended at the footpath. It is too well trodden and it is not possible to see from which direction either came.'

Angel's eyes narrowed as he visualized the scene. 'Where was the kneeler found?'

'By his feet, sir,' Taylor said, pointing to the ground. 'Just tossed there.'

Angel looked down to where Taylor had pointed.

'We've bagged it,' Taylor said. 'For the lab.'

Angel nodded. 'Tell me about it.'

'Well, it's a church kneeler, sir, about twenty inches by nine inches by three inches. It's covered in powder burns on one side and has a hole in the middle with a scorch mark, as you'd expect, where the bullet entered.'

'Mmm. Right.'

Angel heard footsteps behind him. He turned to see the flap of the marquee lifted and Crisp standing there.

'Father Hugo Riley has just turned up, sir,' Crisp said. 'Says he wants to see *you*.'

Angel's eyebrows shot up. 'Oh, does he? I'll be there in one minute, lad,' he said.

Crisp nodded, lowered the flap and went away.

Angel turned back to Taylor, glanced down at the body of Irish John and said, 'Right, Don. Ship him off to the mortuary. Disturb him as little as possible. And search the snow beneath him and around him thoroughly. And look carefully through the waste-bins.'

'We are going to spray the entire area gently with watering cans of warm water. If there's anything there, we'll find it.'

Angel was satisfied they would. He looked slowly round, wondering if there was anything he had forgotten. He couldn't bring anything to mind, so he glanced back at Taylor and said, 'Right, Don. I'm off.'

As he lowered the flap outside, he heard the distinctive Irish voice of Hugo Riley talking to a group of four women on the pavement.

As Angel walked across the yard towards them, he heard him saying, 'Take heart, my dears. This is a time when your faith will sustain you. Let no one be afraid. The Lord is with you. Pray for the poor man's soul, for the forgiveness of his sins and likewise pray for the person who has brought about the man's passing over. *He* needs our prayers too. Then praise the Lord. Give Him thanks for all your blessings. Then pray to Our Lady. Say a decade of Hail Marys. Now go back to your homes. There is nothing to worry about.' Then he made a sign of the cross in front of them, and with an open hand gave a very slow, gentle wave as the women turned away. Then he called after them. 'I will open the church tonight at six o'clock for a special short service of prayers and thanksgiving for the man's soul. Just twenty minutes or so. So spread the word. God bless you. God bless you.'

Angel reached him and said, 'Father Riley.'

The priest turned, and when he saw it was Angel, his hands went into the air and his eyes flashed. 'Just the man I want. Blessed Mother of God, what has happened here, Inspector? A murder in the precincts of my church. It is getting more like Sodom and Gomorrah every day.'

'Can we go somewhere out of this wind?'

Riley pointed towards the presbytery door. 'Come to my house. We can thaw out our bones and partake of a mug of coffee.'

Angel thought it an excellent plan.

Five minutes later, the two men were established in the presbytery sitting room in front of a big orange gas fire, warming their hands around mugs of coffee laced with rum.

Riley said, 'I have been away from the house only two hours on important parish visiting, and when I return I find the remains of a man who has gone to glory at the hand of some wicked person in the back yard of my own church. What is happening?'

Angel's knuckles tightened momentarily round the handle of the coffee mug. 'We are doing our best,' he said.

'Some of my women parishioners are upset and afraid. Not only for themselves but also for their children and their elderly parents, Inspector. Some of them are even afraid for *me*! I pointed out to them that the two priests murdered – God bless them – were both Anglican.'

Angel said, 'You think because you are Catholic that you are not in danger? I wouldn't be so sure, Father. I have evidence that the man seen skulking around your presbytery at the time it was broken into and ransacked, and the man who murdered the Reverend Raymond Gulli and ransacked his vicarage, are one and the same. In fact I now have proof that the white gown he was seen wearing was a scapular.'

Riley gasped. 'Oh.' He shook his head in disbelief then he said, 'A scapular. A most blessed garment. That is sacrilege, Inspector. The man is clearly a heathen. A servant of Beelzebub. This is going to take a lot of prayer.'

'I believe that you escaped being murdered because, luckily, you were not there to try to prevent him.'

Riley glared at him. 'Luck had nothing to do with it, Inspector. There is no such thing as luck. I see the hand of God in this.'

Angel shrugged. 'Maybe. Maybe,' he said.

'I asked your sergeant, Sergeant Crisp, if the body had been identified. He said it had not. As the man's life was taken outside my church, he might be local. I might know him. He could be part of my congregation. Besides I need a name to pray for. Perhaps I might see the body.'

'If we are unable to ID him, I would be most grateful,' Angel said. 'We think he is known locally as Irish John.'

Riley rubbed his chin. 'I know that name from somewhere and it's not from my days in County Cork. Irish John? Of course, I remember. He was on my list of unfortunates who came every month or so for … assistance.'

'You gave him money?'

'I gave him money, and moral support. I tried to give him faith in God as well, as I did all the unfortunates.'

Angel nodded sympathetically. 'What sort of a man was he?'

'Quiet. He never spoke much except when it came to asking for money for a meal.'

'What else can you tell me about him?'

'He didn't want to talk and he didn't want to listen. I daresay he was socially and academically a cut above the general standard of unfortunates wandering the streets. But he was still one of God's creatures. Can't think of anything else, Inspector.'

'Can you think of any reason why anybody would want to murder him?'

'Oh no, Inspector. Certainly not.'

Angel sipped the coffee, looked into the orange-red flame of the gas fire for a few moments then said, 'Was the church locked up later than usual last night, Father?'

Riley's eyebrows shot up. He leaned back in the chair and looked at Angel in surprise. 'It was not locked until after eight o'clock. The church wardens – two admirable ladies – and I stayed over to wash, wrap and pack safely away the figures of the crib, the big red Christmas candles and the tree lights. It should have been done when we took everything down at Epiphany, but it was too cold. But how did you know that?'

'I didn't. Just guessing,' Angel said. 'And where exactly did you do this washing and packing?'

'In the vestry. There's a sink in there.'

'In the vestry, with the door closed, and the church door unlocked?'

'Well, yes, Inspector, why?'

'A hassock was used by the murderer to muffle the sound of the gun.'

'Merciful Father! You are saying that a hassock from this church was used in the murder of … And while we were packing away the holy crib in the vestry, the murderer came into the church and ventured purposely into a pew and stole a hassock to … to …'

'You didn't hear the sound of a gun shot at any time, did you?'

'No, I did not. As it happens we were nearly blown out by the racket from The Fisherman's Rest next door. It's outrageous to have such riotous noise on a Sunday evening, particularly when it is next door to a church.'

'Do you mean somebody was playing loud music?'

'That's what *they* call it. Drums, guitars and a woman screeching something. You could have heard her in Hades.'

Angel rubbed his chin. 'You don't happen to know her name, do you?'

Riley's eyebrows shot up. 'No idea, I'm sure.'

'Anyway, Father, what time did you finish your chores and lock the church door?'

'It must have been a few minutes past eight.'

'Then what did you do?'

Riley stared back at him. He wasn't pleased. He thought the question implied that he was under suspicion. He hesitated a moment before he said, 'I came back here, had my supper, said Compline and was in bed for about ten o'clock.'

'Thank you,' Angel said.

'Even as my head hit the pillow, I could hear that wretched woman with a drum and guitars screaming like a harlot in purgatory.'

'And did you get to sleep all right?'

'Oh yes. But I would have rather fallen asleep in silence in the care of my guardian angel.'

Angel thanked Riley for the coffee and the warm and walked back to the BMW, which he had parked directly in front of The Fisherman's Rest. He glanced at the public house and a small poster in a glass picture frame on the door caught his attention. There was a photograph on the poster of a woman with a lot of fair hair. He made his way through the snow up to the door to see it. As he had thought, the singer who had so disturbed Father Hugo Riley was Felicity Kellerman. She had been appearing at the pub the previous evening, singing and playing her guitar.

Angel rubbed his chin thoughtfully as he returned to the car.

THIRTEEN

When he arrived back at his office, DS Carter was waiting for him.

'Have you a minute, sir?' she said.

'Come in, lass. What have you got?'

'I managed to get to see the CCTV at Heathrow of passengers leaving for San Francisco last Monday afternoon, sir, and I clearly saw the bearded figure of Ben Wizard actually boarding flight 4088 at 1720 hours. So he couldn't have been involved in the murder of Harry Weston, here at 3 p.m., nor the priests subsequently.'

Angel's face tightened. Another suspect was crossed off his metaphorical list.

Carter said: 'I also asked to see the passenger list and it confirmed that he was on that flight.'

Angel nodded. That seemed to be conclusive. That was the end of Ben Wizard.

'It also occurred to me that the person Zoe Costello said she saw was clean shaven, sir,' she said.

'I know, lass. I know,' Angel said. 'But beards can be shaved off and stage beards applied.'

She looked surprised. She hesitated. 'Yes, sir. I suppose so.'

'You have to consider all possibilities.'

'Yes, sir,' she said, 'but—'

The phone rang.

'Just a minute, 'Angel said and reached out for the handset. It was the civilian receptionist.

'There's a Miss Phoebe Wilkinson of St Joseph's Church on the line. Sounds very strange, asking for you, Inspector.'

Angel frowned. He was worried for the old lady.

'Put her through, please,' he said. 'Hello, Miss Wilkinson, are you all right?'

'Perfectly, Inspector Angel, thank you. But I appear to have broken the law, inadvertently, of course, and I don't quite know where to turn. My dear brother Tom would go mad if he knew. He's away, you know, in Rome – doesn't return while next Monday. Then Elaine, my help, suggested that I spoke to you. I wonder if you would be kind enough to call round at your earliest convenience? I would come to you but it is a little difficult. I do not walk very well and I am so slow.'

'I will call on you in about twenty minutes, Miss Wilkinson, if that would be convenient.'

The old lady was delighted and thanked him for his consideration.

He replaced the phone, turned to Flora and was about to say something when the phone rang again. He snatched it up.

Angel knew it was Detective Superintendent Harker on the line because of the raucous sound of a hippopotamus clearing its throat followed by a few quick small coughs and ending with a loud roar, the result of a cough and a sneeze combined.

When it all quietened down, Harker said: 'Ah, Angel. The manager of Cheapo's supermarket has just phoned in to report two young men attempting to rob their outside cash dispensing machines. Their staff are holding one of them. Sort it out, lad.'

Before he could reply, Harker had banged down his handset. Angel tightened his lips back against his teeth, yanked the phone away from his ear and replaced it noisily in its cradle. He relayed the information to Carter then added, 'I have a lot on, Flora. I'll leave it to you to sort out. You might need a bit of muscle. Take John Weightman if he's on duty.'

Carter felt a warm glow in her chest. It was the first case he had entrusted to her since she joined Bromersley force in 2009.

'Right, sir,' she said. She smiled and went out.

Angel was pleased to see that somebody was happy. He assembled all the reports, envelopes and papers on his desk into a pile and put them in the top right-hand drawer of his desk. He reached out for his coat, switched off the light and closed the door.

St Joseph's presbytery. Monday, 18 January 2010. 4.45 p.m.

Elaine Jubb answered the presbytery door. She gave Angel an uncertain smile and then deliberately looked away. He wondered what she had to be cagey about.

'Miss Wilkinson is expecting you,' she mumbled. 'Please come this way.'

She opened the door into the sitting room where Phoebe Wilkinson was seated in the lounger chair facing the two television sets. The screens were black and silent. A tartan car rug was draped over a chair on her left. To her right were two chairs heaped with newspapers.

Miss Wilkinson was holding a large magnifying glass with a carved ivory handle and studiously reading *The Racing Post*.

'It's Inspector Angel,' Elaine said.

The old lady's face brightened when she looked up at him. 'Ah, yes. Thank you for coming so promptly, Inspector,' she said. 'Please sit down. Would you like anything to drink? Elaine will organize some tea, coffee or something stronger?'

'No, thank you, Miss Wilkinson,' he said. He moved the newspapers away on to the other chair and sat down.

The old lady turned to Elaine and said, 'Right, dear. Now you get off to the bookie, dear? He closes at five, doesn't he? And I'll see you in the morning.'

'Righto, Miss Wilkinson, if you're sure there's nothing else you want. The casserole is ready in the oven, don't forget.'

'Thank you, dear,' Miss Wilkinson said.

Elaine Jubb went out.

Angel noted that as soon as the room door was closed and they were on their own, Miss Wilkinson changed. The ready smile and cordiality left her with the speed of a bank robber's getaway car.

'Inspector Angel, I have made a dreadful mistake.'

'Tell me about it, Miss Wilkinson.'

'There was a photograph of an unusual stone- and brown-coloured suitcase in the *Bromersley Chronicle*. The caption said that it was used in the robbery of that security van two weeks ago.'

Something disturbed the sleeping hive of bees in Angel's chest. They suddenly awoke and began to whizz around at speed, creating a regular hot throbbing around his heart.

'Yes. That's right,' he said.

'Did you ever find the suitcase? Did anybody come forward with it?' she said.

His hands shook slightly, then he said, 'No, no. Why?'

'Well, my brother has a suitcase in exactly the same colours and design,' she said. 'Did it have ... did it have money in it?'

Angel stood up. '*Where is it*, Miss Wilkinson?'

Her hand reached out to her left to a tartan car rug across a chair. Then deliberately looking away, she pulled the rug to reveal a stone-and brown-coloured suitcase.

When Angel saw the case, he darted round the back of Miss Wilkinson's chair to reach it. He pressed the two catches on the locks and lifted the lid. It was part filled with twenty pound notes. He didn't touch any of the contents but began to try to estimate how much money there was in there. He saw that the notes were wrapped in fifties in blue sleeves, worth £1,000, and they were packed in bundles of ten in clear polythene and labelled 'Northern Bank. £10,000 in £20 notes'. After a few moments, he stood back, turned to Miss Wilkinson and said, 'It isn't all here. There's a lot missing. There's about two million, at a rough count.'

He closed the case, put it on the floor and sat down.

'That's right. It is exactly half.'

'Where is the rest?'

'In the bank. I took your advice, you know, and opened another account.'

'The money that was in the flour bin?'

Her face brightened. 'Yes. You see, I thought that that was my share of the money.'

His face reddened. 'More than two million pounds, *your* share?' he said.

'I thought it was the money from the sale of Daddy's house, The Grange. You see, in his Will, Daddy left the house in equal shares to my brother Tom and me. The two million in the suitcase was Tom's share. Elaine put it in his study until he got back from Rome. I forgot all about it.'

Angel ran his hand through his hair. 'But Miss Wilkinson, you didn't think the house was going to fetch over four million pounds, did you?'

'I don't know. Its value was never mentioned in my hearing. An actual price wasn't actually discussed. And everybody said what a magnificent estate it was.'

He remembered what a great house and grounds it was, but the country was in the middle of a recession, and property sales were at an all-time low. He couldn't see it selling for that figure.

'How much was the house actually sold for?' he said.

'It *hasn't* been sold, Inspector. That's what alerted me to this mistake.'

Angel blew out a lungful of air through his teeth. 'Well, how much have you in the bank?' he said.

'What? In my own name?'

'In *anybody's* name?'

'It's a bit difficult to give you an exact figure,' she said. 'You see, I have two accounts. One is for what I will call my own account, and then I have a second one that I call my charities account. Also there are cheques in the post that may not yet have been cleared. You see, I have sent £250,000 to Haiti following that dreadful earthquake appeal, £250,000 to Save the Children, £250,000 to the Cancer appeal and £250,000 to the Red Cross.'

Angel gasped. 'That's a ... that's a ... that's a *million* pounds, Miss Wilkinson.'

'Yes,' she said with a big smile. 'Isn't it *great*?'

Angel gulped, ran his hand through his hair again and said, 'So how much have you got left?'

'I have the original capital of two million pounds,' she said.

He sighed.

'Plus today's winnings of about £1,800 from my online betting,' she said.

He nodded.

'And I've £200 to come from Brian, the bookie,' she said.

Angel sighed with relief. 'Is that it?'

Miss Wilkinson's eyebrows shot up. 'Why no. I nearly forgot. There's also my stake money of £10.'

'Of course,' he said with a wry smile as he dipped into his pocket and began to fish around for his mobile. 'You haven't yet told me how you came by the suitcase.'

'Ah yes,' she said. 'Elaine found the suitcase left in the hall by the door one morning and took it into the kitchen. Before he left, my brother had told her to expect the return of some vestments borrowed by a priest from Skiptonthorpe and that they might include a surplice that needing washing. She was quite used to this. It happened from time to time.'

'I see,' Angel said. 'Please excuse me a moment, Miss Wilkinson.'

He tapped a number into his mobile and had a quick muttered conversation with Don Taylor at SOCO. He then ended the call and pocketed the phone.

He turned back to Miss Wilkinson. 'Thank you,' he said. 'And Elaine thought that that was the suitcase?'

'Yes. She opened the case up on the kitchen table, found it full of money and brought it to me. I naturally thought it was the money from the sale of The Grange.'

Angel shook his head. 'Now why on earth would you think that?'

Miss Wilkinson raised herself up and said, 'I had already told Elaine I was expecting a big sum of money. She thought that that was it. We both did. My brother Tom being away, I ... Anyway, I understood The Grange had been sold, and I also heard that some firms wouldn't accept cheques in payment any more. I don't know. I wondered if it was because so many banks have recently been in financial trouble? Fancy! Banks in financial difficulty? My father never trusted banks. So I thought that the solicitors perhaps weren't using banks any more. These are fast-moving days of change that I can hardly keep pace with, Inspector. It was a natural mistake to make, surely?'

'You don't know what happened to the suitcase containing the borrowed vestments, do you?'

She blinked several times. 'Father Robin Roebuck, my brother's locum, would have been the priest who left it here. He must know.'

Angel smiled. 'And how can I reach him, Miss Wilkinson?'

It was 5.45 p.m. when Angel drove the BMW into his garage at 30 Park Street. As he put his key in the back door, he noticed that the house was in darkness except for a light in the back bedroom. The house was comfortably warm but he pulled a face when he noted that there was no sign or smell of any cooking.

He put on some lights, crossed the hall and looked up the stairs. 'Anybody at home?' he called.

'Oh. *Oh*! Is that the time?' Mary said. 'Coming, love. Coming.'

Angel took a small notebook and a pen out of his pocket, hung up his coat, got a beer out of the fridge and sat down in the sitting room. He made out a list. It read: 'Irish John. Ben Wizard. Peter King. A priest.'

He sipped the beer, stared at the list for a few moments then tossed the notebook on to the library table, leaned back in the chair and closed his eyes.

Mary came down the stairs. She saw him in the sitting room and went in. He didn't open his eyes. She looked at him a moment then she leaned over and kissed him on the forehead. 'Are you tired?' she said. 'Dinner won't be long.'

He opened one eye. 'Hello, gorgeous,' he said.

'I've almost finished the wallpapering,' she said and went into the kitchen.

He closed the open eye and fell asleep.

It was almost 7.30 when they finished dinner and returned to the sitting room. Angel carried his beer and Mary's coffee through, put them on the library table between their favourite chairs, sat down, picked up the notebook and stared at it, reading and re-reading the names, while stroking his non-existent beard.

Mary came to the room door. She was wiping her hands on a tea towel. 'That's the pans to soak and I've covered the leftovers.'

Angel grunted his approval without looking up.

Mary put her hands on her hips and said, 'Well, Michael, don't you want to see my wallpapering then? It's nearly finished.'

'I'll look at it when we go to bed.'

Her face changed. She was disappointed. 'You can put Lolly's bed together now, you know. I thought you could do it tonight? There's nothing stopping you. There's nothing on the telly.'

He glanced up. 'I'll do it later, love.'

Mary wasn't pleased but she could see he was distracted. She went out, came back without the tea towel and sat down. She reached out for the coffee and saw him gazing at the notepad.

'What are you doing?'

'Nothing,' he said.

She peered over his shoulder, read it, then looked at him and said, 'It's a list of suspects, isn't it?'

179

He rubbed his chin for a few moments and then said, 'Well, sort of. But there are different reasons why it can't be *any* of them.'

'What do you mean?'

He shook his head, hesitated, blew out a foot of breath and said, 'Well, it's complicated.'

She looked at him. She knew he wanted to talk about it even though he was apparently unforthcoming.

'Well, all right then,' he said, passing her the notebook. 'Take the first one. Irish John. He's dead. It couldn't be him, could it?'

'No, I suppose not,' she said. 'Although he could have murdered that ticket clerk and the two priests, and then somebody else may have shot *him*, maybe in retaliation.'

'It's possible, love. It's possible. But they were all shot with the same gun, in the heart. And a pillow or a cushion was used in the murders of Sam Smart and Raymond Gulli. How would the murderer of Irish John know the MO sufficiently well to improvize with a kneeler, and find and take possession of the same gun and shoot John directly in the identical place in the chest?'

Mary shook her head.

'But it's all possible,' Angel said. 'Then there's Ben Wizard. He had begun his journey to the States when the first victim, Harry Weston, was murdered. Flora Carter has seen a tape of him boarding a plane at Heathrow on that day at a time that meant that he could not possibly have been in Bromersley.'

'That rules him out then, doesn't it?'

'It does if it really *was* him on the plane.'

'Hadn't she seen him?'

'Not in person. Nor have I. We are relying on photographs and a description from Felicity Kellerman. He has a beard and big side-burns, which he could stick on and take off to order.'

'What do the airline say?'

'They confirmed that a man called Ben Wizard got off the plane in Seattle.'

'Isn't their word reliable?' she said. 'US airlines are so nervous these days.'

'Yes,' he said. He sounded more confident. 'That's very true. That probably means he's not the one. He'll be twanging his guitar all round Seattle and Washington State.'

Mary smiled and consulted the notebook. 'Then there's Peter King,' she said. 'Isn't he the one who wants to go to prison?'

'Oh yes, and he wants to be in the headlines of all the papers for something horribly gory, sexual and macho.'

Mary frowned.

Angel thought about King a moment, shook his head and said, 'Even though he tried hard to be picked out in an ID parade by the only witness we have, Zoe Costello, she still passed him by and declined to identify him.'

'It won't be him then.'

'Probably not.'

Mary squinted at the notebook. 'What's this last one? Your writing is getting worse.'

'A priest,' he said.

'A priest? Which one?'

'I don't know which one. I find it hard to believe that it could be a priest at all, but there's so much evidence,' he said. 'It was a man in a dog collar – priest or not – who shot Harry Weston. We now know it was a man in a scapular – priest or not – who murdered the two priests Sam Smart and Raymond Gulli. Also a man in the same or similar garb was seen before gaining access to and inflicting havoc on Father Hugo Riley's house and church.'

Mary pursed her lips and looked at him. 'I see what you mean,' she said.

Angel said, 'Why would a priest want to kill his brother priests and search through their places? I mean, what about his vows as a priest? And what was he looking for?'

'The two priests who were murdered were both Anglican, weren't they? Father Riley is Roman Catholic isn't he? *He* wasn't attacked. Do you think the fact they were different denominations has anything to do with it?'

'I don't know. I wouldn't have thought so. There are a lot fewer differences than there used to be. The ministers of the Methodists, the Baptists, the Pentecostals and the other free churches have not been attacked either. If the murderer is an accredited minister or priest, he must have gone completely off his chump. Why also would he murder a ticket clerk and a man of the road? I tell you, that man, whoever he is, has a private room waiting for him in Broadmoor. I've got to catch him, Mary,' he said, running his hand through his hair, 'before he murders anybody else. I am running out of lines of inquiry. This case has got me licked.'

'No it hasn't,' she said, patting him on the hand. 'You've always solved your cases in the end, but you are now probably too close to it. What you need to do now, love, is to rest *that* part of your mind and involve yourself in something entirely different.'

Angel narrowed his eyes. He looked at her and said, 'Like what?'

Mary's face brightened. 'Well, there's Lolly's bed that needs putting together.'

Angel wrinkled his nose.

It was almost nine o'clock when he went upstairs, into the back bedroom, and switched on the glaring, shadeless lightbulb. It shone down brightly on the new, clean wallpaper.

Mary followed him in, looking proudly around at her handiwork.

'Well?' she said, looking at Angel expectantly.

He didn't notice her or the walls. He went straight to the bed, still fastened with paper tape to the long box, tore it away and opened it. There was an A4 leaflet listing the parts and four diagrams in the form of exploded line drawings illustrating how some parts should be assembled but with no words of explanation. He looked at it, pulled a face and tipped the contents out on to the carpet. All the parts were packed in separate polythene bags. He carefully checked them off against the leaflet: 64 x 2cm bolts, 64 x 2cm washers, 64 x 2cm nuts, 108 x 8cm springs, 72 x 12cm springs, 8 x 10.2cm bolts, 216 x 6.5cm double-ended wire connectors, 144 x 4cm single-ended connectors, 8 Y pieces, 4 Z pieces.

He stood up, looked at the leaflet and the polythene bags, and rubbed his chin. It was like doing the cloudless blue sky in a jigsaw puzzle.

Mary watched him from the door, hesitated and said, 'Well, aren't you going to put it together?'

'Nay, it's complicated, Mary. There's a lot to it,' he said.

She was not pleased. 'It's not *that* difficult, surely,' she said.

'I'm not used to this sort of thing,' he said as he leaned down and began to put the polythene bags back in the box. 'It's a job that will need a lot of time. It's best done when I can get a good run at it – three or fours hours at a continuous stretch.'

'Lolly's coming the day after tomorrow, you know.'

'Well, I'm sorry, love. I can't do it tonight. It's a bit late and I'm tired.'

'Michael!'

The phone rang.

Angel reached out for it. It was Mac.

'Good morning, Michael,' he said. 'This character we are calling Irish John – he's turning out to be full of surprises. I thought you'd like to know that there is nothing in his pockets. Nothing at all. He has obviously been thoroughly searched and his pockets emptied. The linings of his trouser pockets were actually hanging out.'

Furrowed lines formed on Angel's forehead. 'Unusual,' he said.

Mac said, 'The murderer was anxious to conceal the victim's identity?'

'Maybe,' Angel said. 'Maybe. Anything else?'

'Oh yes,' Mac said. 'A lot more. This character has £400 on him. £20 notes … £200 in each boot.'

Angel blinked. Now that *was* a surprise. '£400?'

'Yes. Neatly packed under the insoles, Michael. I haven't finished the PM yet. Should be done by about lunchtime. But I thought you'd like to know.'

'Yes indeed. Thanks, Mac.'

Angel replaced the phone. How could a man of the road come by £400? It was a lot of money to a man who ostensibly had no regular income and was on the cadge from the church. It could have been his life savings, of course. Or he could have stolen it. It looked as if the murderer knew he was in possession of the money, maybe told him to hand it over, Irish John refused, the murderer shot him, searched his body … but didn't think of looking in his boots. It sounded a feasible explanation.

There was a knock at the door. Angel looked up. 'Come in.'

It was Trevor Crisp.

'Good morning, sir. Knocked on all the houses visible from the back of All Saints and Martyrs Church and nobody saw or heard anything unusual, sir. And I went in The Fisherman's Rest, spoke to the landlord – nobody saw or heard anything, Sunday evening. He did happen to say that between about nine and ten, Felicity

Kellerman was on stage singing. She brought her own mike and amplifier kit, so it would have been a bit noisy.'

'That was within the time range that Mac says Irish John was shot. He was probably shot while she was in the pub screaming her head off.'

'She sings country and western. She's rather nice. I like her.'

Angel shook his head. 'You like anything in a skirt, lad. You need pills for it.'

Crisp grinned.

Angel told him what Mac had said about Irish John.

'It's strange that the victims are so different, sir,' Crisp said. 'A ticket office clerk, two Anglican clergymen and now a rich tramp. And we have no proof that the same murderer has killed all four, have we?'

'The MO is similar. The gun used is the same gun. All victims were shot through the heart. It is very likely but there is no absolute certainty, no. We've no motive for the first three murders. If we knew that, we could make real progress. The way Mac found Irish John suggests that the motive in his case was robbery.'

'Or *attempted* robbery,' Crisp said, 'considering he didn't actually find the money.'

'All right,' Angel conceded, 'but his pockets may have been emptied purely to conceal his identity and delay our investigation.'

Crisp nodded.

'Well, he's somebody's son,' Angel said, 'as my mother would have said. He'll have to be given a decent burial.'

'It won't have to be a pauper's, sir. There's funds there to do it.'

'Aye. But see if you can find his next of kin. That had better be your next job but one.'

Crisp peered at Angel. 'Next job but one?'

'Aye. I want you to chase Don Taylor and get the shoe size and a print of the pattern of the soles of the murderer's shoes from the footprints found at the scene of the crime, then print off copies for distribution to the squad. All right?'

'Right, sir,' Crisp said. He got up and made for the door.

Angel looked down at the desk and shook his head. He leaned back in the chair and closed his eyes. While he had been flat out trying to find the serial killer, the pile of files, envelopes and loose papers on his desk had grown and grown. They had grown like the pots in the sink to be washed when Mary used to leave him to go away and visit her mother. And that reminded him, he had promised her (well, he had been ambushed by her) that he would assemble that bed tonight for her sister, Lolly. He had no idea how to do it. He didn't want to do it and it was such a bore. He wondered how he had gotten himself into making such a promise.

There was a knock at the door.

He opened his eyes, eased the chair forward and said, 'Come in.'

It was Flora Carter. Her face was glowing, her eyes intense.

'What's the matter, Flora?'

'That job you sent me on, sir. Two young men were trying to rob Cheapo's outside cash machines by blowing them up.'

Angel's mouth dropped open. 'Blowing them up? What with?'

She shrugged. 'Don't know, sir. Boys will be boys. They broke into a lock-up garage and they took an old van from outside the pub.'

Angel rubbed his chin thoughtfully.

'I've got one of the lads in the interview room, with his mother,' she said.

'His mother?' he said. He pulled a face and shook his head. He didn't like interviewing young villains when their mothers were present. 'How old is he?'

'Eighteen.'

He frowned. 'Eighteen? In the eyes of the law, he's a man. Has he any form?'

'No, sir. I thought you would want to interview him?'

Angel looked up at her, eyebrows raised. He rubbed his mouth roughly several times. 'You know, Flora, I haven't really time for this. I am up to my eyes. *You* interview him.'

'Right, sir,' she said, making for the door. 'Just keeping you posted.'

He nodded.

She opened the door.

'Get his own solicitor, if he has one, or Edwin Bloomfield, to sit in, lass,' he called.

But Flora Carter knew all about conducting a formal interview.

'I know, sir,' she said, flouncing out and banging the door.

He looked up in surprise. His lips displayed the smallest possible smile.

There was an immediate knock and the door was reopened. It was DC Scrivens. 'Have you a minute, sir?'

'Aye. Come in, Ted,' he said. 'This place is busier than a prison on visitors' day.'

Scrivens was carrying a screwdriver. 'These screwdrivers, sir, with this logo,' he said, pointing to the design on the handle. 'I phoned up the patent office, then sent them a drawing of it, and I had an email from them yesterday morning. The logo was registered in 1986 to Maestro Organs. Of course, if you look at it right, sir, it's some white notes and some black notes as on a keyboard with the letter M and O superimposed on it.'

'Yes. Yes. Yes,' he said quickly.

'Well, Maestro Organs used to sell and distribute electronic organs around Yorkshire and Lincolnshire,' Scrivens said. 'Their address was 111/113 Bulstrode Way, Leeds. I tried to reach them on the phone but discovered that they went bust in 2002. Fortunately they didn't pay their council tax so from their records Leeds Council Tax office was able to tell me the name of the solicitor's practice who represented Maestro Organs during the winding-up process. In turn, I spoke to the partner who dealt with them. He couldn't recall much detail, but remembered the name of the warehouse manager of Maestro Organs, who is now retired. I traced him and he said that when the company folded, there wasn't much left, but all the surplus bits and pieces and oddments, such as these advertising screwdrivers, were sold by a firm of auctioneers. Incidentally, he also told me that these screwdrivers were given away. They were packed individually in a fancy box with "Maestro Organs" plastered all over it. They were used to assemble the larger organs and the bench seats that were often delivered in flatpacks. The screwdriver might be used by the delivery men and then left behind intentionally as an advertising gift. Good idea, sir. Nobody throws a screwdriver away, do they?'

Angel said, 'But did you find out who bought the screwdrivers from the auctioneers then?'

'Well, no, sir,' Scrivens said. 'I hadn't thought about taking it any further after all this time?'

'Why not?' Angel said. 'You know what a difficult case this is. You know how I've been scratching away for a clue, a hint, a sniff, and nothing has come up. Everything so far has led to a dead end.'

'Well, the auctioneer may not have any record after all this time.'

Angel's eyes flashed. 'True. He might be dead. He may have emigrated to Zanzibar, living in the jungle and be impossible to trace. Maybe eaten by a lion. He may still have the records but be suffering from amnesia and not know where he has put them. He may have dropped his sandwiches on them and covered them in jam so that we can't read them. The cat may have used them, to make a nest to have kittens in. There is also a slight risk, isn't there, that he may still be in business, have those records to hand, be able to tell us who bought those screwdrivers and that could lead us to making an arrest for the armed robbery of four million from First Security Delivery Services. Now, I know it's a long shot, Ted, but it's all we've got, and after all, that's what detective work is all about, isn't it?'

Scrivens was surprised at Angel's outburst. 'Yes, sir. I suppose so.'

'There's no *suppose so* about it,' Angel said. 'It *is* so. Do you know the name of the auctioneer and the approximate date of the auction?'

'Yes, sir. The warehouse manager said October or November 2002, and the name of the auctioneer was Bird. It was Bird's of Leeds.'

'Well, take wing, fly off and see if you can get him to tweet the buyer.'

Scrivens duly left for Leeds, and Angel began to work on the accumulation of paperwork on his desk.

FOURTEEN

Later that morning, there was a knock on the door.
'Come in,' Angel said.

It was Flora Carter, all smiles.

'What have you to be so happy about?' he asked, pointing to the chair.

'The lad admitted everything, sir,' she said, taking the chair. 'When he heard that there was CCTV covering all the outside areas of Cheapo's, he had little choice. Besides, his mother would have killed him if he hadn't come clean.'

Angel nodded.

'Told us the other lad's name and everything,' she said.

'Good. You said that they were planning to *blow* up the cash machines, didn't you?'

'Yes, sir. He said that they had broken into a garage and found some sticks of dynamite in a box. That's what gave them the idea.'

'Dynamite?' Angel said, looking up. A glow suddenly developed in his chest and it began to pulsate like 10,000 ants making toast. 'Do you know where this garage is?'

'Well, yes, sir. It's being guarded by PC Weightman while SOCO and the Wakefield explosives unit go through it.'

'You've charged the lad, and you're looking for his accomplice?'

'Yes, sir,' she said. 'I've issued a warrant for his arrest, and I've sent a team to his home address to pick him up.'

She seemed to have covered everything. He rubbed his chin.

Her mouth tightened. 'I know what to do, sir,' she said.

She was beginning to read his mind.

'Great,' he said with a sniff. 'That's great. Now I want to go to this garage. I want to see this dynamite. Take me there.'

Ten minutes later he was standing at the door of a garage in a row of thirty-one other garages at the back of Mount Street off Wakefield Road. It had the number nineteen daubed crudely on the door with the remains of somebody's 'Serenity White' Dulux gloss, probably left over from the decoration of their bathroom.

PC John Weightman was opening the battered old door. There wasn't much in the tiny garage. There were four tyres without tread hanging from brackets on the wall, and two dusty cardboard boxes and a box of tools on the floor, but no car.

Angel turned to Flora Carter and said, 'Where is the dynamite?'

She pointed to one of the two cardboard boxes on the floor.

Angel glanced at it and pulled a slim white envelope from his pocket, tore off the end and took out a pair of rubber gloves. Then he crouched down in front of the cardboard box, and with gloved fingertips he eased open one of the flaps of the box to reveal several cellophane-wrapped cream-coloured sticks of the powerful explosive.

Both he and Carter sighed. Then he gently closed the box flap and stood up.

'What's in that other box?' he said.

'Don't know, sir. I was prepared to wait until after SOCO had done their bit.'

She was right, of course, from the point of procedure, but Angel was always one for breaking the rules and hoping to gain an advantage. He crouched down again and carefully lifted the flap of the box and peered inside. He saw long, narrow, brightly coloured printed boxes. He thought they might contain long knives of some sort. Then he saw the word 'Maestro' and part of an organ keyboard and he knew exactly what he was looking at. He promptly dropped the box flap and stood up.

'They are exactly like the screwdrivers used by the armed robbers to puncture the tyres on that furniture van and to jump-start the giant crane.'

His pulse was throbbing with excitement.

Carter said, 'Found with the dynamite used by the robbers to blow open the safe on the security van would be powerful evidence.'

He turned to Carter and said, 'Whose garage is this, Flora? We've got to find out whose garage this is.'

'I've been unable to find that out, sir.'

'You can easily find out who pays the rates or community charge on the damned place.'

'I know. I know that, sir. And I would have been at the town hall at this very moment if you hadn't asked me to accompany you here.'

He looked at her with a furrowed brow.

'All right. All right, lass,' he said. 'Let me know as soon you find out. And don't get agitated. You've got a lot of mouth on you for a young 'un.'

Blood rushed to her cheeks. She was furious. She strutted out of the garage, turned to face him, and stood there in the service road, head up, bosom out, arms straight down her sides, looking like a Hollywood film star and breathing at twice her regular speed.

Angel came out of the garage deep in thought. He glanced at her, took in the situation, peeled off the rubber gloves, and said, 'We'll leave the rest to SOCO. There'll be prints off those boxes. If we have them on file we can charge him or them with armed robbery.'

She gave him the slightest nod.

'Keep me posted,' he said, then he got into the BMW and drove away. He felt ten inches taller and as light as champagne.

He went straight to his office and found DC Scrivens waiting for him.

The young detective's eyes were bright, he was standing upright and seemed at ease. Angel assumed that, for a welcome change, he was the bearer of good news.

'Come in, lad. Sit down,' Angel said. 'I take it you have found the auctioneers and discovered who bought the screwdrivers?'

'Yes, sir. The auction was in Bird and Co's saleroom on Tuesday, October 15, 2002. Mr Bird eventually found the sales sheet he used on that day, and pointed out the entry of the lot number, the description of the lot, the price bid and the buyer's name. He confirmed that it was in his own handwriting, so I copied down the line exactly as it was written.' Scrivens then took out a notebook from his inside jacket pocket and began to shuffle through the pages.

Angel breathed in impatiently and said, 'All right, lad, don't waste time. What did it say?'

Scrivens hurriedly found the page and read from it: 'It said, "lot number 124, box of approx. thirty advertising screwdrivers, £4, Rossi".'

Angel nodded, then pursed his lips. 'Rossi. Angus Rossi,' he said heavily. 'We've *got you.*'

Scrivens nodded.

Angel said, 'Get a warrant out for his arrest for armed robbery. There will be other charges, but that will do for starters. Off you go. Take a couple of men with you.'

Scrivens' eyes shone and he went out briskly.

As the door opened, Trevor Crisp came in. He was clutching a handful of A4 printed leaflets.

Angel saw them and said, 'Are those leaflets showing the sole of the boot of the gunman taken in the snow?'

'Yes, sir,' Crisp said with a smile.

'It's taken you long enough,' Angel said. 'What's the shoe size?'

'Nine, sir.'

Angel explained briefly how they had deduced that Rossi was leader of the armed gang that had robbed the security van.

'I've sent Ted to get a warrant to arrest him,' Angel said. 'When he's done that, follow him into Rossi's house and see if you can find any footwear there that matches that print. If you do, we've got him for four murders as well!'

Crisp's eyes opened wider and he nodded several times quickly. 'Right, sir,' he said.

'In the meantime, distribute those leaflets. See that everybody on my team gets one. And don't throw it at him. Put it into his dirty, sticky hand and *tell* him about it.'

'Right, sir,' he said and turned to go.

'Tell Ahmed I want him.'

'Right, sir,' he said and dashed off.

A few minutes later there was a knock at Angel's door.

'Come in,' Angel said. 'Sit down a minute. I want you to do something a bit artistic.'

Ahmed blinked. 'Artistic, sir?'

He had never thought of himself or any policeman being in any way artistic.

'Angus Rossi is being arrested for armed robbery,' Angel said. 'When he is brought in and being processed, I want you to get a photograph of his face and neck and superimpose it on to a picture of a priest wearing a dog collar and a black shirt front. Can you do that, lad?'

Ahmed frowned briefly then suddenly looked up. 'You think that Angus Rossi was also the serial murderer.'

Angel nodded then he said, 'It's a possibility, lad.'

'Yes, sir. It wouldn't be difficult. I would have to find a photo of a priest dressed like that from somewhere. There are probably some on a website I can pinch one from.'

'I have plenty of friends in the church who can supply one or even pose expressly for you, if needs be.'

He nodded quickly. 'Right, sir,' he said.

'I need it today, so get weaving.'

Ahmed went out.

Angel picked up the phone and tapped in a number. It rang out a few moments and then a woman's voice answered. 'Hello?'

'Ah, Miss Costello,' he said. 'Inspector Angel here. I wonder if ...'

Later that morning, DC Scrivens walked into Angel's office. 'We've got Angus Rossi down in the cells, sir,' he said. 'He's been processed and is protesting noisily. He insists he is innocent.'

Angel shrugged. 'Have you advised his solicitor?'

'Yes, sir. It's Mr Bloomberg, of course. He's on his way.'

'Right, lad. Let me know as soon as they're ready and I'll come through.'

Scrivens nodded and went out as Carter came in.

'I've got some good news, sir,' she said.

'Ah yes, Flora. Sit down and tell me about it.'

'I have confirmation from SOCO, sir,' Carter said, 'that the prints on both the screwdriver box and the dynamite box in the lock-up *are* those of Angus Rossi.'

Angel's eyebrows eased slowly upwards. He smiled and said, 'Good. There's nothing like scientific proof that can't be disputed to warm the cockles of your heart on a cold winter's day.'

'There's more, sir,' she said. 'That box which now contains thirty-two sticks *is* the box that originally contained thirty-six sticks of dynamite that was stolen from South Creekman quarry in North Derbyshire overnight November 5th to the 6th last year.'

'Great. Well, four sticks were used to blow the back off the First Security Delivery Services van.'

There was a knock at the door.

It was Crisp. 'Can I come in, sir?'

'Yes, lad,' Angel said. 'Come in. Flora's brought evidence that Rossi handled both the dynamite and the screwdrivers.'

Crisp grinned, looked at Carter and said, 'That's great, Flora.'

Angel turned back to Carter. 'And what about the lock-up garage, Flora? Does Rossi own it?'

'No, sir. All that row of garages and lots of other small buildings around Bromersley are owned by a London property company, Catania and Modica.'

Angel rubbed his chin. 'Never heard of them. Sound foreign to me.'

'I'll try and find out about them, sir.'

Angel nodded.

She smiled at him and Crisp and then went out.

Crisp was smiling. He watched her go.

Angel noticed how Crisp's eyes followed her out of the room, and that the smile stayed on his face even after the door had closed.

Angel shook his head and said, 'You've got the hots for her, haven't you?'

Crisp looked at Angel, still smiling. He was thinking about what to say.

'If I were her,' Angel said, 'I wouldn't give *you* the time of day. Look here, Trevor, I don't mind you chasing lasses in your own time. Indeed, you would be right to say it was none of my business, but I don't want you billing and cooing in this station or when you're out on police work. I want you with your mind a hundred per cent on finding criminals and locking them up. That's what we're paid for. You understand?'

The smile vanished. 'Oh yes, sir,' Crisp said. 'I understand that. Don't worry about it.'

Angel wasn't convinced. 'I think there's something wrong with you. You're always taking lasses out, going to the pictures, out for a meal, going away for weekends and so on, but you never actually finish up marrying any of them.'

'One of these days I am going to surprise you,' Crisp said, and he seemed to mean it.

'I know she's a cracker,' Angel said, rubbing his chin.

Crisp's eyes shone. 'More beautiful than Cheryl Cole, sir,' he said.

Angel thought about it for a moment. Then suddenly his face changed. He looked up at him and said, 'Look, we're not here to discuss pop stars. What did you come in for?' He ran his hand through his hair then his face brightened. 'I know,' he said. 'You have come to tell me about Rossi's footwear?'

'That's right, sir.'

'Well, let's have it.'

'Yes sir, well, it's not good news, sir. I checked all the shoes in the house against the leaflet. There were only three pairs, and none matched.'

'You looked everywhere? Upstairs in the wardrobes? In the cellar? Nooks and crannies, particularly around the back door?'

'I looked everywhere, sir. It's only a small house, as you know.'

Angel wrinkled his nose.

Crisp said, 'But his shoe size *is* nine.'

'That's good. Yes. That's the right size.'

'And I suppose he could easily have thrown those shoes away.'

'Of course he could. In the River Don or the canal or a tip, but I wouldn't know where to start looking.' Then he suddenly said, 'You *did* check the shoes he's been arrested in, didn't you?'

Crisp's mouth dropped open. 'No, sir. I didn't.'

Angel dug his fingernails into the chair arms. 'Well, do it now,' he said.

Crisp rushed out and closed the door.

Angel looked down at the pile of envelopes and reports beckoning his attention. He began looking through them.

Suddenly, his office door was brusquely opened and thrown back so hard that it crashed noisily into a chair against the wall.

He looked up to see the figure of Detective Superintendent Harker framed in the doorway.

Angel's mouth opened. He sucked in a lungful of air and leaped to his feet. 'What's the matter, sir?' he said.

Harker waved an impatient hand and said, 'Control room have just had a triple nine from a female cashier at that petrol and diesel filling station on Wakefield Road ... the one near the roundabout. She said that a man has been violently attacked in his van on the forecourt by a gang with guns. Get off down there and see what you can do.'

Angel's pulse was racing. He reached out for his coat. He hoped it was not another murder. That would be *too* much.

'There is a patrol car on its way there,' Harker said. 'I will contact Asquith promptly and get him to divert some more uniform from town centre duties.'

Angel passed him at the door. 'Right, sir.'

'Approach with caution. Report to me as soon as you have the facts.'

The service station was on the fringe of the town on the Wakefield side. It took Angel only five or six minutes to reach it. He pulled on to the forecourt and immediately saw the damaged vehicle. He recognized it as a retail ice-cream van of Grogan's, battered almost out of existence and parked next to one of the pumps. It looked as if it had been driven under a bridge only a metre high. All the glass windows were broken and the bodywork had been severely battered. Broken glass was scattered around the forecourt.

Angel's heart sunk. He expected to find another body.

Several customers were on the forecourt, standing by their cars with pump nozzles in their hands, looking at the unattended wreck and then up to the cashier's office window.

A police patrol car was parked by the pay office door. Angel parked his BMW behind it and got out. He dashed across to the wrecked ice-cream van and looked inside at the crumpled mess, expecting to see a victim in a sea of blood. There was no body there and no sign of any blood. There was only broken glass, twisted metalwork, a towel and empty ice-cream cones scattered over the driver's seat and in the footwell. There was no sign of any armed men anywhere.

He breathed out heavily. He was relieved there was no corpse. He turned towards the pay office. Then his mobile phone rang out. He wasn't pleased. He reached into his pocket and checked the LCD. It was Ahmed. He briefly considered whether to ignore it or not. He clicked the button. 'What is it, lad? Make it quick.'

Ahmed was taken aback. 'It's … there's something on, sir,' he said.

'Something on? What do you mean?'

'Everybody's been put on standby, sir. We've been ordered not to move out of the building and not to make outgoing phone calls. I'm not supposed to be phoning you.'

Angel's screwed up his face. 'Who says?'

'The super says ... something to do with security. I thought you'd want to know.'

This was a new experience. It had never happened to Angel before. That sort of order was usually reserved for the announcement of the outbreak of a war, but on that morning's radio news there had not been any hint that any kind of national emergency was imminent. He knew a General Election was expected to be called soon but he couldn't think that that had anything to do with it. He pursed his lips. It must surely then be something local but very important.

'Yes. Right, lad, thank you. If you find out anything else, give me a ring, if you can.' He pocketed the phone and rubbed his chin.

While he had been on the phone, a police patrolman had noticed him and had run out of the office and across the forecourt towards him.

Angel recognized him. It was PC Donohue. 'Any injuries, Sean?' Angel said.

'No, sir. The cashier was scared but I think she's all right now. The van is the only casualty here,' Donohue said, pointing at it. 'They certainly meant business.'

Angel glanced back at it, pursed his lips and blew out a length of air. 'What happened?'

'The cashier said that the driver of the ice-cream van drove up to that pump, got out and then disappeared. Shortly afterwards, four men in black balaclavas and gloves came in here and demanded to know where he was, and threatened her with a gun. The cashier said she didn't know. So they left her and set about attacking the van with iron bars and hammers and in a minute or so they reduced it to that. Then they ran off. Then the cashier locked the office door, switched off the pumps and dialled 999.'

Angel saw two more police Range Rovers arrive and several uniformed policemen on foot.

'Right, Sean,' he said. 'Liaise with the other lads and ask those customers – politely – if they saw anything. If they didn't, ask them to leave. And tape off the entrance and exit. There might be some closed signs you can put up. Then see if you can see anything around that might have belonged to the vandals – weapons, balaclavas, gloves or anything they might have dropped or discarded.'

'Right, sir,' he said and dashed off.

Angel went back across the forecourt up to the pay-office door, opened it and went inside.

He saw a young woman standing behind the counter talking on the phone. She nervously looked across at him and frowned. Her hands were shaking and her face was white – whiter than the walls in the loos at Strangeways.

'I don't care about all that,' she said into the phone. 'I want my money up to date and my cards. I'm leaving and I'm leaving *tonight*.' Then she banged the phone down into the cradle.

'Who are you?' she said.

Angel held up his warrant card and badge and said, 'I'm Detective Inspector Angel, miss. What's your name?'

She looked at the warrant card, nodded and said, 'Another policeman! Julia Makepeace.'

'What exactly happened, Julia?'

'I've already been through it twice.'

He smiled at her gently and said, 'I know, Julia. I know. But this is absolutely necessary, I assure you. You want us to catch the thugs, don't you?'

She shrugged awkwardly then said, 'I s'pose.'

Then she began to tell him just what PC Sean Donohue had said, but more colourfully.

Angel rubbed his chin and said, 'Did you know the driver of the van?'

'I never actually saw him, Inspector. I saw the van arrive and stop at pump number two. I noticed it was one of Grogan's vans. Then a customer came in to pay. I attended to her. When I looked back, he was not around. Couldn't see him anywhere. Then those thugs arrived. At first they crowded round the van, looking at each other, then they started crossing the forecourt in this direction. I was terrified. They came in here. It was horrifying. They came through that door ... all in black, their eyes and lips showing through the knitted balaclavas, one of them carrying a gun.' She shuddered.

Angel nodded. He understood how frightened she must have been.

'Then what happened, Julia?' he said.

'The one with the gun wanted to know where the driver was. I couldn't speak, I was that scared. He screamed the question at me again and waved the gun in front of my face. Eventually, I managed to get out that I didn't know.'

'Do you remember the exact words he used, Julia? It could be important.'

She narrowed her eyes and said, 'Yes. I'm pretty certain he said, "Where's the driver of Grogan's van?"'

'You're sure?'

'Yes. He yelled it out loud two or three times. "Where's the driver of Grogan's van?"'

Angel nodded. 'Was there anything unusual about his voice or his clothes or any of the other men's clothes and voices?'

'The one with the gun was the only one who spoke,' she said. 'He wasn't from round here. I'm pretty sure it was a cockney accent.'

Angel nodded. 'Then what happened?'

'They ran out of here and began to trash the van.'

Angel rubbed his chin. After a few moments, he glanced over the counter at the cash till. He pointed at it with his thumb and said, 'There'll be a few quid in there, I expect, Julia?'

'Over a thousand pounds,' she said.

'Didn't your friends in the balaclavas show any interest in it at all?' Angel said, raising his eyebrows.

'No. I thought that that's what they wanted when they came into the office, but no. And for all I care, Inspector, they could have had it too. I'm not brave. I'm not paid for dealing with men with guns.'

'Did you see if they had a car?'

'No. They seemed to arrive from nowhere, did what they did and then dashed off. I don't know which way they went. I was too scared to look.'

Angel wasn't learning much. The villains had pretty well covered themselves.

He thanked Julia Makepeace for her patience and left the office. He noticed that the uniformed constables had cleared the forecourt of the general public, taped off the area and formed a line of eight, and were methodically crossing the forecourt with their heads down, searching for clues. He nodded approvingly and crossed the forecourt to reach the constables just as they had completed their search.

He looked at PC Donohue and said, 'Did you find anything, Sean?'

'No, sir.'

He wasn't surprised.

'Well, thanks anyway, lads,' he said. 'Wait until SOCO get here with DS Taylor then return to your normal duties. I'll get off.'

He turned and made the few steps across the forecourt to his car. He had just fastened the seatbelt and was reaching for the ignition when his mobile rang. It was Harker. He sounded strange. His voice was an octave higher than usual.

'Ah yes, Angel,' he said. 'The chief constable has declared that Bromersley Constabulary is formally on standby. You are to stay exactly where you are until you receive further instructions. And you are to keep your phone line open to receive further orders. So carry on working on your cases, but stay put, so that I know exactly where to find you. All right?'

Angel blinked. 'Yes, sir,' he said. 'But why is—'

Harker had gone. The line was dead.

Angel closed the phone and dropped it into his pocket. Those were exactly the orders Ahmed told him that he had received in the CID office. Angel frowned. It wasn't likely that the authority of Bromersley Constabulary had been rescinded. Bromersley was a totally responsible force with a high success rate. It must be some significant political or criminal activity that needed the intervention of other specialized organizations such as MI5 or the army.

Angel's mobile rang again. His hand shook as he opened it. It was Ahmed.

'What's happening?' Angel said.

'I've got this from a constable in the control room, sir. It should be reliable. Apparently, at about nine o'clock this morning there were several big explosions at Grogan's ice-cream factory. There was a lot of damage to the building and the plant, and there were some injuries and some dead, including Mr Grogan himself. The chief constable promptly decided to bring in the Special Unit of Operations. It was apparently the SUO's directive that for our own safety we were to keep well away from the site and continue with our routine work. Some members of the gang responsible for the explosions are thought to be still in the building, and the SUO have brought in a team of armed men, track vehicles, even a helicopter. And I understand that there are fire engines from all over ... Barnsley, Rotherham and Sheffield. And ambulances from Bromersley General and Barnsley General. And that's about it, sir.'

Angel looked through the windscreen along the grey bonnet of the car and slowly shook his head. It was a sad day.

'Does anybody know why?' he said.

'No, sir. They don't know anything more in the control room.'

Angel rubbed his chin, then said, 'And did you say Raphael Grogan was dead?'

'Yes, sir.'

Angel said, 'Right, lad. Thanks very much.'

He closed the phone and slowly dropped it into his pocket. He sighed deeply. His mind was racing as he assimilated the amazing news. He needed to know what was happening. All the action was at Grogan's ice-cream factory. Although he had been ordered to stay at the service station his investigation there was completed and he had no intention of hanging around wasting time.

He pulled the seatbelt round and clicked the chromium plated lip into position. Then he reached forward, turned on the ignition and the car engine purred into life. He let in the clutch and drove the BMW towards the exit and the blue and white DO NOT CROSS tape. A constable lifted the tape for the car to pass under and then threw up a salute. Angel waved a hand of thanks and pressed on across the pavement and into the main Wakefield Road.

FIFTEEN

As Angel drove the BMW up Wakefield Road towards the Fitzallan Trading Estate he saw a black funnel-shaped cloud directly over the area. The sight made him gasp. As he got nearer, he could see the upward movement of a black column of smoke and then the billowing out creating a mushroom shape. He turned on to the ring road then soon reached the short road on to the Fitzallan Trading Estate. He passed the signboards showing the layout of the estate and the 10mph speed restriction sign. Ahead he heard a short burst of four shots from a gun or a rifle.

His heart began to thump.

He slowly turned the curve in the road and saw an unbelievable sight. Grogan's factory lay in ruins. Some of the walls were reduced to piles of bricks, the building had no roof and there were black holes where windows and doors had been. The stream of black smoke generating in the middle of the building continued to ascend into the sky. He heard another burst of four rifle shots followed by a response of seven or eight. He couldn't see the source of the exchange.

Three firemen's ladders were suspended over the factory roof directing water hoses into the middle of the factory. There were two cars and two three-ton lorries in khaki livery parked on the front of the neighbouring factory unit. A Daimler track vehicle with tin helmets bobbing out of the top of it raced past the side of Grogan's factory, ripping up the carefully maintained turf. Near them, a group of men were sheltering behind an armoured car. Some of them seemed to be consulting a map, while others had their rifles set in firing positions.

Angel bit his lip uneasily as he sat there, mesmerized by the sight. He pulled the car over to the side of the road and cut his speed.

Suddenly from nowhere out stepped a man in an army uniform gripping a rifle. He briefly put out a hand with palm facing to indicate that he wanted Angel to stop.

Angel braked and saw that the man was fully kitted in army khaki, a steel helmet and holding a menacingly dangerous SA80 A2 Heckler and Koch rifle.

Angel lowered the car window.

The soldier kept his eyes on him and ambled round the car to it. 'No entry here, sir,' he said. 'You'll have to turn round.'

Angel said, 'I am a police officer. Detective Inspector Angel, Bromersley Police.' He pulled out the leather holder that held his warrant card and badge and showed it to the soldier.

The man merely nodded towards it and said, 'I don't care if you're Ann Widdecombe, sir. You can't come past this point.'

Angel pocketed the leather case and said, 'Why, what's happened?'

The soldier shook his head. 'A gang of villains has blown up a factory and we're clearing up after them, that's all. Now just turn round and go away, sir,' he said, with a wave of the rifle. '*Please.*'

The sound of a distant siren grew louder. An ambulance was coming straight towards them from the direction of Grogan's factory. The soldier dashed round the back of the BMW to give it more room as it roared past.

The soldier watched it go, then took up a position in the middle of the road in front of the car. He readjusted the helmet strap under his chin, stared at Angel and alternately tightened then slackened his fingers round the grips on the rifle.

Angel could see that he had no alternative but to take his leave. He reversed back a short way to a junction and turned round. When he was out of sight of the soldier and could see the ring road ahead, he stopped the car and pulled on the handbrake. He rubbed his chin as he gazed out at the brown fields on each side. There was nothing he would be allowed to do at Grogan's factory so he may just as well leave. He would have liked to return to his office but Harker had rather put that out of bounds. The superintendent believed that he was at the service station on Wakefield Road but it was pointless going back there. Everything that he could do had been done. He could go home but Mary would insist that he got that bed assembled in time for Lolly's visit. She was arriving the following day, and he feared the bed would not be assembled in time. Even so, he wasn't up for doing it.

What a ridiculous state of affairs.

He gazed out of the windscreen. The snow had almost melted away but there were still strips of the dirty white stuff in the prickly, black hedge bottom.

Suddenly, he thought he saw something moving. He focussed his eyes on it. It was on his left about forty metres away, close to the hedge bottom. At first he thought it was a fox or a dog, crawling slowly along, as if it was injured, but then it stood up, looked around, probably saw the BMW and quickly flopped back down full length into the snow and stayed motionless. Angel realized it was a man, a man who didn't want to be seen. The man didn't stay still for long, and began to crawl slowly further along. Angel assumed that he was making for the ring road. He could see an aluminium gate on the corner of the field that he should easily be able to open or climb over, then a few steps and he would be at the side of the ring road. Angel estimated that at the man's present rate of progress, he would be there in three minutes and he decided to act as a reception committee and meet him at the kerbside.

At due time, Angel started the BMW and drove the short distance out of the estate and on to the ring road where he stopped, turned off the ignition, took out the keys, then ran round the front of the car and up to the aluminium gate.

The man seemed to be well dressed in a suit, collar and tie with a thin dark raincoat on top. However, he was soaking wet and his face and head as well as his clothes were daubed with streaks of mud. He didn't speak even though he must have felt Angel's grip. He pulled the man over the gate, carefully arranging to have his right arm up his back when his feet landed on the ground.

'Are you in a hurry, sir?' Angel said.

'Let go of me, for goodness' sake, Angel,' the man said. 'I'm Raphael Grogan.'

Angel stared at the man. The voice was right. But he had been told he was dead. He released the hold. 'I'm terribly sorry, Mr Grogan. Didn't recognize you under all that mud … Come along. I'll give you a lift. You must have had a terrible time.' He pointed to the car. 'Jump in.'

It was then that Angel saw blood on the fingers of his left hand and realized that he must have caught it from some place on Grogan.

Grogan saw the blood and said, 'I have a cut on my shoulder from a big piece of plaster that fell on me. It's nothing much. Nothing at all to worry about.'

Angel assisted Grogan into the car and got into the driving seat. Grogan was having difficulty fastening his seatbelt because of the injured shoulder, so Angel pulled it across him and pressed the tab home.

'I have some tissues somewhere,' Angel said and he began searching the glove shelf behind the steering wheel. 'Clean you up a bit.'

Grogan smiled. 'Thank you, Inspector. That would be nice.'

Angel shook his head as he fiddled with some dusters and a sign with the word POLICE printed on it and a pair of handcuffs.

'Don't know where they are,' he said. 'Will you look in the glove box in front of you, Mr Grogan? That might be where I put them.'

Grogan nodded, leaned forward, pressed the catch and busied himself among maps, charts and police pamphlets with titles such as: 'BROMERSLEY POLICE PROCEDURE. Leaflet No. 465 – procedure on being in collision with wild animals such as tiger, lion, elephant, et cetera. Note: this does not apply to wolves or foxes under two years of age or over twelve years of age.'

'I have them, Mr Grogan,' Angel said, pulling a big box of Kleenex tissues off the shelf, waving them in triumph and handing them to him. 'They were behind the tachometer all the time.'

Grogan took the box and thanked him.

Angel then started the car.

'I'll take you straight to the hospital,' Angel said. 'Have that shoulder seen to, a general check-up and a wash, and if you're all right, then I'll take you home.'

'No thanks, Inspector,' Grogan said. 'It's very considerate of you but it is nothing, I assure you. Would you please take me to the railway station?'

Angel frowned, shook his head and said, 'The railway station? I couldn't do that, Mr Grogan. You must have been through a terrible time. Please don't worry. I will see you right.'

Angel turned off the ring road on to a short link road called Wells

Road. Bromersley General Hospital was on a crossroads off Wells Road.

Grogan said, 'Well, then, if you won't take me to the railway station, please stop and let me out here.'

'Can't do that, Mr Grogan. You are in my custody. You are wanted for the murder of four men, for armed robbery and for dealing in cocaine.'

Grogan stared at him; his jaw dropped. 'Ridiculous. You must be out of your mind.'

'But I wouldn't want you to die on us from septicaemia before you are tried, so we are going to the hospital to have that bullet taken out of your shoulder before we go straight to the station.'

'There is no bullet in my shoulder! I told you it was—'

'Come on, Grogan. You can't fool me. If it was a flesh wound it wouldn't be bleeding so profusely. It has never stopped since you got in the car. It's a good job this upholstery is genuine plastic. Besides, you have a small hole in your raincoat that exactly matches that of a bullet hole.'

Angel pulled on to the frontage of the hospital and began looking for a place to park. It was very busy. An ambulance man at the Accident and Emergency entrance was delivering an elderly man on a stretcher. Two nurses were getting an elderly woman out of a car. There were NO WAITING signs everywhere.

Angel looked round in every direction. There was simply nowhere to park the BMW.

Grogan's eyes were shining like landing lights on a 747. Suddenly, he reached into his left-hand raincoat pocket, pulled something out and pointed it Angel.

Angel noticed the movement and turned to see what was happening. He found himself looking down the barrel of a gun. His eyebrows shot up. His heart began to thump like a steam hammer.

'I see that you know what this is,' Grogan said, shaking the gun at him.

Angel nodded. 'A Walther PPK/S .32 automatic.'

'Good. Now drive me out of this frigging place. I told you I didn't want to be here, and I frigging well don't. I want to get well away from here and it now looks like you have frigging well volunteered to be my frigging chauffeur.'

Angel breathed deeply several times. He noticed how Grogan had changed. He sounded different. He even looked different. Deadly, awful and brutal.

Angel drove the BMW round the semi-circle past the main doors of the hospital and stopped at the exit road.

'Turn right,' Grogan said.

Angel pulled the wheel round to the right. 'Where are we going?' he said.

'I'll tell you all you need to know,' Grogan said.

Angel drove the car along the road in silence. He drove straight ahead unless told otherwise. They seemed to be headed for Barnsley.

After a few minutes, Grogan said, 'What made you think I was dealing in cocaine?'

'I first got the idea when we had notice that 250 boxes of cocaine in the form of biscuits were heading for a customer in Barnsley.'

'That didn't have to be me.'

'No, it didn't. But when I saw that many of your teenage customers were indiscriminately dumping your exceedingly delicious ice cream and the cones on paths and grass, it got me thinking. Cones are, of course, biscuits. Maybe the 250 boxes of cocaine in the form of biscuits were delivered to you, and maybe in the bottom of each ice-cream cone was a twist of cocaine, so that it could be distributed discreetly and in a big way. That would explain why your ice-cream salesmen could still find it worthwhile to stand outside a school or a park in the middle of winter and still make a profit.'

'Ridiculous. You will have to prove it.'

Angel smiled. 'When the judge and jury find out that your salesmen are mostly unemployable crooks, such as Angus Rossi and the lad who stood outside the park last Saturday afternoon, Johnny Oxford, it won't be difficult. That name only came to me this morning. He did three years for handling stolen goods – I put him away myself. Were the rest of your salesmen ex cons?'

'They worked cheap, Angel. And they kept their frigging traps frigging shut.'

Angel came to a junction. The sign ahead said 'Barnsley 4 miles'. Angel drove the BMW straight on.

'Something else has just occurred to me,' Angel said. '250 boxes of 500 ice-cream cones to a box, with a twist of cocaine in each cone, would amount to a huge amount of money ... in the region of four million?'

Grogan said nothing.

'And if you were dependent on the proceeds of the raid on the First Security Delivery Services van to *pay* for it, and you lost those proceeds, you would make some unsavoury people very, very unhappy – so unhappy they might want to murder you and your gang and blow up your factory.'

Grogan said, 'You will have to prove this, you know.'

Angel shrugged. Then his eyes shone briefly. 'That explains something else. That's why you are hell bent on getting as far away from here as possible. That's not an MI5 or a Special Unit of Operations bullet in your shoulder, it's come from one of your Colombian friends. I suppose you are lucky to escape with your life.'

'It's another frigging figment of your imagination,' Grogan said.

The traffic lights on Market Hill in the centre of Barnsley had just turned to red as Angel drove the BMW up to them. He pulled on the handbrake and looked up at the shops, the bank, the town hall. This was familiar territory. But contact was denied him. Angel had a quick look down at the Walther being held steadily in Grogan's left hand and he sighed. The muscles of his jaw tightened. He looked thoughtfully along the bonnet of the BMW. If he had reached for the door handle he would have been dead in seconds.

'Get on to the M1,' Grogan said.

The traffic lights went to green. Angel eased off the handbrake, let in the clutch and turned the corner. Ten minutes later, they were on the M1 travelling northwards at 60mph. Angel had no idea of Grogan's destination or how much longer they would be travelling. He hoped, however, that throughout the time he would be able to keep Grogan talking.

After a few minutes, he said, 'I suppose you hand-picked four of those poor bent souls to assist in the robbery of the First Security Delivery Services van.'

Grogan laughed. 'What makes you think I had anything to do with that?'

'It was the work of a genius,' Angel said. Flattery often opens the most stubborn doors. 'A masterstroke.'

Grogan smiled. 'It was, wasn't it? How are you proposing to try to frigging well hang it on me?'

'Well, you know the screwdrivers used on the job?'

Grogan frowned. His face changed and it was not to a happy expression. 'There weren't any fingerprints on them, were there? I warned Angus Rossi and Johnny Oxford to wipe them well. We all wore gloves. Did you know that?'

'Oh yes. We have a witness who saw the robbery, the whole thing.'

'I didn't see anybody.'

'She was in a building on an upper floor. She had a ringside seat.'

'But we all wore balaclavas.'

'She didn't see your faces until afterwards when you took them off and you were walking away with the suitcase full of money.'

'She saw my face?'

'Just a glance, but I'll be able to prove your gang did the job because of the screwdrivers. We traced them back to Rossi, your employee and number one henchman, who bought them in an auction in Leeds in 2002.'

Grogan's face went scarlet. 'He said no one would be able to frigging well trace them!'

Angel said nothing. He kept his foot squarely on the accelerator. This interview was proceeding better in the car than it would have done at the station.

Grogan sighed then said, 'So what. That's eight years ago, Angel. There were a lot of those around.'

Angel shrugged. 'The stealing of the dynamite used can be traced back to a robbery last November in Derbyshire, and that can also be traced back to Rossi and you.'

He turned down his lower lip like a child denied a toy. 'Why me? How can you trace it back to me? I wasn't even there.'

'Do you know of a property company called Catania and Modica Limited?'

Grogan's eyelids lowered halfway as he wondered what Angel was going to say next. 'Yes, yes. Of course I do.'

'I have a colleague looking into it.'

Grogan pulled a face and said, 'It's a frigging holding company wholly owned by me.'

'Well, then, that completes the link, Grogan,' Angel said. 'Both the dynamite and the screwdrivers were found in a lock-up owned by Catania and Modica Limited.'

'You will have to prove that Catania and Modica *knew* that the dynamite and screwdrivers were in their lock-up.'

'Maybe, maybe,' Angel said. 'But as Angus Rossi's prints were all over both boxes, and as he rented the place from Catania and Modica, which is you, I don't think that it will be too difficult a connection for a jury to make, do you?'

Grogan sniffed. 'What a load of frigging crap. A frigging good barrister would make nonsense of all that. Besides, I didn't take the money.'

'You were seen,' Angel roared. 'My witness saw you.'

The pupils of Grogan's eyes rose up and came down again. He'd been caught in a blatant lie.

'What I meant was I haven't got the frigging money,' he said. 'If I haven't got the frigging money, how can you charge me with stealing it? A good barrister would have that frigging charge of robbery or attempted robbery removed altogether.'

Angel didn't think so. But he didn't want to rile him any more than necessary. He was the one with the Walther. The one he had used to kill four men, maybe more. And Angel must keep him talking.

'It must have felt good,' Angel said. 'Walking off with four million in that case.'

'It felt frigging good, Angel. I can tell you.'

'So you walked down to the railway station, went up to the ticket window and bought a ticket.'

'How do you know that? I suppose you have another witness?'

There *was* no other witness. Angel just smiled as if he knew a lot more than he was saying, but he had only said what he thought must have happened. It wasn't differential calculus.

'Where was the ticket to?' Angel said.

Grogan stuck out his chest. 'There was another frigging aspect of my genius,' he said. 'I knew you frigging police would be sniffing all over, like pimps round a virgin, expecting us to be making our escape by frigging car, so I planned it so that the lads would leave on foot in different directions, and I would leave with the suitcase by train. And it worked. I bought a ticket to the next station down the line, Skiptonthorpe.'

'And that's where it went wrong.'

Grogan pulled a face. 'I was queuing at the ticket window, standing in front of a frigging idiot in a dog collar and a black shirt. I wouldn't normally have noticed him but almost every person that passed spoke to him in a friendly way and he answered them. He seemed well known and as popular as sex.'

'But he picked up the wrong suitcase,' Angel said.

Grogan's face went scarlet as the memory of the incident returned to him. 'The frigging stupid bastard!' he yelled. 'Yes. He picked up the wrong frigging suitcase.'

'And you didn't find that out until you reached the gents toilet at Skiptonthorpe?' Angel said.

Grogan was still fuming. 'The frigging stupid bastard,' he said. Then he suddenly caught up with Angel's question. 'Don't tell me you had a witness in the frigging bog?'

Angel shook his head. 'So you put on the dog collar and black shirt front from out of the case you had taken. You thought it would make you popular as well as make it easier for you to talk to people. You also thought it would make it easier to find the priest who had taken your case.'

'Yeah, Angel. Exactly.'

'You had to get the money back,' Angel said. 'You had to pay for the cocaine. It was four million quid. It had to be paid. You were desperate. You took the next train back to Bromersley, and you asked the lad in the ticket office, Harry Weston, for information about the priest who had been standing behind you. His reply wasn't helpful, probably cheeky or offhand. You were so angry and frantic, you threatened him and you shot him.'

'No.'

'Then you dashed out of the station and hid on the floor of one of your own ice-cream sales vans which happened to be standing by the station entrance.'

'No. It's not true. You'd never prove it. Anyway, Rossi would deny it.'

'Then you murdered two priests and harassed others in your desperate search for the suitcase and the money. Unfortunately for you and them and their families, you never found the right priest.'

'That's absolute frigging rubbish.'

'Inside the suitcase you found a white garment which you put on because you thought it would be an appropriate garment to wear to visit 'brother' priests in their homes, when they are off duty, so to speak. You thought it would give you immediate acceptable access. What you didn't know was that that garment was a scapular, only worn in the church on certain days specified in the church's calendar, almost only when bread and wine are being consecrated.'

He frowned. 'What?' he said.

'Never mind,' Angel said. He didn't want to try and explain. Grogan clearly had had no experience of Christian church culture. Angel wanted to change the subject and he noticed that they passed the sign at the slip road exit of junction 40 to Wakefield. 'How far north are we going, Grogan?'

'I'll tell you when,' he said. 'You said I murdered *four* men. Who was the fourth?'

'You know full well it was Irish John.'

'The tramp?' Grogan said. 'Was that the frigger's name? He deserved to die.'

'He was blackmailing you.'

'He was hanging round St Mary's Church. He heard the frigging gunshot, he watched me come out and followed me home. He assumed that I'd shot the vicar in there, and threatened to tell the police. I gave him money. But he was never satisfied.'

'You tried to get it back. It was £400.'

Grogan's eyes opened wide. 'How do you know that?'

'But you didn't find it.'

'How do you know that? How could you possibly know that? He was frigging crafty. Where was it? Tell me, Angel, where was it?'

'There was £200 in each boot.'

'In his boots? The crafty sod.'

'What size shoes do you wear, Grogan?'

'Size nine, why? What's that got to do with it?'

'That's the size Irish John's murderer wore.'

'Well, it wasn't me. You prove it, Angel. Just you frigging well prove it. Millions of people are a size nine.'

'We will. The money was still in the Northern Bank sleeves. The sleeves were date stamped and initialled by the cashier who paid it out. If your bank statement shows a withdrawal of £400 or more on that date …'

'Huh. The cashier will never frigging well remember. I'm on safe ground there, Angel.'

Angel shook his head. Bank records were usually a hundred per cent reliable.

He noticed they were approaching the slip road for junction 42.

Grogan suddenly looked ahead out of the windscreen. 'Where are we? You're putting me off.' He looked up at the signs. He sucked in air and said, 'It's the M62. You want to be on the slip road; bear left quickly.'

Angel touched the stalk control and switched on the flashers, checked his mirror and moved left off the M1.

'And take the road on the M62 east in the direction of Hull.'

Angel did as he was directed. He had little choice. But he did notice that as determined to watch him as Grogan has been, he had briefly lost his concentration and taken his eyes off him looking for road signs. It must have been for two long seconds. He reckoned that it would have been long enough for him to have wrenched the gun away from him. At sixty miles an hour it would have undoubtedly been risky, but it would have been a risk worth taking. He thought about this in silence as he drove the BMW further and further along the motorway.

He reckoned that he was about the same weight as Grogan and several inches taller. Grogan had a bullet in his shoulder. Sticky blood was still seeping out through his coat on to the upholstery, which Angel reasoned must be weakening him. But Grogan was also in possession of a .32 automatic, which was pointed straight at his head.

Angel knew that he would have to make a challenge of some sort before he delivered Grogan to his destination – wherever it was – because he seriously didn't expect Grogan to let him live, knowing that he had all that mostly indisputable evidence piled up against him. After all, what was another killing to a man who had murdered four men in the past three days?

Angel's brain was operating at top speed. He knew he would have to create his own opportunity. He couldn't rely on providence to save his life. He couldn't leave it to lady luck. He wasn't ready for his wings yet. There was too much to live for. And he couldn't possibly leave Mary behind ...

He glanced down at Grogan. He glared back at him and gripped the Walther tighter and tilted it upwards at Angel's head.

'What *you* looking at?' Grogan said.

'Just wondered how much further to go?'

'You'll find out soon enough.'

'Do I just keep straight on this road? Don't we turn off anywhere?'

'I'll tell you where and when,' Grogan said. 'Just keep your eye on the road.'

Angel pressed the BMW harder and faster until the motorway ended and the road ran into the A63, where he reduced speed appreciably.

Suddenly Grogan said: 'Take the next turn right.'

Angel carefully pulled into the middle of the road. There was a lot of traffic in both directions, heavy wagons taking and delivering goods to the docks in Hull only a few miles away. Eventually a gap appeared and he turned carefully into a side road. It was more of a cart track. Ahead he could see the River Humber, which leads to the North Sea. He must be very close to the end of his journey. He knew he had to make an early bid.

He remembered that there was a switch under the edge of the carpet by the driver's seat which was an immobilizer switch. It could be operated by contact with the heel of his right shoe if he pulled it back far enough. It was put on all Bromersley police vehicles to prevent a car being stolen when, for some reason, it may have to be parked in an unsafe area. He wondered if he could make use of it on this occasion. He had a plan.

As he meandered down the cart track, Angel developed a cough. It seemed to be nothing, but it persisted, so eventually, he reached down with his right hand to his trouser pocket.

Grogan started. He reared up and said, 'What you doing? Show me your hand, *slowly.*'

Angel's heart began to thump at the speed of the Ritual Fire Dance. He brought up his hand to show that he held only a plain white handkerchief.

Grogan eyed it suspiciously then said, 'All right.'

Angel nodded and coughed into it. He held it in his hand for a little while. The cough seemed to subside so he returned the handkerchief to the same pocket. Seconds later the cough returned. He reached down for the handkerchief.

Grogan said, 'All right, but don't try anything clever or I'll blow your frigging head off.'

Angel's hand returned with the handkerchief. He coughed into it. He repeated the cough. He sounded genuinely ill.

Grogan stared up at Angel's face.

While his attention was diverted, Angel brought back his right foot, knocked the switch under the carpet with the heel of his shoe, and the engine stopped abruptly, causing the car to jerk to a halt.

Grogan glanced round. 'What's happened?'

'Don't know,' Angel said.

'Are you out of petrol?'

Angel knew the tank was a quarter full. 'No,' he said.

Grogan tried to reach back to click off his seatbelt. He couldn't do it. 'Unfasten me,' he said.

Angel realized he intended walking down the lane. Their destination couldn't be far because the river was only a few hundred yards away. He knew his life would be at an end if he didn't act soon.

Angel released Grogan's seatbelt catch. The belt zipped away across him. Then Grogan reached up with the gun in his hand to the door handle. There was Angel's chance. There was the valuable two seconds. Angel reached over Grogan's chest and with both hands leaped on his left hand and reached out to the gun. A shot rang out. It was deafening and so close. Hot lead landed somewhere.

The gun was in Angel's hand.

Angel then saw a hole in the car roof. He blew out a big breath in surprise and relief. The bullet had missed him by inches.

Grogan nursed the fingers of his left hand and said, 'You frigging bastard.'

Angel knew he would have to move fast. If Grogan had supporters waiting for him with a boat at the water's edge, the gunshot may have alerted them and they might turn up looking for him.

Angel got out of the car, rushed round to Grogan's door, yanked it open then stepped several paces back. He released the clip on the

Walther and counted three rounds, then pushed it back. A full clip held eight. Grogan had murdered four men and attempted to murder him; that was five. Five from eight, three. Correct.

'Get out of the car,' Angel said. '*Move*. Turn round. Put your hands on the car roof.'

He noted the great mess of blood on the car seat and Grogan's raincoat. He patted him down. He was looking for any other weapons. There weren't any but there were sealed, plastic packs of £1000 worth of £20 notes in every pocket. He snatched them out and threw them on the ledge under the windscreen. There were about twenty-five packs altogether.

'What's this, Grogan?' Angel said. 'Pocket money?'

'Mind your own frigging business.'

He waved the gun at Grogan and said, 'Stay there.'

Angel dashed back to the driver's side of the car and fished around on the glove shelf looking for his handcuffs. He was going to handcuff Grogan and then fasten him with rope to the backseat of the car where he could do no harm, then quietly investigate the end of the lane.

He hadn't reached the car door when a small white pick-up truck came racing towards him from the direction of the dock. There were two men standing in the back of the truck, aiming rifles at him, and in the cab were two others. He thought he recognized the driver.

Angel's heart sank. He reached into his pocket for the Walther. Even with the luck of a lottery winner, he couldn't possibly manage four of them and Grogan as well with three rounds.

The truck stopped close up to him, several feet from the BMW. The driver was Johnny Oxford, one of Grogan's gang. He was pointing a revolver out of the window at him, 'Put them up, Angel.'

He had no option but to obey. He raised his hands, his right hand still holding the Walther.

The men piled out of the truck.

Grogan rushed round the BMW, smiling and holding out his hands. He snatched the Walther out of Angel's raised hand.

Oxford gave Grogan a bear hug and said, 'Raphael, Raphael.'

Grogan said, 'Johnny.'

'You're wounded, boss.'

'Got caught by a stray bullet as I was trying to get out. I must get it seen to. Is everybody here?'

'Yeah. Yeah.'

One of the men said, 'Angus hasn't turned up.'

'He won't be coming,' Grogan said. He glanced back at Angel and said, 'This frigging bastard has got him locked up at Bromersley nick.'

The five men glared at Angel.

Angel was worried. Seriously worried.

'The boat ready?' Grogan said.

'Ready and waiting,' Oxford said. He pointed at Angel and said, 'What you going to do with the copper?'

'We can't take him with us,' said one of the others.

'Well, we can't leave him here,' Grogan said. 'He knows too much.'

He looked round at the gang.

They all stared back at him.

'Leave it to me.'

Angel felt a shiver run down his spine, his legs and his arms, down to his fingertips. He wanted to run but he knew it would only serve to entertain Grogan's gang and prolong the agony of his certain death.

Grogan looked at him with cold, unfeeling eyes. There was no pity in them. 'Angel,' he said, and he pointed the barrel of the Walther towards the river. 'Walk down the lane.'

Angel didn't move. He couldn't move. His body felt numb. He wanted to pray but he also wanted to stay alert, in case there was a way of avoiding this final scene. This wasn't the way he had ever thought he would leave this earth. He had considered the possibility that he might die in a gun fight, but he had always thought that he would at least have had a gun in his hand. He had certainly not expected to be shot like a dog.

'Go on,' Grogan said, 'walk down the lane.'

Angel kept his ground. He looked at Grogan with a fixed stare.

'Walk down the lane, Angel,' Grogan said. 'Go on.'

Grogan raised the gun.

Angel saw his finger tighten round the trigger.

There was a loud gunshot and a tiny shower of earth exploded six inches in front of Angel and landed on his shoes.

'If you won't walk, then run, you frigging bastard.'

The other members of the gang laughed.

Grogan looked round at them, smiled and raised the gun again.

Then they heard a voice through a police megaphone say, 'Put that gun down. You are surrounded. You are all under arrest.'

The gang looked round but they couldn't see anybody. They defiantly raised their weapons.

'Put your weapons on the ground now or you will be shot,' the voice said.

More than thirty armed men in army uniforms, with bits of twigs and greenery projecting from their uniforms, suddenly appeared from behind the bushes, coming up the lane from the river and down the lane from the main road.

The gang hesitated.

'Put your weapons on the ground now or you will be shot,' the voice said. 'This is your last chance.'

The four men and Grogan dropped their weapons and raised their hands to show they were empty.

Angel lowered his hands, sighed and gawped at them in surprise.

An unmarked police car he recognized turned off the main road, turned down the lane and stopped behind the BMW.

Out jumped Flora Carter. She had a big smile on her face. She ran up to him.

'Are you all right, sir?' she said brightly.

'Of course,' he said, rolling his shoulders and arms round to relax them. 'You took your time.'

'Your text message, "With Grogan. Follow. Inform SUO," was a bit cryptic, sir, to say the least.'

'It was the best I could do. Grogan was watching me, and I was watching him. I had to do it when I was looking for tissues for him, to clean him up.'

'And you drove very fast, sir.'

'The vehicle tracking device works regardless of speed, Flora,' he said. 'It just takes a bit longer to catch up, that's all.'

'Yes, sir. Have we enough to hold Grogan, sir?' she said.

'There's plenty,' Angel said. He reached into the BMW through the open window, picked up a small white box from the glove shelf and said, 'Thanks to modern technology, Flora, absolutely everything is recorded on there.' He put the box in his pocket and tapped it safely. He looked round.

'Hey. Do these chaps know there are probably a few more of Grogan's gang at the bottom of this lane?'

'There were two, sir,' Carter said. 'They mopped them up first. They were in a small boat – a cobble I think they call it – with a trunk full of money. They were waiting for Grogan and any others in the gang who had survived the attack.'

'They presumably had a rendezvous with a sea-going boat to who knows where.'

Angel saw Grogan, and the other members of the gang, hand-cuffed behind their backs, being pushed up the lane.

'Well, come on, Flora. Might as well get off. These Special Unit of Operations lads seem to know what they are doing. They can finish up here.'

SIXTEEN

Angel arrived back at the station at a few minutes past four o'clock. Ahmed followed him into his office carrying a blue message pad.

'Everything all right now, Ahmed? The emergency over?'

'Yes, sir.'

'Thank you for telling me what was going on. I realize that you could have been in trouble.'

He smiled. 'That's all right, sir.' He referred to the blue pad he was holding. 'I've got three messages for you.'

'Right, lad, what are they?'

'Inspector Trickett from Leeds Central phoned just to keep you in the loop about Peter King,' Ahmed said. 'The inspector said that a cardigan has turned up belonging to that schoolgirl who was raped and murdered just before Christmas. It has been tested for DNA and semen stains on it showed that they are from Peter King, so he's been re-arrested and charged.'

'He'll be pleased.' Angel said.

'Who will?' Ahmed said.

'Both,' Angel said. 'It'll get him out of our way for a bit. What else?'

'Superintendent Harker wants to see you, sir,' he said, 'as soon as you come in.'

Angel frowned. He didn't want to know about it. It was always trouble. 'What about, lad? Have you any idea?'

'It might be that you weren't at that service station when he'd specifically told you to stay there, sir.'

Angel wrinkled his nose and thought about it for a moment then said, 'Aye, it might. And if I *had* stayed there, Grogan might be on his way to Morocco or somewhere more exotic, that has no extradition agreement with the UK, with four million quid belonging to other people.' He sighed. 'All right, lad. I'll go up there. I'll sort it. Thank you. Anything else?'

'Your wife rang, sir. She said would you phone her back. She said it was important.'

Angel pulled a face. 'That bloody bed,' he said.

Ahmed peered at him. 'What's that, sir?'

Angel looked up. He hadn't intended speaking out loud. 'Oh? Nothing. Right, lad. Thank you.'

Ahmed went out.

Angel's nose went up and the corners of his mouth turned down. He hadn't assembled that bed yet and Lolly was supposed to be arriving tomorrow. It was such a tedious puzzle. He didn't mind a mental puzzle but a physical puzzle was beyond him. It would take him all that evening to assemble it. And there was the fancy bedhead to assemble and then fix. He reached out for the phone and tapped in the number.

'Hello, love,' he said. 'Are all right? Ahmed said you wanted me urgently. What's the matter?'

'It's Lolly,' she said.

He thought she sounded as if she'd been crying.

'What about her?'

'She's not coming,' she said. 'After all I've done – *we've* done. She's *not* coming.'

Angel was delighted but he said nothing.

'You wouldn't believe it,' Mary said. 'You know that she was originally coming to us to get out of the smell of paint because she had the decorator in to do the whole place? Well, the decorator is very artistic. She said he hasn't just slapped paint on and papered clean bright new wallpaper. Here and there he has painted frescos. Anyway, he is quite mature and unmarried, a bit younger than her … well, eighteen years younger than her, actually … He's finished decorating the house and, well, they're going off to Nice together for three weeks. Staying in his sister's seafront flat. And if it works out all right, they might get married. He's already asked her. She says he's a terrific physique. Runs on the beach every day. Has a great suntan and a great eight-pack. Personally, I think it's disgusting. I don't know what you think. Of course, you take a far more liberated attitude to carryings on like that. You'll probably approve of what she's going to do. I tried to talk her out of it but she wasn't having any. She's been married three times and each one of them has ended in disaster. I reminded her that I was the elder sister but that didn't make any difference. Well, what do you think? If my mother was alive, she'd turn in her grave. Well, what do you think? Just a minute, there's somebody at the door. Hold on, love. I will have to answer it. Hold on.'

Angel smiled. He didn't care if Lolly married Nicolas Sarkozy or even Angela Merkel if he didn't have to put that wretched bed together.

Suddenly he heard her voice again. 'Hello, Michael. Are you there?'

'Yes, love. Who was it?'

'Josh from next door,' she said sounding mysterious. 'He took a little package in from the postman for us when I was out shopping this morning. It's only small but it's too big, whichever way you try it, to go through our letterbox. It's quite heavy for its size. Shall I open it? Are you expecting anything? Can I open it now?'

'For goodness' sake, open it,' Angel said. 'Put yourself out of your misery.'

'Hold on then. I've got a knife here.'

Angel heard the rustle of paper and then sounds of mystification, then more rustling of paper, more mystification then a sound of delight. 'Oh, Michael. It's beautiful. Amethyst. Natural amethyst. The way it picks up the light. Lolly would have been delighted to have had that in her bedroom. All those blues and purples. Oh, you are a darling. Thank you, sweetheart. As she is not coming I'll put it at the side of the bed ... *my* side. Is that all right, Michael?'

'Yes, love,' he said.

It would be from Felicity Kellerman. She had said she would send him a piece of amethyst, which he had politely declined. But it was very kind of her.

'Will you be late tonight, darling?' Mary said.

His ears pricked up. She hardly ever called him darling. 'I don't expect so, love,' he said, warily. 'Why?'

'I've missed you, you fool. It's been a long day. And I want to thank you for the beautiful amethyst. You can be so romantic when you want to be.'

He smiled. 'No, I won't be late, Mary,' he said. 'Goodbye, sweetheart.' He replaced the phone, smiling. There was a bit of good news. Great. He continued to sit at his desk, smiling, until he heard it. That bluebottle had started up its monotonous buzzing again. Then he saw it. It zigzagged across his desk and made for the closed window. He leaped up, reached out for the *Police Review*, rolled it up and lunged into attack. He made several swipes to the left and then the right. Then it suddenly went very quiet. He wondered if he had made a direct hit. He looked carefully round the window but he could not see it. The buzzing suddenly started up behind him. He turned round. It was flying round the lampshade. He made swipe after swipe and was sure he had caught it at least once, but it continued to make that annoying buzzing sound. Then it disappeared again and the buzzing stopped.

Angel looked everywhere for it but he couldn't see it. He stood there a few moments in silence, shrugged, threw down the *Police Review*, reached out for his coat and went home.